Praise for 4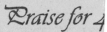

FATHER AND CHILD
"…great, one-sitting romantic suspense that will keep readers on the edge of the seats from start to finish."*

FOR YOUR EYES ONLY
"Few write suspense like Rebecca York."‡

FACE TO FACE
"Harlequin's first lady of suspense…a marvelous storyteller, Ms. York cleverly develops an intricate plotted romance to challenge our imaginations and warm our hearts."†

PRINCE OF TIME
"Get ready for the time of your life…. Breathtaking excitement and exotic romance…in the most thrilling 43 Light Street adventure yet!"†

TILL DEATH US DO PART
"Readers will delight in every page."‡

TANGLED VOWS
"A bravura performance by one of the best writers ever of quality romantic suspense."†

MIDNIGHT KISS
"A sizzling, seductive tale of dark mystery and brooding passion."†

*Harriet Klausner, Amazon.com
†Melinda Helfer, *Romantic Times*
‡Debbie Richardson, *Romantic Times*

Dear Reader,

I'm often asked which book in the 43 LIGHT STREET series I like best. It's hard to pick an absolute favorite, but over the years there have been books that were near and dear to my heart. *Nowhere Man* is one of these. It's the poignant story of a man named Hunter condemned to a kind of living hell, through no fault of his own, and a woman named Kathryn determined to save him. But reaching out to him is fraught with emotional and physical danger. *Nowhere Man* is also about the misuse of power, about ruthless men with deep secrets who have put themselves above the laws of God and man.

Over the years I've developed a strong image of what a 43 LIGHT STREET book should be. I'm particularly proud of recent ones such as *Prince of Time, For Your Eyes Only* and *Father and Child.* And I'm excited to follow them with *Nowhere Man,* the first book written by Ruth Glick, aka Rebecca York. It's one of many more 43 LIGHT STREET novels I want to write, novels embodying my personal concept of romantic suspense—the blending of an emotion-charged love story with heart-pounding suspense.

Next will be *Shattered Lullaby.* It's about a man on the run, whose only hope of survival is to hide his identity. He can't afford emotional involvement because anyone who helps him is likely to wind up dead. But he doesn't reckon with the courage of one strong woman determined to save him. And he doesn't know how much danger he's put her in until he discovers she's carrying his child.

I hope you enjoy *Nowhere Man* and the many future 43 LIGHT STREET books.

Sincerely,

Rebecca

Ruth Glick writing as Rebecca York

Rebecca York

NOWHERE MAN

Ruth Glick writing as Rebecca York

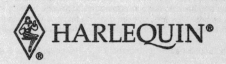

HARLEQUIN®

TORONTO • NEW YORK • LONDON
AMSTERDAM • PARIS • SYDNEY • HAMBURG
STOCKHOLM • ATHENS • TOKYO • MILAN • MADRID
PRAGUE • WARSAW • BUDAPEST • AUCKLAND

ISBN 0-373-22473-7

NOWHERE MAN

Copyright © 1998 by Ruth Glick

Directory
4 3 L I G H T S T R E E T

	Room
ADVENTURES IN TRAVEL	204
ABIGAIL FRANKLIN, Ph.D.	509
KATHRYN KELLEY, Ph.D.	
Clinical Psychology	
BIRTH DATA, INC.	322
INNER HARBOR PRODUCTIONS	404
THE LIGHT STREET FOUNDATION	322
KATHRYN MARTIN-McQUADE, M.D.	515
Branch Office, Medizone Labs	
O'MALLEY & LANCER	518
Detective Agency	
LAURA ROSWELL, LL.B.	311
Attorney at Law	
SABRINA'S FANCY	Lobby
STRUCTURAL DESIGN GROUP	407
NOEL ZACHARIAS	311
Paralegal Service	
L. ROSSINI	Lower Level
Superintendent	

CAST OF CHARACTERS

Kathryn Kelley—Fear drove her to Stratford Creek, but the only man who made her feel safe there was supposed to be a criminal.

Hunter—Why did he have no memories before waking up at Stratford Creek?

William Emerson—Chief of operations, he hired Kathryn to work for him, but was he telling the truth about her assignment?

Chip McCourt—Did the assistant chief of security advance his career through murder?

Jerome Beckton—He was chief of training, but he abused his power once too often.

Sam Winslow—Was Beckton's assistant simply doing his job or obstructing Kathryn's?

Dr. Jules Kolb—How did the physician fit into the power structure?

Dr. Avery Swinton—The chief of research and the brains behind the frightening secret of Stratford Creek. How far would he go to safeguard his project?

Dr. Roger Anderson—Was Swinton's assistant secretly warning Kathryn to be careful?

Ken Reid—He and Kathryn developed an instant dislike.

Don't miss the next 43 Light Street:
Shattered Lullaby
January 1999

Prologue

Kathryn Kelley, a small figure dwarfed by the silent, eerie space beyond, hesitated in the doorway to the darkened room. Where were the lights, she wondered, her gaze probing the inky blackness. She could see almost nothing, but felt thick, chemical-tinged mist wafting toward her. It sent shivers over her skin as it collided with the cooler air of the hallway. Trying to dispel the sudden chill, she rubbed her hands along the thick sleeves of her robe.

It was Friday evening, and since the moment she'd opened her eyes last Monday, she'd sensed that something was wrong. She'd tried to ignore the oppressive sensation, but it was like a storm gathering around her. The feeling of apprehension made her glance quickly over her shoulder to confirm that the corridor behind her was empty.

Of course it was empty! She made a wry face, annoyed at the tricks her mind was playing on her.

"What's *wrong* with you?" she asked, her voice echoing in the darkness beyond the door. With a quick decisive movement, she switched on the lights and marched inside. Shrugging out of her robe, she secured her mane of red hair with a band at the nape of her neck, kicked off her shoes, and executed a perfect dive into the turquoise water of the swimming pool below her.

The cold was a momentary shock to her system as she

shot downward into the pool, then came up to blink water out of her blue eyes. Straightening her limber body, she began a rapid crawl stroke. Ever since high school, when she was on the swim team, swimming had remained her exercise of choice. In fact, she'd selected her Baltimore apartment because the sixties renovation of the Cecil Arms had included a pool on the top floor.

Ten-thirty was late for a solitary swim. Actually, the pool was supposed to be closed to tenants at that hour. But she'd negotiated a lease that allowed her to use the facility after hours. Willing the tension out of her muscles, she cut rapidly through the water. Still, she couldn't outdistance the demons of the day. She'd appeared as an expert witness in a child custody trial that afternoon. Although she'd kept her cool on the stand, her testimony about the abuse of a ten-year-old boy by his father had made her stomach knot.

The mere thought of the man made her lose the rhythm of her strokes. With this child, she'd slipped over the line of professional detachment—once again. Lately it was getting harder to maintain an objective distance from other people's pain. So she swam in the Cecil Arms pool like the victim of a shipwreck flailing toward an unreachable shore, while her mind wandered to fantasies of trading in her psychology practice for a flower shop like the guy in *Bed of Roses*. Maybe the management at 43 Light Street would rent her space in the lobby.

She didn't hear the door open. But a jolt went through her as she saw the overhead lights and the ones along the side of the pool wink out. Stopping dead, she held her breath, barely treading water, as her gaze scanned the floor-to-ceiling windows along the far wall. Below her, lights twinkled in other North Baltimore apartment buildings, yet this room at the top of the Cecil Arms was dark.

"Is somebody there?" She could hear her pulse pounding in her ears and the reverberations of her voice from the walls and ceiling of the large room.

When no one answered, goose bumps rose on her arms. She wanted to believe someone was playing a cruel practical joke on the lady who went swimming in the evening. The explanation didn't wash. In a blinding moment of panic, all the anxiety of the week coalesced into a terrible moment of certainty. On a gut level she knew who had turned off the lights, knew who had been stalking her. Now it all made sense.

"James?" she quavered.

He made her beg for the answer.

"James."

"Got ya!" a familiar, low voice echoed off the water.

She had been hoping against hope it wasn't true. Now she pictured a slender man with blond hair and blue eyes standing between her and the only door, the only escape route.

James Harrison. He had a charming smile and an easy manner, unless you looked below the surface to the rotten core carefully hidden inside.

She hadn't wanted to believe he was back. Yet deep in her subconscious she must have known. Three years ago he'd been confined to the Indiana Institution for the Criminally Insane, and he'd sworn to get even with Dr. Kelley for helping put him there.

She'd moved away, started over again in a new place with a new job and new friends. And time had dulled the memory of the curses he'd hurled at her. She'd felt safe—until this week.

A splash told her he was in the water. She dragged in a lungful of air and dove deep, praying she had a chance to escape. Surfacing at the edge of the pool near the door, she felt for the metal ladder and began to scramble up. But he must have been planning this carefully, must have studied the layout of the pool, for strong hands closed around her thighs and dragged her back down.

Kathryn had time for only a quick gasp of air before he

pulled her under, pushing her below with the weight of his body. Trapped, she flailed in panic. But the watery world muted the impact of her blows. All she could do was rake her nails across his ribs. The attack didn't have any apparent effect.

Frantically, she tried to struggle upward, but cruel hands held her under. Then for a moment he let her up, long enough for her to get a blessed gasp of oxygen before he pulled her down into the dark water again.

She knew then that he was toying with her, prolonging her agony for his own sick satisfaction. With all her strength, she tried to pull free. She tried to hit him. He only shifted her in his grasp, his fingers like tentacles on her water-slick flesh. Someone had told her once that drowning wasn't such a bad death. Now she took no comfort in the snatch of memory.

Her chest was bursting, and bright dots danced before her eyes. Soon it would be impossible to hold her breath, and the water would fill her lungs. James Harrison would finally get his wish—her death.

Yet she kept fighting him. Her flailing hand brushed the edge of his swim suit. She followed the fabric downward until she encountered sensitive male flesh, then dug her nails into him with all her remaining strength. Through the muffling water, she heard him scream. As his grasp loosened she wrenched away and broke the surface, dragging in life-giving air.

He cursed and made a grab for her, his fingers grazing her shoulder. Hardly able to think, Kathryn maneuvered into open water, heading for the opposite ladder. When his hand grazed her foot, she screamed and kicked harder.

Before he could catch up again, the lights flashed on and a voice boomed over the water. "What the hell's going on in here?"

Reaching the ladder, Kathryn gave a heartfelt cry of thanks and scrambled up. But she didn't get any farther.

As the air hit her body, she crumpled and lay panting on the cold cement. In the glow from the overhead lights, all her eyes could make out was an indistinct figure standing in the doorway.

"Listen up. You'd better have a good explanation, or I'm going to call the police."

Even with the echo bouncing off the walls, she recognized the voice. It was Mr. Clemson, the building superintendent. "God, yes, call the police," she croaked.

A flash of movement on the other side of the pool made her cringe toward the wall. She saw James vault out of the water, hurtle toward Clemson, and give him a mighty shove before charging through the door and disappearing.

Barely finding her legs, Kathryn wobbled toward the wall phone and dialed 911.

Chapter One

She was in a prison.

No, she had *chosen* to come to this place called Stratford Creek on a deserted stretch of road in Western Maryland, where the mountain scenery took your breath away and the security was tight as a federal penitentiary. But this wasn't a jail, and Kathryn Kelley wasn't a prisoner. She could leave any time she wanted, she reminded herself as the door to the cell-like gatehouse slammed closed behind her.

"I have an appointment with Mr. Emerson," she said, addressing a man in gray slacks and a blue shirt who stood behind a low counter. He was muscular, with a square jaw, square shoulders, and a crew cut. His unobtrusive plastic tag said his name was McCourt, and he kept his steely gaze fixed on her.

"Please hand me your purse and step through the metal detector." He waved toward a security entrance much like the ones that were now a fact of life to anyone who regularly used the nation's airports.

Kathryn complied, then watched him paw through the contents of her pocketbook as if he thought her lipstick was a miniaturized bomb. Satisfied, he handed back the purse and gestured toward a small wooden table. "You're on the schedule. Have a seat. May I see two forms of identification?"

"Of course," she answered, trying to match the coolness of his voice. But her hand tremored as she pulled out the chair behind the table and sat down.

He's just using standard intimidation techniques, she told herself. But she wasn't in good enough shape to keep from reacting. At least he hadn't searched her for hidden weapons.

When she thumbed her driver's license out of her wallet, he made her wait with it in her outstretched hand while he got a clipboard from the wall in back of him. As he turned, she saw the bulge of a gun riding discreetly at his waist.

Feeling like she'd caught him with his fly open, she looked quickly away and unfolded the fax she'd received yesterday evening. "This is my authorization letter from Mr. Emerson," she said, handing it across the desk.

In fact, it was one of the strangest job offers she'd ever received—and accepted. She'd be temporarily working for the Defense Department, but the orders didn't specify exactly what her duties would be, although she'd been assured during several phone interviews that her background and experience were perfect for the assignment.

As McCourt perused the fax, she tried to gather her composure. Any other time, she would have been better prepared for his subtle little power game. But she was still trying to cope with the emotional aftermath of the attack in the swimming pool two weeks ago, not to mention the police interviews and the dawning realization that Baltimore's finest couldn't guarantee her safety. Her attacker, James Harrison, was still at large, probably in the area. The Indiana authorities hadn't warned her he was coming because they'd thought he was dead. Apparently he'd set fire to the maximum-security unit at the hospital where he was being held and escaped in the confusion, making sure there was a body in his bunk burned beyond recognition.

After almost killing her in the Cecil Arms pool, Harrison had disappeared into the night, and she had gone downstairs to her apartment only long enough to pack some clothes. For the past two weeks, she'd been staying with various friends and shutting down her private practice—since the cops had no idea where to find her lunatic stalker. He'd already proved himself frighteningly resourceful, and she wasn't willing to wait around like a tethered goat for him to pounce on her again.

Finished with the fax, McCourt compared her to the blue-eyed redhead in the photograph on her driver's license and pulled a folder from a drawer behind the counter. "Your temporary clearance is in order."

"It shouldn't be temporary. I had it updated when I did some work at Randolph Electronics."

"Yes, but we have additional requirements here."

Before she could make any further objections, he handed her a form and said, "Sign here."

When she'd written her name, along with the date and time, he initialed the entry.

"I'm Chip McCourt. Glad to have you with us," he said, obviously still withholding judgment. "I'll take you to the headquarters building, Dr. Kelley."

Kathryn pushed back her chair. "I can find my way if you'll just give me directions."

"I am required to escort you," he said firmly.

Her fingers tightened on the strap of her purse as she fought the impulse to blurt out that she'd changed her mind. She was only a few hours away from Baltimore. She could turn around and drive back. But then what? She wouldn't feel safe in her apartment. Or her office. And she couldn't camp out permanently at her friends' houses. Instead of resenting the security here, she told herself, she should be grateful.

With a sigh, she stood and let him usher her outside, where he stopped and conferred briefly with another man who had arrived in a Jeep Cherokee.

"All set," he said, turning back to her.

Manufacturing a smile, she led the way to her car, thankful that McCourt slid into the passenger seat instead of demanding her keys.

Her escort wasn't much for small talk, simply giving her toneless directions. So she took stock of what had been described as the Stratford Creek campus as he copiloted her up a winding road lined with white pine trees, then past low, redbrick buildings that might have been constructed as a garden apartment complex in the fifties or sixties. Some campus. The lawns were half dirt and the wood trim on a number of the buildings was flaking. Although she'd been assured by Mr. Emerson that Stratford Creek was well funded, apparently the U.S. government wasn't putting much money into exterior maintenance.

Many of the windows had a dusty blankness that told her some of the offices were empty. Adding to the ghost-town atmosphere was the lack of traffic. She met no other cars, and as she rounded a corner, she made the mistake of turning her head to look at the remains of a flower bed in the center of a weed-choked lawn.

As she turned back to the road, she caught a blur of motion to her left. With a start, she realized that a man had materialized from behind a nearby stand of bushy pines and was on a collision course with her car.

McCourt shouted a warning as Kathryn slammed on the brakes, bringing the vehicle to a bouncing halt. But the man must have had lightning reflexes, because he'd already halted.

Time seemed to slow as she stared at him. He stood on the balls of his feet, breathing hard, his body glowing with a fine sheen of perspiration and his hands flexed at his sides as if he were ready for an attack. A myriad impressions assaulted her at once, the way they often did when she was meeting someone who sparked her interest. She let the perceptions flow, hoping she could sort them out later.

Physically, he was magnificent. His damp T-shirt was

stretched across a broad, well-muscled chest, and his running shorts showcased impressive masculine details beneath the skimpy fabric. Below the shorts were the long, muscular legs of an athlete.

He moved his hand to swipe a lock of dark hair away from his forehead, drawing her gaze to his chiseled face. It was all sharp angles and acute planes that were arresting in themselves. But it was his fierce, deep-set eyes that captured her attention as they regarded her with a kind of uncensored curiosity.

They were the darkest eyes she'd ever seen as they found hers through the windshield, telegraphing a message that he needed nothing from her or anyone else. He stood alone, which should mean nothing in itself. Yet something about the look on his lean features conveyed a sense of isolation that made her breath catch painfully.

She couldn't analyze the feeling. For several heartbeats she was held by the currents she sensed flowing below the surface of the dark eyes. He broke the spell by moving his hands to his shoulders, easing a pair of straps, and she realized that he was wearing a heavy-looking backpack.

Her attention was so totally focused on the runner that she forgot all about McCourt sitting next to her. Apparently he had been as transfixed as she—until the man took a step toward the car. Then her passenger reached for the door handle.

"Who is that?" she managed.

Without answering, McCourt climbed out and stepped around the car, his face set in harsh lines. From her vantage point behind the wheel, Kathryn watched the dynamics with fascination.

"What the hell are you doing on this part of the grounds?" McCourt demanded, yet the question came out more wary than authoritative.

The runner shifted his stance. Although he kept his face carefully neutral, there was something about the angle of his firm jaw that sent a shiver up her spine. When he spoke his voice was low, controlled. "Training exercise," he answered in measured syllables, using only the precise number of words he needed to convey his meaning. "Ten-mile run. Fifty-pound pack." His voice was rough, rusty, with a kind of unused quality.

Kathryn goggled as she tried to imagine the stamina it would take to run ten miles carrying that much weight.

"You're not supposed to be here," McCourt growled.

The man drew himself up taller. "The trails are wet," he said in his gritty voice, then took a step toward McCourt who backed up the same amount of space.

"Stay away from me," he warned, a quaver in his voice as his hand inched toward the gun at his waist.

Kathryn could see he was badly rattled by the chance encounter. My God, was he capable of shooting the man for being in the wrong place at the wrong time? What kind of place was this, anyway?

She looked around. The grounds were as deserted as before. She was the only witness.

Her heart started to pound. Before she quite realized what she was doing, she stepped out of the car and joined the two men.

McCourt heard the car door open and glanced back at her. He swore under his breath. "Stay out of his reach. He'll beat the tar out of you as soon as look at you."

The runner shook his head in strong denial, then switched his attention from the lieutenant to her, apparently dismissing the other man as if he had ceased to exist. Yet she had the feeling that if McCourt made a sudden move for his gun, it would be knocked out of his hand before he could raise it into firing position.

"I will not hurt you," the runner said to her with an absolute finality that she felt as well as heard.

"I believe you," Kathryn replied, lifting her eyes to meet his.

His gaze locked with hers. "Thank you." He spoke the simple phrase with deep sincerity, giving the impression that he rarely had the opportunity to thank anyone.

"I never lie," he added.

It wasn't a boast, she decided. It was a simple statement of fact.

"Who are you?" she asked, in as steady a voice as she could manage.

It was a straightforward request for information, yet he appeared to give it deep consideration, and she had the strange feeling that perhaps nobody had ever bothered to ask the question before.

"Nobody," he finally answered with a half shrug of his shoulders.

"You must have a name."

He tugged for a moment at his left earlobe, as if the gesture helped him think. "I am called John Doe," he recited, the syllables running together into one word. From someone else, it might have been a joke or a sarcastic attempt to cut off the conversation, but the serious look on his face belied any attempt at humor or irony.

He didn't ask her name, yet she offered it anyway. "Kathryn Kelley. Kelley with an extra *e* before the *y*," the way she always said it, even as she pondered the combination of a first and last name that had very little chance of being real.

"Kathryn Kelley," he repeated in a thoughtful voice. "You are different."

"How?"

He considered the question. "Many ways. Your hair." He reached out a hand toward her red curls, his fingers making the barest contact, like a man afraid to harm something of great value. The touch was gentle, yet it sent a vibration traveling along her nerve endings.

"I—remember—" He stopped, looked perplexed.

Her breath stilled as she gazed into his eyes. He was

waiting for something, and she didn't know what. Slowly, as if controlled by some outside force, she raised her hand so that her fingers were pressed to his. She could feel the blood pounding in her fingers and wondered if he felt it, too.

Neither of them moved, and she saw a look of wonder fill his dark eyes. It was replaced almost instantly by an utter bleakness that brought an answering tightness in her chest. "You are not afraid of me like the others," he said in that same gritty voice as he pulled his hand back.

"What did you do to make them afraid?" she asked.

He shrugged, his face going as blank as a window when the shades are abruptly drawn.

Kathryn had utterly dismissed McCourt from her mind during the exchange. Now he made his presence felt with a muttered expletive. "That's enough," he snapped. "How many miles are left in your run?" he asked John Doe.

The answer came back without hesitation. "Two."

"Then finish up. And do an extra two miles to make up for the interruption."

"Yes, sir." He acknowledged the order crisply, though there was an undertone of insolence that she was sure McCourt couldn't miss.

Before she could ask any more questions, the man who called himself John Doe crossed the road and started across the scraggly lawn, his long, muscular legs pumping. He picked up speed as he went, until he was moving in a blur of motion that seemed beyond the capacity of anybody but an Olympic sprinter. Yet he was settling into the fast pace for what was still a long run. In a few more seconds he was out of sight.

Kathryn stared after him, but her attention snapped back to McCourt as he swore under his breath.

"Is he being punished?" Kathryn asked.

"Like he said, he's being trained," her escort snapped. Pulling a cell phone out of his pocket, he began to punch in numbers. Then he turned his back to Kathryn, stepped to the far side of the car, and began to speak in a strained, rapid voice.

"Give me Beckton," he demanded, then glanced in her direction and lowered his voice. Yet she still caught the tone of annoyance.

Unfortunately, the rest of his conversation was muffled. When she realized she was standing in the middle of the road straining her ears to hear what he was saying, she grimaced and moved to the side of the car, resting her hips against the fender. The wind rustled her hair, and she smiled slightly as she remembered the caress of John Doe's fingers. He was strong, yet his touch had been gentle, like a man stroking a wild bird. Something she didn't understand had transpired during the few minutes they'd spent together. All she could say for sure was that she'd met a man who was so out of her realm of experience that he seemed to have dropped to earth from another planet. At the very least, she thought as she recalled his alternately clipped and formal sentence patterns, he sounded like someone who was still learning English.

Yet the two of them hadn't needed brilliant conversation to make contact on a very human level. On the other hand, he hadn't smiled the whole time they had talked, and she was hard put to imagine the harsh lines of his face softening into a smile.

Feeling suddenly sad, she swiped her hand through her hair, brushing it back from her face.

Who was he? What was he doing in this strangely controlled environment? She wanted some answers before she agreed to remain on this base.

McCourt terminated the conversation and dialed a second number. This time he spoke in a more deferential tone. As she watched him, she had ample time to start wondering if she was building fantasies around the encounter on the road. She'd hardly spent five minutes with the man who called himself John Doe. She shouldn't be jumping to so many conclusions.

McCourt shoved the phone back into his pocket and returned to the car. Silently, they both climbed inside and closed the doors.

"John Doe isn't really his name, is it?" she asked as she sat with her hands wrapped around the wheel, making no move to start the engine. "Who is he?"

"I'm not authorized to give you that information. You'll have to address your questions to Mr. Emerson," he said in a clipped voice.

"But—"

"God help you, you'll find out soon enough. And God help me if I don't have you in the office of the chief of operations in the next five minutes."

HIS POWERFUL LEGS PUMPED and his feet pounded the ground, eating up the miles between himself and the woman with the red hair and the gentle expression in her blue eyes. She had looked at him with a kind of interest that was different from Swinton and Beckton and the rest.

Kathryn Kelley. Kelley with an extra *e* before the *y*, she had told him. She was of no importance to his mission. He should wipe her from his mind.

But his pace faltered as details bombarded him. Hair of flame. Blue eyes like still water. The rounded curve of breasts and hips. The hem of her skirt where it brushed the tops of her knees. The images licked at his nerve endings like the fire of her hair.

Somewhere…somewhere he had seen her before. In a dream. It couldn't be in real life.

His hands clenched into fists as he forced the distracting visual images from his mind. Immediately they were replaced by words. His words to her. Her words to him. Every detail of the brief conversation was branded into his mind.

She had talked with a soft voice, but she could hurt him—worse than the others.

She had made him feel a strange light-headedness. It came again, and he almost stumbled. With renewed concentration, he got the rhythm back and managed not to dwell on her for a full thirty seconds. When she tiptoed back into his mind, he reminded himself sternly that she was not part of his world. He would never see her again. So he could stop thinking about her.

But she stayed with him. She had stirred up something inside him, something that had been buried deep. Like the memory of a scent that would sometimes tickle the back of his throat, then drift out of reach. Or the music that rose to the surface of his mind the way mist rose from a pond in the woods and swirled in thick currents. He had never heard that music in real life. It was nothing like the classic rock Beckton played on the radio. Or the country-and-western songs some of the men liked. Yet it must come from somewhere.

His feet assaulted the blacktop as he picked up the pace in time to the music in his head. The familiar rhythm helped soothe him, and he forced his mind to more important matters. Logic. His work, Project Sandstorm.

He ran toward that goal. It was burned into him. Everything he did was focused on completing the assignment he had been given. Sandstorm was important. Essential. The reason for his existence. He must carry out the job for which he had been preparing all these months—or he would die trying.

Then it would be over. The drills on hand-to-hand combat. The survival classes. And all the other details that spelled the difference between success and failure.

His instructors, Beckton and Winslow and the rest of them, would not be there. None of the scientists or the lab technicians would travel with him to a country halfway around the world. He would be on his own. He would have to make all the decisions on weapons, logistics, deployment. And he would have to calculate the odds of success, weigh each individual detail—like the number of guards at each entrance to the general's palace.

It seemed as if he had been training for this assignment all his life. It was his destiny. And going over the details brought him a feeling that bordered on serenity. Yet complete peace eluded him.

On a deep, instinctive level he sensed that something important inside his brain had been changed. He didn't understand what had happened, exactly. And he wasn't ready to cope with it. Yet he had learned above all else to accept the world as he found it. And he knew that his feeling of inner harmony had been shaken in those few minutes when he had encountered Kathryn Kelley—when he had looked at her, talked with her.

But there was a balance to the equation. If he had lost something, he had gained something as well—an important component, he realized now, that he had lacked. It was still too unfamiliar for him to name. And he didn't know exactly what had changed or how it would affect his behavior. Yet he sensed, as he put more distance between himself and the woman, that nothing would be the same again.

Chapter Two

There was nothing besides a modest white sign with black letters to set the administrative offices apart from the rest of the buildings, Kathryn thought as McCourt directed her to a visitor's parking space near one of the drab redbrick structures. Like the gatehouse, the entrance was equipped with a metal detector—in case she'd acquired a gun on the drive from the entrance.

"William Emerson's office is the third one on the right," McCourt told her.

She couldn't stop herself from saying, "Thank you for taking such good care of me."

"Just doing my job," he returned crisply.

She immediately regretted the sarcasm. It was a bad idea to start a new job by sniping at other staff members. But the man had been rubbing her wrong at every opportunity.

He stayed in the small lobby, keeping his eye on her as she headed down the dull gray corridor. Not until she opened the door marked Chief of Operations did he abandon the guard duty.

A petite brunette secretary who looked like she could chew nails in an emergency asked her to take a seat. Kathryn sank onto one of the worn leather couches in the anteroom. As the minutes ticked by, she thought about the way she'd been approached for this job. Emerson had called her out of the blue and offered her a lot of money to accept a short-term assignment at Stratford Creek. When she'd initially turned him down, he'd upped the pay to a figure that had made her blink. At the same time, his insistence had stirred a responsive wariness, and she knew she wouldn't be here at all if James Harrison hadn't scared the spit out of her.

Emerson had been so anxious to get her to Western Maryland that she'd expected to be ushered into his office the moment she set foot in the anteroom. In fact, he kept her cooling her heels for a good twenty minutes.

She was paging through a battered copy of *Newsweek* when he finally appeared.

"Dr. Kelley. Bill Emerson," he said, holding out his hand.

She rose, working to hide her annoyance as they shook hands. "Nice to meet you."

"Sorry to keep you waiting," he apologized.

"Not at all." Her first thought was that Emerson and McCourt must have the same barber, since their crew cuts looked identical—although Emerson's was gray instead of sandy blond. He was dressed in a blazer and slacks, but he looked as if he'd be more at home in a military uniform.

He was probably in his late fifties and was only a few inches taller than Kathryn's own five foot seven, she judged. But he appeared taller because he stood with his shoulders thrown back as if expecting a surprise visit from the secretary of defense.

When he ushered her into his office, the plaques and photographs on his wall confirmed the hypothesis that he'd been in the military.

"You've recently left the army?" she asked.

He smiled. "Yes. I'm a retired colonel. But I couldn't stand playing golf and trading war stories at the Army Navy Club. When they asked me to head up this project, I jumped at the chance."

As she scanned the framed citations and plaques, she gathered that he was proud of his achievements. If she were given a chance to study the memorabilia, she could probably reconstruct a good part of his service record, she thought.

Had he been given the Stratford Creek assignment as a reward, or because the project needed a strong hand at the helm, she wondered.

"I'm glad you were able to join us," he said with a satisfied smile. "I've been perusing your record again, and it's very impressive."

"Thank you," she answered, as she sat down in a visitor's chairs.

"We're a little off the beaten track. Did you have any trouble finding us?" Emerson asked, reclaiming his seat behind the desk.

"No, but the security measures here are a bit intimidating."

"They have to be. We're doing highly classified work. Once you get used to us, I'm sure you'll appreciate being a member of the team."

"Actually, I've reserved judgment on taking the assignment until we could meet in person, and you could tell me what I'd be doing," she said in an even voice.

His face registered a flash of anger that he quickly masked. "We've gone to a great deal of trouble to expedite your hiring."

"I appreciate that."

"And I thought your personal situation was an urgent consideration," he added.

"It is," she conceded. "But coming here has raised some questions."

"About...?"

"I'd like to know more about the man McCourt and I met on the road."

''John Doe?'' he asked in a tone that turned the question into a statement.

''News travels fast around here.''

''I had a report from McCourt.''

''Of course,'' she said. So that had been the deferential phone call. She should have known.

''What did you think of him?''

''McCourt?''

''John Doe.''

The question took her by surprise, and she came out with the first impression she'd formed. ''He was very fit.''

Emerson laughed as if enjoying a private joke. ''Hmm. Yes. What else did you observe?''

''Well, he appears to speak English as if he's just learned it,'' she answered, embarrassed to voice one of the more personal observations she'd made.

''You have well-developed powers of observation.''

Another compliment. She should be pleased. Instead the man's intense scrutiny made her feel suffocated.

''He's a convict who has volunteered for a special assignment.''

Kathryn blinked, completely thrown. ''That's hard to believe,'' she murmured.

''Why?''

''I've worked with criminals. He doesn't behave like one.'' If she'd been asked to justify the statement, it would have been difficult to come up with supporting details based on her brief encounter with the man. It was more a feeling than a professional observation.

Luckily, Emerson didn't challenge her, but his tone was emphatic as he continued, ''We've changed him a lot since he arrived. He was serving a life sentence for murder.''

The unexpected words hit her like a blow to the stomach, and she gasped in a startled breath of air.

A little smile played around Emerson's lips. At first she thought he was enjoying her shock. Yet as his gaze slid away from hers, she saw something more disturbing. His eyes gave him away. For some reason, he was telling her a lie. Or he was filtering the truth.

To find out which, she'd have to encourage him to keep talking. "Is that the big secret up here? You're using behavior modification techniques the rest of us haven't discovered yet?"

"No. Our Dr. Swinton is conducting experiments which are on the cutting edge of biological research. We're doing sociobiological engineering using tools unavailable just a few years ago." Warming to the subject, he continued, "We've developed a protocol for the complete rehabilitation of criminals, if you will."

"Complete rehabilitation. That's hard to believe," Kathryn ventured, recalling the many experiments she'd read about. The success rate for preventing recidivism was abysmally low, even with the most ambitious programs—which required strong incentives for offenders to change their view of the world. John Doe didn't seem to be enjoying any special incentives.

Emerson lowered his voice and leaned across the desk as if a hidden microphone from miles down the road could pick up his words. "Dr. Swinton has used a completely new approach. John Doe won't repeat his criminal activity, because we've been able to erase the antisocial memories from his mind."

She goggled. "How?"

"Through intensive drug therapy that interrupts the flow of neurotransmitters and scrubs away previous behavior patterns and learned responses."

He was apparently unaware of the effect he was having on Kathryn as she tried to imagine someone who would want to do that to a human being.

"Are you telling me you've given him mind-altering drugs that wiped out his memory?" she managed.

"That's right. Which is why we need to have you work with him."

"Me?" she asked in a choked voice.

"Yes." He shook his head. "Sorry. I forgot you haven't been given the whole picture. During phase two of our project, he absorbed a great deal of technical information and acquired impressive physical expertise. But his social development is lagging way behind. Your assignment will be to bring him up to speed on people skills."

She was trying to come to grips with that when a loud buzzer sounded in the room, making her jump.

"What now?" he muttered in annoyance, reaching for the telephone.

She couldn't hear any of the conversation on the other end of the line, but she could tell from the rush of words and the thunderous response on Emerson's face that the news was bad.

"When?" he asked. Then, "How in the hell did that happen?"

He listened to the answer, then cursed. "Well, try not to damage him. I'll be right there." Standing, he moved around the desk. "John Doe assaulted one of his instructors and is tearing the gym apart."

"He couldn't have," Kathryn protested, wanting to be right.

Emerson gave her a dark look. "Dammit to hell. I thought this time we'd done it."

"I'm good in a crisis situation," she answered. "Let me see what I can do." Without waiting for an answer, she hurried after Emerson out the door and down the hall, moving in double time to keep up.

A government-issue brown Chevrolet was parked outside the back door.

His lips pressed grimly together, Emerson climbed behind the wheel. Kathryn slid into the passenger seat. He didn't wait for her to fasten her seat belt before shooting backwards out of the space, reversing with a screech of tires, and barreling down the hill.

She braced her hand against the dashboard, trying to keep from being flung about by the wild motion of the car and at the same time trying to understand everything she'd just heard. All her instincts screamed that Emerson's claims about John Doe's background were untrue. He couldn't be a criminal. And they couldn't have cold-bloodedly wiped out his memories. Yet she had no other information to go on. And no explanation for why he'd gone berserk.

As she struggled to keep her seat, an ambulance with siren blaring passed them in the opposite direction. She'd almost worked out a system for staying in place when they skidded to a stop in front of a large building with a curved roof.

Emerson jumped out of the car and took the cracked sidewalk at a run. Kathryn trotted after him.

A small crowd of men was grouped around the door. Some were cut from the same mold as McCourt. Others wore lab coats. And a sizable contingent were dressed in blue uniforms, like a private security force. Most of them eyed her curiously as she came to a halt behind the chief of operations.

"Where is he?" Emerson demanded.

"In the locker room." The answer came from a broad-shouldered black man who stepped forward. His name tag identified him as Winslow.

Emerson glanced around at the crowd. "Get back to your duties," he said in a voice that demanded compliance.

The group immediately began to disperse.

"Inside," he said to Winslow.

Deciding she was included in the terse invitation, Kathryn followed them into a small lobby.

"Let's have it," Emerson demanded after pushing the door shut.

Winslow stood with his arms stiffly at his sides. "He

was late from his run. Beckton was angry because he'd been waiting for the hand-to-hand combat session. He shoved him around a little bit the way he does when he's riled up."

"And then what?" Emerson demanded.

"Doe said he was given an extra two miles by McCourt. Beckton told him to shut up and punched him on the arm. Doe got this strange look on his face and turned and socked Beckton in the gut. Beckton went down. He got up cursing and went in low, but Doe kept at him. A couple of guys dived in and tried to pull him off. He decked them and retreated into the locker room. We were able to pull Beckton out. He was unconscious when they took him away."

"What happened today that was different from past sessions?" Emerson demanded.

Winslow looked flustered. "Nothing, sir. Beckton's been rough with him before."

"Has anyone tried to get Doe out of the locker room?" Emerson asked.

"No, sir. We were waiting for your direct orders. We have Reid standing by with a tazzer. Or we can use the tranq gun. I assume you don't want to terminate the subject," Winslow added in a low voice.

Kathryn felt the blood freeze in her veins. They were discussing the man she'd met as if he were a dangerous animal that had escaped from a zoo—or a homicidal maniac.

"Certainly not!" Emerson shot back. "We've gotten further with him than any of the others."

"Let me talk to him," she said.

The men's heads snapped toward her.

"I don't think that would be such a good idea, ma'am," Winslow said.

"I'm Dr. Kathryn Kelley," she answered. "I was hired to work with Doe."

"*You're* Dr. Kelley?" he asked, and she got the impression he'd been expecting her to be ten feet tall and built like a Sherman tank.

She squared her shoulders. "I believe I'm up to the job."

Emerson nodded. "She and McCourt encountered Doe on his run. McCourt said they had quite a conversation—for Doe. She seemed to click with him."

Winslow looked from her to Emerson and back again. "What the hell did you say to him?"

"I—" She stopped, shrugged. "Not much. I asked his name. He said I was different from the other people here." She related a few more lines of the conversation, knowing she hadn't conveyed the flavor of the experience. Too much of it had been on a nonverbal level.

Was it possible she had anything to do with his aberrant behavior? Maybe. Or maybe it was simply a coincidence. Before Winslow could say anything else, or she could change her mind, she pulled open the door behind him and stepped into a large room with a wooden floor, a basketball hoop, and a track marked off around the perimeter.

"Come back, you damn little fool," he called.

Emerson said nothing. He was a pragmatist, and he was probably thinking that he didn't have anything to lose by letting his new recruit try her luck. If she got herself killed, he could hire somebody else.

She looked around at the gym, searching for signs of a madman on a rampage. The indications were minimal. A clipboard lay on the floor with the pages ruffled. A few feet away was a service revolver and ballpoint pen with a crushed barrel.

Still, as her gaze zeroed in on some red droplets spattering the floor, she knew she was viewing the evidence of the fight. Was she out of her mind to be in here?

Slowly she turned and found that Emerson had followed her into the gym. "Don't let anybody else come in unless I call for assistance," she said in a firm voice.

"Do we have a live microphone in there?" he asked Winslow through the partially opened door.

"It's shorted out."

"Damn."

She was only wasting time, she told herself as her gaze swept the room. At the far end was an exit to the outside of the building. Through the glass she could see several of the men in blue uniforms standing guard. So presumably Doe hadn't escaped.

Trying to ignore the pulse pounding in her temple, she marched to the door on her right, pulled it open, and found herself facing an ordinary dressing room, about fourteen feet square. Gray metal lockers lined two of the walls, and wooden benches were positioned in front of them. The air smelled like damp towels and male bodies, but the room was empty. The only exit was an archway at the back from which she saw steam billowing and heard the sound of running water.

It appeared that John Doe had beaten one man unconscious and decked several others—and now he was calmly taking a shower.

Before she could change her mind, she stepped into the locker room and felt the door swing shut behind her. Seconds later, she heard the water stop. God, what was she doing? she suddenly wondered, glancing from the shower room to closed the door and back again. Coming in here alone might be the most dangerous thing she'd ever done.

She wanted to bolt from the room. But she remembered the face of the man on the road. She'd seen a bleakness behind his eyes that had wrenched at her heart. No wonder, when you considered the implications of Emerson and Winslow's callous conversation.

Instead of running away, she crossed the tile floor on unsteady legs and dropped quickly onto one of the benches.

There was no noise from inside the shower room besides

the steady dripping of water. And she could see nothing beyond the billowing steam.

"Hello?" she called.

No answer.

"Hello. It's Kathryn Kelley. Do you remember me? We met while you were on your run. I'm in the locker room."

She sat staring into the mist, wondering if he had heard. Or if he even remembered her, for that matter, she thought with a jolt. If they'd been feeding him mind-altering drugs, there was no telling what they'd done to him.

After several seconds she saw a form moving indistinctly in the vapor. A tall, man-shaped form. Moving closer... moving slowly on feet that were silent as a cat. Then he stepped through the doorway and into the locker room, and she couldn't hold back a gasp. Except for a towel draped across his shoulders, he was as naked as the day he was born.

She saw her own feeling of shock mirrored on his face as he came to an abrupt halt, staring at her with a mixture of recognition and astonishment. Well, he remembered her, all right. Apparently their meeting had been as unique for him as it had been for her.

The disbelief vanished as he continued to regard her, standing comfortably with his feet several inches apart. He was tall and intimidating, towering over her where she huddled on the bench. Droplets of water clung to his skin. His dark hair was wet, making it look almost black.

"You were with McCourt," he said, his features filling with a roiling mixture of emotions before he got control of them.

She struggled to keep her posture relaxed as she looked up at him. He had been compelling in running shorts and a T-shirt. Naked he reminded her of Michelangelo's David. And he stood with the same unconscious nobility, as if nudity were the norm. His shoulders were broad, his hips lean, his stomach flat, and his sex was proportioned to inspire some very erotic fantasies.

But this was no time for fantasies or recklessness. One wrong move and she could be in serious trouble.

She swallowed hard, resisting the impulse to put more space between them. Dragging her eyes upward, she saw a narrow slash along his ribs that looked like a recent knife wound. There were other injuries to his olive-colored flesh, all of which appeared to have been inflicted within the past few months, judging from their color. He'd taken a lot of physical punishment, and the knowledge made her throat tighten.

She wasn't sure what she expected him to say. When he spoke, his words were a shock. "Why are you sad?" he asked, picking up on the emotion she had neglected to hide. She knew then, that whatever else he was, he was very good at reading people.

Her gaze moved higher still and collided with his dark, almost black eyes. They held a kind of aching vulnerability that made her fingers curl around the edge of the bench. "I—I was thinking about how you got all those injuries."

"Fighting. Or sometimes they hit me," he said, his voice even, as if his words were of no importance.

She winced. "Like Beckton?"

He nodded gravely.

"This time he made you angry?"

The naked man didn't answer. But she could tell he was considering the question as his gaze turned inward.

Seconds ticked by. Her mind raced as she remembered what Emerson had said about him. She didn't want to accept the claim that he was a criminal. But she could believe the parts about his memories having been stolen. His present behavior was enough to convince her that he lacked a basic understanding of the social interactions of Western society. Either that, or he was a master at faking total unconcern for his state of undress.

While it might be natural for him to be conducting an extended conversation in his birthday suit, it was hardly the norm for her.

"You have to put some clothes on," she said, watching his face. It was as innocent as a child's.

"Why?"

"It's not polite to be naked in front of a woman."

She watched as he moved the towel briskly across his shoulders, then down his lean but muscular body. When she realized she was still staring, she pivoted her body in the other direction.

It dawned on her that she'd just turned her back on someone who had sent a man to the hospital a short time ago. She should be afraid, but she didn't brace for an attack.

Behind her, the locker door opened. She heard the sound of the towel, then the rustling of clothing. When she turned back, he had pulled on a pair of jeans. His chest was still bare, and he was rubbing the towel vigorously across his head. Then he ran his hands through the long strands of his hair, combing them back from his face before reaching inside the locker for a dark green knit shirt and pulling it over his head.

As he sat down to pull on socks and running shoes, she framed and rejected several questions.

Again, he took the initiative from her. "The men are afraid to come in here. Yet you are small and—" he stopped and searched for the right word "—defenseless, and you found the courage."

"It didn't take so much courage."

He looked up in the act of tying his shoe. "You are not telling me the truth."

She was shocked at the bluntness of his observation.

"Okay. I was afraid at first. Then I knew you wouldn't hurt me."

"How?"

"Your eyes," she said.

He narrowed them, making his expression harder. She wasn't fooled by the feigned look of aggression.

"I'm not afraid of you. But I'm afraid of what Mr. Emerson might do to you if he doesn't hear from me soon. I'm going to open the door and tell him I'm all right. Okay?"

Seconds ticked by before he nodded.

She crossed to the door and pulled it open. Emerson and Winslow were where she'd left them—on the far side of the gym. "We're fine in here," she called out.

"Bring him out," Emerson ordered.

"Not yet."

"Bring him out, or we're coming in."

"Give me a few minutes to talk to him." She closed the door firmly and turned to find John Doe watching her intently.

"Why did you come here?" he asked.

"I want to help you."

He tipped his head to one side, examining her from a slightly different angle. "Nobody wants to help me," he said in a flat voice. "They want to train me, like an animal who can do tricks. I have many tricks."

The harsh words and the level tone sent a great wave of anguish crashing over her. Her face contorted, and unconsciously, she reached out a hand toward him. "I want to be your friend," she said, realizing that it wasn't just a ploy to get him to trust her. It was the truth. If anyone had ever needed a friend, it was this man.

He searched her eyes, slipped one hand into his pocket and said nothing more. His posture, his face told her that he wasn't prepared to believe her.

She asked herself briefly why she cared. Or why she desperately needed to prove the truth of her words. She had no answers, except that she wanted to make contact with him as one human being who takes responsibility for another. Going on blind instinct, she stood and crossed the room. Warily he watched her progress, but she didn't stop until she was standing about a foot away. Reaching out, she touched his forearm. She felt the muscles under the fabric of his shirt quiver, otherwise he stood very still, like an animal sniffing the air for danger.

She moved her hand, the barest caress and heard him draw in a deep breath.

"That feels good," he said, and she heard the wonder in his voice. It was like a little boy on Christmas morning finding the floor under the tree unexpectedly piled with presents. Yet it had taken only the touch of her hand on his arm to elicit the response.

She felt a strange fluttering around her heart. At that moment she was achingly convinced that he had no recent memory of any gentle touch. It was the strongest proof yet that Bill Emerson wasn't lying about his past history. If it was true, though, the implications were staggering. Was this really a man without memories of human interaction— good or bad?

God, what would that be like? Maybe a little like having amnesia.

If she stopped to examine the logic of the situation, she was lost. This encounter was like nothing she had ever experienced in her life. He was like no one she had ever met. They could have been two people from different galaxies making first contact. Two people trying to find common ground that would let them understand each other.

"Why do they call you John Doe?" she asked in a low voice.

It was a simple question, but more seconds ticked by while he thought about the answer. Finally he shrugged.

"If you could pick a name, what would it be?"

He considered her question. "Hunter," he finally said.

"Why Hunter?"

"That is what I am."

She didn't know him well enough to follow his reasoning, but she nodded. "I like that name."

"Then I will tell them I am Hunter."

"Yes." She liked the way he said it, his tone clear and decisive. "You chose it yourself."

He nodded, a look of pride on his face. It brought a subtle change to his features

Such a little thing, she thought with a surge of wonder. A name. Yet it made an enormous difference to him. As she gazed at him, she felt an invisible net tightening around her, pulling her toward this man who needed her more than anybody had ever needed her before. It was empowering, yet frightening. She sensed that he had let her past a barrier no other person had crossed. He was so open to her. Vulnerable. She could hurt him badly if she didn't handle things in the right way.

He watched her eyes intently as he lifted his hand and very gently ran his thumb over her cheek, down to her lips. The pad of his thumb was rough.

"Your skin is soft," he said in a barely audible voice. "I touched a yellow flower in the field once. You are soft— like the petals."

The way he said it made a shiver go through her. All she could do was nod. The emotional turmoil of the past few days had been staggering. She had come to Stratford Creek because she thought she'd be safe—that she could stop worrying about being stalked. But nothing that had happened so far had been what she expected. She hadn't met anyone here who made her feel safe. Except, oddly enough, a man who was supposed to be a criminal.

A sense of unsteadiness, of confusion, made her heart beat faster. The effort of holding herself together was suddenly too much. Without conscious thought she let her head drift to his broad shoulder. It was solid and strong. Closing her eyes, she allowed her mind to conjure a little fantasy.

If she delivered herself into this man's hands, he would shield her from harm.

The notion was deeply appealing, and she sighed. So did he.

"Where did we meet before?" he asked.

"On the road."

"Before that. I do not know when it was. All I know is that it is important to remember," he continued in an urgent voice. "More important than the music. Or the other things."

"What other things?" She raised her head and stared at him.

He tugged on his left earlobe the way he had done before, thinking. "The things that come to me. A color. Or a sound. A smell. The sunset over the desert at night. They flit into my mind like a moth. Then they escape into the darkness."

"You remember things?" she asked, suddenly hoping for proof that Emerson had been lying.

"I...do not know for sure. What is the difference between memories and wishing?"

She had no answer, for she knew that it was perfectly possible, under the right circumstances, for people to remember things that hadn't happened. But the mixture of uncertainty and longing on his face tore at her, and she raised her hand to his cheek. For a long moment, neither of them moved, then he turned his head so that his lips brushed her fingers, so lightly she wondered if she imagined it.

"Another thing I remember...the touch of soft flesh against my flesh. Or perhaps I want to think it is true," he said wistfully.

His voice was husky with emotion she suspected had been bottled up inside him for a long time. She wanted to turn and gather him to her. Then she remembered that Emerson and a squad of security men were waiting outside.

Straightening, she cleared her throat. Although it wasn't easy to make herself pull back, she took a small step away from him. "I told Mr. Emerson I'd find out about what happened with Beckton," she said.

His expression hardened. "He asked why I was late. I told him. He said I was lying, and he punched me. I do not lie."

She tried to keep her voice neutral. "He hit you before, and you didn't hurt him. Why was this time different?"

"It just was."

"Why?"

His brows knit. Seconds ticked by. "You," he finally said. "Seeing you. And talking."

"I don't understand. What does it have to do with me?"

"You made me want to be different," he said, then looked startled by the revelation.

"What do you mean?" she persisted in a shaky voice.

"I—" Before he could finish the sentence, the sound of running feet echoed through the gym.

Hunter's gaze shot from her to the door through which she'd entered. He gave her a look that was equal parts hurt and anger. Then his face went blank. Whirling, he crouched in a defensive stance, just as the door opened and a swarm of men wearing riot gear poured into the locker room.

Chapter Three

Kathryn screamed as the riot squad swarmed over Hunter like predators fighting over fresh meat. With remarkable strength, he was able to defend himself with several well-placed martial-arts moves, but there were six of them and only one of him. She saw them landing blow after blow, then, as if on an unspoken signal, a man in the back calmly lifted a gun with a needle-shaped barrel and fired into Hunter's shoulder.

Even as her mind registered that it must be a tranquilizer gun, an anguished gasp tore from her lips.

She saw consciousness slipping from him, but he fought to stay awake. Raising his head, he scanned the room for something. He was looking for her, she realized with a start as his dark gaze cleared for a moment, boring into her with the force of a drill bit gouging through solid rock. Anger blazed in the depths of his eyes like cold fire. Suddenly she was thankful that four men were restraining him.

"You...tricked...me," he flung at her, fighting to get the words out as the dart did its insidious work.

"No!"

"You came here...with soft words...so they could..." The effort to speak sapped the last of his strength, and his body sagged.

"No," she repeated, shaking her head violently, still protesting her innocence even as he lost the effort to keep his eyes open.

The four men hanging on to him were left supporting his dead weight. Even as he slipped toward the floor, the man with the gun uttered a vile curse.

"Get him out of here, Reid," Emerson ordered.

"Where should we put him?" the man asked. "In a cell?"

"In his bedroom," Kathryn interjected.

Emerson turned in her direction, his expression indicating he'd forgotten she was on the scene.

"Are you afraid of an unconscious man?" she asked in as detached a voice as she could manage.

"He'll come around in a couple of hours," Reid said. "Then we'll have a mess on our hands."

"If you're afraid to deal with the consequences, I can be there to manage him," she answered, deliberately trying to use a word they would respect. "In fact, I was managing him very well until you came bursting into the room."

The men ignored her, waiting for orders from Emerson. "Take him to his quarters," he said.

"And don't hit him again," Kathryn added. "That's counterproductive."

"He needs to be knocked upside the head," Reid growled.

"You've already done enough of that."

"We weren't having any trouble with him until you showed up," a familiar voice said from the doorway.

She turned and saw Chip McCourt watching her with interest.

"No trouble?" she asked, her voice edged with sarcasm. "Then why did you say he'd beat me up if I got close to him?"

The man's face darkened, and she realized her jangled nerves had resulted in another tactical error.

"We haven't had an incident for a while," he mumbled. "But you obviously triggered regressive behavior."

"Maybe it was more mature behavior—in some private context of his own," she countered.

"Oh, come on!"

"I'll be better equipped to make judgments when I'm up to speed on his previous history," she said, retreating into her role as newly hired psychologist. "Perhaps we should have a strategy session before he wakes up. Those who are working with him can fill me in on what I need to know, so I won't make any mistakes."

McCourt's expression told her he thought she'd already made plenty of mistakes.

"That's an excellent idea," Emerson agreed. He turned to McCourt. "Be in my office in half an hour. You and the rest of the senior staff. Winslow, Kolb, Swinton." He paused for a moment. "And Anderson."

"Yes, sir." McCourt wheeled and left the room.

Emerson strode back into the gym.

Kathryn followed him to the car, still haunted by the mixture of anger and anguish in Hunter's eyes—and by the cryptic statement he'd made just before the security men had grabbed him.

He'd told her the two of them had met before. But he was too striking, too remarkable for her to have forgotten him. It made more sense to assume that he had dredged up a half-buried memory and inserted her into it as part of a defense mechanism to cope with a situation any sane person would find untenable. Yet even as she struggled for an explanation, she felt a kind of truth to his words deep inside herself, as sure as the pounding of her heart and the blood rushing through her veins. Perhaps they hadn't laid eyes on each other before today, but something remarkable had happened between them.

She sensed he'd told her things—private things—he had never shared with anyone else. He would have told her more, except that the cavalry had charged into the room, and he thought she'd abused his trust. Unfortunately, there was a grain of truth to his assumption. The chief of operations had been using her to make Hunter relax his defenses—so he could bring in the riot troops.

The car started, and she swung her head toward the window, feigning a deep interest in the redbrick buildings when what she really wanted to do was round on Emerson and shout out her outrage and frustration. Instead, she kept her lips pressed together. No more unavoidable errors, she warned herself. No emotional outbursts. She had to stay cool and figure out how to work within the system that had been established here if she was going to help Hunter. And she was going to help him, she silently promised herself, because in her professional career, she'd never seen anything that disturbed her as much as what they'd just done to him.

Was he really being subjected to cruel and unusual punishment as part of an official U.S. Government project? It was hard to believe, yet she had to assume from her own observations that it was true. What if she could gather enough information to write up a report that would close down Stratford Creek? Though the plan had appeal, it would be risky—both to herself and Hunter, she suspected.

She worried her lower lip between her teeth, acknowledging the all too familiar symptoms in herself. She was getting involved again—opening herself to the depths of someone else's pain. But this time was different, she realized. It was stronger, sharper, suffused with a sense of urgency she'd never felt before. She had never met a man quite like Hunter and never been affected on quite such a personal level.

Bill Emerson's voice pierced her thoughts.

"You've been through quite an ordeal," he said, and she realized that as he drove he'd been covertly observing the play of emotions on her face.

"I'm fine," she lied, clamping down on the need to press a hand to her temple, which had begun to throb.

"Well, I'm impressed with the way you came in here cold and figured out what needed to be done. I was worried we might damage him."

The casually delivered comment made her lower her hand so that he wouldn't see it tremble. "Damage," she repeated. "You sound like you're referring to a piece of equipment."

"Yes. Sorry. Habits die hard." He paused for a fraction of a second. "We've thought of John Doe as a test subject for so long that it's difficult to shift our attitudes."

"Perhaps it would help if you told me what he's being trained to do," she said in as nonconfrontational a voice as she could manage.

"Yes, I was about to fill you in on some pertinent background when we were so rudely interrupted. Our subject has volunteered for a dangerous mission in a foreign country. He has to go in by himself, maybe set up a temporary base of operations, which means he's got to function in a public setting without drawing suspicion to himself. In other words, he needs a crash course in acceptable social behavior. That's where your expertise will be needed."

Several pointed observations flitted through Kathryn's mind. The first was that Hunter was backward socially because he was living with a bunch of jerks. The second was that it was a bit unfair to be undertaking a dangerous assignment when you couldn't remember having volunteered. All she said was, "What kind of mission?"

"You don't need to know any more than I've told you." Emerson answered crisply. "You just have to make sure he's ready to go."

The way he said it made her blood run cold. But she only gave him a little nod of acknowledgment.

Emerson pulled into the same parking slot in back of the administration building. However, instead of taking her to his office, he showed her into an adjoining conference room.

"Take a few minutes to relax before the meeting starts," he advised before leaving her alone.

She didn't have any problem following his advice. The moment he closed the door behind her, she slumped in one of the seats around the conference table. She'd only gotten a few moments of blessed repose when a disturbing thought drifted into her mind. Emerson had mentioned that the surveillance equipment in the locker room was broken. What if he had a recording system in here? Sitting up, she looked around, seeing nothing as obvious as a camera. Maybe it was hidden behind a picture—like in Orwell's *1984,* she thought with a grim little twinge as she inspected a landscape on the opposite wall. Well, she'd have to learn to adapt to the conditions here, she told herself, and knew she'd made the decision to stay.

Minutes later, the brunette secretary bustled into the room with a tray of sandwiches and muffins and a pot of coffee.

Kathryn tried to eat, but an image of Hunter being dragged away by the security team flashed into her mind. Dropping her sandwich on the paper plate in front of her, she rose from her seat, seized with the irrational notion that if she could make physical contact with him—grasp his hand or something—she could somehow make him understand that she'd hadn't tricked him. But she didn't even know where to find him, she conceded as she sank back into her chair. Even if she did, she'd only be demonstrating an unprofessional personal involvement with the Stratford Creek research subject. Not a smart move, under the circumstances.

At that moment, the door opened and Winslow strode in. After several seconds' hesitation, he gave her a curt nod and took a seat across the table—where he could keep an eye on her? Or did he want to make it clear they weren't allies?

"How is he?" she couldn't stop herself from asking.

"Sleeping. Dr. Kolb is checking him out."

At least that was something. Before she could ask any more questions, McCourt arrived. To her surprise, he turned out to be the assistant chief of security. What was he, the boy wonder?

Other men followed, each introducing himself and briefly filling her in on his job. Sam Winslow worked under Jerome Beckton, the chief of training. Doug Granger, who looked like a college wrestling champion, with bulging muscles and a ruddy complexion, was also on the training staff. As Emerson had already mentioned, Dr. Swinton was chief of research. Dr. Kolb, the facility's physician, a small man with a pale complexion and a deeply lined face, came hurrying in last.

Like Emerson, everyone was dressed in civilian clothing. But as she studied the men he'd referred to as the senior staff, she noted that they all projected a military bearing, except for the tall, balding Dr. Swinton. She pegged him as an academic type when she spotted his white socks and plastic pocket protector stuffed full of ballpoint pens. Of the men in the room, he looked the most uncomfortable in her presence. Maybe he was sensing her antipathy to his line of research.

Of the group, she found Dr. Kolb the most unsettling. His bloodshot eyes kept swinging in her direction when he thought she wasn't looking, as if he had a special interest in her, but didn't want her to know.

Emerson came in late, poured himself a cup of coffee and snagged a ham sandwich before taking the place at the head of the table. "Where's Anderson?" he asked.

"My assistant had other duties," Dr. Swinton answered, making it sound as if he didn't feel Anderson was entitled to a place at the table.

Emerson gave a curt nod, then turned abruptly to Dr. Kolb. "How is John Doe?"

The doctor jumped. "Uh…his vital signs are normal, under the circumstances, Colonel."

"Good." Emerson took in the information, then addressed the rest of the men. "I trust you've all met Dr. Kelley, our newly hired psychologist, and that you are all familiar with her excellent background in working with various types of disadvantaged individuals."

There was a chorus of murmurs around the table.

So he'd already circulated her résumé, Kathryn thought. Fast work.

"As you know, Dr. Kelley was added to the Project Sandstorm team as an outgrowth of the monthly progress evaluation being made of our subject—our prison volunteer, John Doe."

Project Sandstorm, she mused. It conjured up a stealth attack in the desert. Was that where he was going?

"When it was determined that our subject's lack of social skills was affecting the timetable of the project," Emerson continued, "various remedial solutions were suggested."

As Kathryn listened to the convoluted speech, she noted that the men around the table were judging her reaction.

Why? Everyone here surely knew they were experimenting with a prison volunteer, so what was the point of emphasizing the man's peculiar status? Unless the chief of operations was subtly reminding them of something else. She found herself conjuring an entirely different scenario. Suppose Emerson was lying about how they'd acquired the services of the man they called John Doe. Suppose their "volunteer" had met with an unfortunate accident that had wiped out his memory, and the Stratford Creek team was capitalizing on the circumstances. Suppose they were using a cover story about a prison volunteer until they thought she was inculcated with their ideas and could be trusted with the truth.

She could well be jumping to unwarranted conclusions. Yet intuition and training both told her that the colonel was twisting the truth again.

Emerson stopped talking, and she realized with a start that he was waiting for a response from her.

Straightening in her chair, she gave him an encouraging smile. "I could see you were having problems with him the moment I met him on the road."

From his place down the table, McCourt nodded, and she knew she'd given the right answer as far as the security man was concerned.

"And I think I've already begun the process of speeding up his socialization," she said, hoping she was still on the right track.

"How?" Winslow demanded.

"By making him feel more accepted. No disrespect intended, but the use of the name John Doe appears to be a deliberate attempt on the part of the staff to distance yourselves from him as an individual. However, he can hardly learn interpersonal relationships without experiencing them," she said, leaning heavily on professional jargon.

"Bingo," Dr. Kolb muttered, and earned a dirty look from the research director.

She noted the not-so-friendly byplay between the two senior staffers as she continued. "In the locker room, I suggested that he give himself a more agreeable name. He chose Hunter. After that, it was easier to communicate with him."

Mixed reactions erupted around the table—from guarded approval on the part of Dr. Kolb to undisguised hostility from Sam Winslow.

"Hunter? Where did that come from?" Dr. Swinton demanded.

She kept her reply conversational. "He says he's a hunter."

The chief of operations laughed appreciatively. "Yes. I guess it fits."

Granger managed to echo his commander's chuckle. McCourt didn't bother to mask his disapproval.

Swinton had taken out one of his ballpoint pens and was twisting it in his fingers, staining them with an occasional slash of blue ink. "I'm not sure socialization should be one of our goals," he said.

Kolb ignored him and asked, "First or last name?"

"First," she answered, hoping she'd read Hunter's intention correctly. "I think it would be beneficial if you can all start using it."

They swung their heads in unison toward Emerson like spectators at a tennis match, and he gave a little nod.

"And I have some other ideas that might help solve your problems," she added, only steps away from improvising. "Most people learn their early socialization during years of interacting in a family setting. Because Hunter doesn't remember a home life, he is seriously handicapped in his ability to interact on a meaningful level."

"He doesn't have to interact on a meaningful level," McCourt growled. "He only has to remember to zip his fly when he comes out of the men's room. And close his mouth when he chews."

Several of the group laughed again. But Swinton pushed back his chair as if to leave. Apparently thinking better of the gesture, he sat down again. "This is ridiculous," he growled. "From the reports I've heard, it appears to me that Dr. Kelley's interactions with the subject have only set his training back."

Kathryn tried to jump in. "I'm sorry if—"

But he plowed on, drowning out the end of her sentence. "I want to see a copy of Dr. Kelley's Omega clearance before she has any additional access to the subject."

"You know that hasn't arrived yet," Emerson answered. "She just got here."

"It's procedure, and I demand that we follow procedure."

For several seconds there was silence in the room. Then Emerson cleared his throat. "I will make sure that Dr. Kelley's paperwork is expedited. But until the proper forms arrive, she will be restricted to alternate duties." Standing, he left the room.

Kathryn sat there stunned, aware that most of the men were coldly judging her reaction again. God, what a callous bunch of bastards. It was clear they didn't give a damn about Hunter's welfare. They were just doing a job. Which one of them had told Swinton so much about her interaction with Hunter? Or did he have some other spy in the training department or on the security force?

"I've been instructed to take your things to guest cottage 3," McCourt said, breaking into her thoughts.

She wanted to tell him she wasn't at Stratford Creek as a guest. Instead, she nodded politely.

CAMERON RANDOLPH TURNED from the window of his home office and walked back to his desk where he shuffled through the papers spread across the blotter. The CEO of a multimillion-dollar electronics firm, he would have preferred to spend his time in the lab, tinkering with inventions. Tonight he was up late, worrying about Kathryn Kelley, who had asked for his advice about taking a job at Stratford Creek.

Hearing footsteps in the hall, he automatically pushed the papers into a pile and slid them into the folder from which they'd emerged.

He looked up guiltily as his wife came in, obviously ready for bed.

"Are you coming up?" Jo asked in a hopeful voice.

"Sorry. I was just finishing."

She gave him a considering look. "If you wanted to keep things secret from your wife, you shouldn't have married a private detective," she said in a mild voice.

He grinned. "I wasn't trying to keep secrets. I was trying not to bother you until tomorrow."

"Bother me about what?" she demanded as she sat down in the comfortable leather chair across from his cluttered desk.

He sighed. "All right. I knew Kathryn was in a hurry to get out of Baltimore after that mess with James Harrison, but I advised her not to accept an assignment at Stratford Creek until I got a full report on the place."

"And now you have the scoop?" she said, gesturing toward the folder.

"Well, I know more."

Jo kept her expression neutral, but he knew she'd been worried about her friend since the attack in the swimming pool.

"None of my Defense Department contacts will talk about the project Bill Emerson is running up there. Either they don't know how he's spending a couple of million dollars, or they won't admit they know."

"A lot of *your* research projects are secret," she pointed out. "That's not necessarily a reason to worry."

He nodded. "Secrecy is one thing. Hiring a bunch of guys I wouldn't want to meet in a dark alley is another."

"What?"

He tapped the folder. "I've gotten a list of the Stratford Creek personnel. Starting with William Emerson, U.S. Army, retired. He's a real superpatriot type, the kind of guy who can justify breaking laws if he thinks he's acting in the interests of national security. If he gets caught, he puts the evidence in the paper shredder."

"That's a bad combination," Jo murmured.

"And the rest of the staff—" He grimaced. "Either

they've got Emerson's attitude, or they've gotten in trouble on other assignments.''

Jo's eyes narrowed as she stared at the sheets of paper spread across his desk. ''How do you know all this?''

''I called in a couple of favors.'' He pulled out the papers and leafed through them. ''One of the worst of the bunch is the also retired Lieutenant Chip McCourt. Emerson rescued him from being court-martialed for assaulting a civilian worker on the base in Wiesbaden, Germany. He was allowed to leave the army with an honorable discharge.''

Jo's eyes widened.

Cam plowed on. ''The doctor, Jules Kolb, would have been sued for medical malpractice if he hadn't been at a V. A. Hospital. The head of training, Jerome Beckton, has been jailed for several bar fights.''

''And you're saving the worst for last,'' Jo guessed.

''Yes. Dr. Avery Swinton. His specialty is biological research. On human subjects. He lost a research grant at Berkeley for illegally experimenting with human fetal tissue. After that he dropped out of sight. Now he's at Stratford Creek—doing God knows what under the shield Emerson has provided.''

''Just great!'' Jo gave her husband a direct look. ''We've got to tell Kathryn what she's dealing with.''

''I put in a call to her a couple of hours ago, but they told me she was unavailable. I could keep trying, but judging from this crowd's past, they're not going to let me get away with saying much over the phone. I need to find a way to get the information about these guys to her. And maybe arrange to pull her out of there if she wants to leave.''

''But how?'' Jo asked.

''That's the sixty-four-thousand-dollar question.''

WIPING A TRICKLE of perspiration off her forehead, Kathryn climbed the steps of guest cottage 3, a stone-and-wood bungalow set about twenty yards back from one of the winding Stratford Creek roads. This was the third time in two days that she'd been out for a jog, ostensibly familiarizing herself with the grounds. But she was also working off her frustration. Since the scene in the locker room, she hadn't been allowed to see Hunter. She didn't even know how he was or what they were doing to him.

So she was reduced to the dim hope that she might run into him. But he wasn't jogging. She told herself it was for security reasons, not because he was suffering any ill effects of the tranquilizers.

A surge of helplessness welled up inside her. She'd had plenty of time to replay the staff meeting over and over in her mind—and also her two previous meetings with Hunter. She always came back to the awful moment when he'd stared at her with such fury.

More than ever, she wanted the chance to show him that somebody cared. But so far she was batting zero. Of course, she'd tried to talk to Emerson about gaining access to Hunter. But the chief of operations had been unavailable to her. And her only assignment over the past two days had been the boring task of flagging personnel with below-average performance appraisals. Talk about wasting a nice fat government salary on diddly-squat, she thought with a snort. If she could only send a message to the *Washington Post*, they'd be up here in a minute to do an exposé on government waste.

Only she wasn't going to be contacting the *Post* anytime soon. One of the disturbing things she'd found out was that new personnel were restricted to Stratford Creek grounds for the first two weeks. And only emergency phone calls were allowed. She bitterly resented the restriction to her freedom, but until she talked to Emerson, there seemed to be nothing she could do to change the situation.

Squaring her shoulders, she marched through the living room of the little house. The place was comfortable but not plush, with two bedrooms in the back, both with standard hotel-room furnishings. She'd taken the one on the right, which had a window overlooking the street and a sliding glass door that opened onto a small cement patio in the weed-choked backyard.

While she showered and dressed, she planned a sort of stealth attack on Dr. Swinton. Pulling out the copy of the Stratford Creek phone directory that had been issued with her information packet, she found the address of the research center. Swinton's office was in room 101. Perhaps if she went over there, she could act interested in the project, flatter him, and get some background information on Hunter.

Of course, she was supposed to be working on the vitally important performance appraisals, she reminded herself. But she'd bet her first month's paycheck that she wouldn't be missed.

There were few cars parked in front of the research center, she noted as she pulled into a prime space near the front door. The lobby was deserted, and she was looking for a directory board when a thin, stoop-shouldered man with wispy brown hair and horn-rimmed glasses approached. Apparently deep in thought, he was carrying a can of soda and a bag of cheese twists.

He almost ran into her, then looked up, startled.

"Sorry—" she apologized. "I was trying to find Dr. Swinton's office."

"He's out of the building at the moment."

She struggled with a surge of disappointment.

"You must be Dr. Kelley. The psychologist," he said. "Sorry I couldn't be at the strategy meeting the other day. I'm Dr. Roger Anderson, the deputy director of research. I'd offer you my hand, but, um—" He held up the soda can.

She nodded her understanding, then switched smoothly

to plan B. "I'm sorry I didn't get to meet you the other day."

"Likewise. I had some things to take care of. Why don't you come down the hall and we can have a chat?"

"Thank you." She followed him to a small office furnished with a government-issue metal desk and swivel chair. The computer beside the desk, however, was a state-of-the-art model.

He set down his food and gestured toward the guest chair. "Do you mind if I drink my soda? I've been here since early in the morning."

"That's fine," she assured him.

He opened the bag of cheese twists and took a bite before asking, "So what can we do for you?"

"I guess you know that I've been prohibited from working with your research subject—Hunter—until my clearance comes through."

"Um, yes. Sorry about that." He lowered his voice. "Dr. Swinton is a stickler for procedure."

The response was better than she had expected. Making a helpless gesture, she said, "I feel like I'm marking time. I'd be very grateful if I could get some background information on the subject, so I'll be up to speed when we start working together."

"Um," Anderson mused, around another mouthful of junk food.

"It would help if I could see the kind of progress he's already made."

Taking a thoughtful swallow of soda, he leaned back in his chair and studied her with blue eyes that held all the charm of a cat watching a goldfinch.

She tried to pretend he wasn't making her nervous.

"Yes, well," he finally said, "I'd have to ask Dr. Swinton's approval to give you written reports. However, there are some videos we've made of selected training sessions. I don't see why you couldn't look at them."

"Thank you," she answered with feeling.

He let his legs thump to the floor and stood. "Come on down to the video room."

She followed him down the hall into a comfortably furnished lounge with a couch and several easy chairs facing a thirty-inch television.

"If you'll sit down, I'll make some selections," he said.

She sat in one of the chairs, watching while he unlocked a metal cabinet crammed with hundreds of videotapes, neatly stacked and labeled. *Quite a collection,* she thought, watching him pick and choose among the offerings.

Finally he closed the door and clicked the lock on the cabinet before setting several boxes on the table in front of her. "I have to get back to work, so just leave these here when you finish."

She heaved a sigh of relief when he left the room. He'd been helpful, but he made her edgy, she thought as she put a tape into the slot.

When she hit the play button, a picture of Hunter flashed onto the screen. He looked as fit and tan as when she'd first encountered him on the road. But that didn't prove anything, she reminded herself. Undoubtedly the video had been made before she met him.

Still, it was impossible not to look carefully for clues to his state of health. Physically, that wasn't hard to determine, since he was wearing a pair of tight-fitting black swimming trunks that gave her a wonderful view of the lithe, well-muscled body she remembered.

As she stared at him, a feeling of pent-up anguish caught her in the solar plexus. "Hunter," she whispered, "I'm sorry."

There was no reply from the video image. But, strangely, the expression on his face told her he doubted her apology.

He turned from the camera, gazed into the turquoise water of a swimming pool, then executed a perfect racing dive and began to swim with a powerful crawl stroke to the other end of the pool.

As a swimmer herself, she could admire his speed and form. And she could also appreciate his stamina. But after ten minutes of watching him do laps, she fast-forwarded the tape.

The next activity was more interesting. There was still no sound, but this time, at least, Hunter was involved in a contact sport—wrestling. His opponent was the solidly built Doug Granger, whose massive body must have outweighed Hunter's by at least fifty pounds. In the first shots, the heavier man seemed to take a kind of childish delight in getting the drop on his less-skilled opponent, using superior knowledge of the sport to slam Hunter onto the mat again and again. Her hands clenched into fists as she saw how much punishment he was taking. Another man might have given up or gotten angry or seized the initiative by biting his opponent's ear. Instead, Hunter stuck to the rules and kept doggedly getting up after each defeat. And she noted with satisfaction that his form and technique were getting better as the match progressed. He was smart, resourceful and well-coordinated. By the end of the session he was claiming most of the victories, and she was cheering him on with a grin and little exclamations of approval.

She looked closely at the two men's faces. Hunter's expression was for the most part neutral, but if she paid careful attention she could tell that he was secretly gratified. Granger, on the other hand, was less successful at hiding his feelings. He was angry. When he started using obviously illegal moves to give himself an edge, she wanted to leap up and pull him off Hunter.

Thankfully, someone else must have noticed what was going on. Granger turned as if in response to a command spoken by an unseen superior. With set lips, he marched off the mat, leaving Hunter standing with his hands on his hips, breathing hard.

The scene cut off, and she eagerly looked for another revealing session. Mostly it was more routine stuff, and she began to think that she'd been had by Anderson. Probably he'd called Emerson to report that he was keeping her busy with the world's most boring home videos. Then the view on the current tape abruptly switched, and she saw Hunter standing at the bottom of a metal pit. He was dressed in slacks and a knit shirt, much like the outfit he had put on in the locker room.

Again, the video was without sound. But from Hunter's shocked reaction, she could see that he'd heard a sudden noise from above—and discovered that something bad was about to happen.

He ducked and covered his head with his hands, and she watched in horror as an ocean of water began to rain down on him.

Her fingers curled around the edge of the chair cushion, dug in as the pit filled. At first there was so much water pouring in that she could barely see anyone. When the flood eased a little, Hunter began to pull himself up a set of rungs fastened to the side of the tank. But he couldn't climb fast enough to stay ahead of the deluge. The water rose to his chest, then higher, and she found she was gasping for breath as waves lapped at his face, then covered his head.

Logically she knew he had gotten out of the death trap. Yet that didn't stop her pulse from pounding and perspiration from drenching her body. She rose from her seat as if she could come to his rescue, then fell back, her knees like straw.

"Hunter, please," she begged. "Pull yourself up. Please."

She saw the top of his dark head. Then he gave a mighty heave and hoisted himself up, hand over hand, staying just ahead of the water. Finally, he flopped out onto a metal deck and lay on his back, panting. Turning his head, he lifted his hand, obviously appealing to someone she couldn't see, someone who might have come to aid him. When no one appeared, she felt hot tears blur her vision.

Her own breath came in ragged gasps as if she was the one who had struggled out of the death trap.

God, what kind of sadist would treat a fellow human being that way? And coldly record it on videotape. Maybe there was some justification for what had happened in the locker room. The security men had been angry and upset. But this was cold-blooded torture.

Rage overpowered her—a pure abiding rage that brought with it an almost physical pain. She wanted to smash something. Smash the television screen that had shown her the dreadful scene. But she was too rational. Instead she sat in the chair, clasping the armrests in a death grip and trying to get her emotions under control.

It took several minutes before she could stanch the tears running down her cheeks as she replayed the scene in her mind, saw again his shocked expression before the water hit him. Nobody had told him what was going to happen. They'd taken him by surprise—and given her a vivid insight into why he found it difficult to trust her or anybody else.

She glanced over her shoulder, almost expecting to find Anderson standing in the doorway watching her with his coldly speculative eyes.

Why had he included this revealing scene with the tapes, she wondered. Had she misread him? Was he alerting her to the kind of inhuman experiments they were doing in this hellhole with the bucolic name of Stratford Creek? Or was he warning her not to interfere? Maybe the surprise viewing had simply been an accident.

With shaky fingers, she pressed the rewind button and waited impatiently until the machine stopped whirring. Ejecting the videotape, she juggled it in her hand. She wanted to remove it as evidence, knew that wasn't an option. The tape would be missed—either by Anderson or someone else. So she ducked into a ladies' room and splashed water on her heated face, trying to make herself look normal again before she left the building.

Chapter Four

Kathryn pictured herself driving straight to the administration building, pushing past Emerson's tough little receptionist, and bursting into his office. But coming at him breathing fire was hardly the way to get what she wanted.

She'd been part of enough bureaucracies to know that it was almost impossible to get anything done unless you worked within the system. But the training center was off limits. Swinton had control over Hunter's records. And she didn't know whether Anderson was a friend or a foe. If she'd had the option, she would have driven through the front gate of Stratford Creek and back to Baltimore, where she could get some aid and comfort from her friends at 43 Light Street.

But that wasn't an option, she reminded herself.

When she reached her car, her eyes widened as she spotted a piece of paper neatly rolled into a tube and stuffed under the door handle. Probably not an advertisement for a new pizza parlor at the local shopping center, she thought as she unwound it free.

MEDICAL CENTER. ONE-FIFTEEN. CARDIOVASCULAR UNIT.
HUNTER WILL BE AVAILABLE TO YOU.

There was no signature and no way of knowing who wanted her to come to the medical facility. Or why. This might be the chance she'd been waiting for, she thought with suppressed excitement. What if she had an ally at Stratford Creek—someone who didn't want to announce his support for her at a staff meeting?

The euphoria faded quickly. It was equally possible that McCourt or maybe Winslow was setting her up to get caught disobeying orders. Or someone could simply be playing mind games with her.

But at least she could give herself a legitimate excuse for being in the wrong place at the wrong time. She'd been putting off surrendering the standard medical forms that she'd been given. Now was the perfect time to turn them in.

Quickly she glanced at her watch. She was going to be late if she didn't hurry.

After picking up the forms at the cottage, she drove to the medical center. As she stepped inside the front door of the building, a nurse looked up. "May I help you?"

"I'm fine," she said, then turned to locate the cardio-vascular unit on the directory. First floor, right wing.

Sailing around the corner, she pushed open the door to the unit and found herself in a waiting area with a desk and three orange plastic chairs. The room was empty, and she felt a surge of disappointment as she decided someone was probably playing games after all.

But she wasn't going to give up yet. Crossing the room, she pushed open an inner door and stepped into a dimly lit hallway. All she could hear as she tiptoed forward was the sound of her pulse pounding in her ears. One door near the end of the hall was open, and she thought she saw the shadow of a tall man standing inside. As she stared at it, she couldn't stop herself from thinking about Chip Mc-Court again, this time with a sardonic grin on his face.

But what if it was Hunter?

Before she could lose her nerve, she crossed the remaining distance and stepped into the little room.

With a sense of relief, she took in the dark hair, broad shoulders, and narrow hips of the man standing a few feet away. Even from the back she recognized Hunter instantly.

Her initial surge of relief gave way almost immediately to gnawing tension in the pit of her stomach. He'd left her in anger. He was supposed to be dangerous. And they were alone again.

Dressed in a gray T-shirt, sweatpants and gym shoes, he was facing the window, gazing toward men on riding mowers cutting the straggly grass. He looked as if he wanted to escape from confinement—run free across the expanse of grass and into the woods beyond.

"Hunter? It's Kathryn," she said with a little tremble in her voice. "Kathryn Kelley."

His back stiffened, but he didn't move.

Before she could stop herself, she closed the door and approached him. The room was small, and she found herself only a few feet from him, angling her gaze upward to compensate for the disparity in their height. "Are you angry?" she asked.

No answer.

"Angry at me?"

The question got more reaction than her previous tries. He turned and stared at her, his features as tight as his knotted muscles. She started to lift her hand toward him but let it fall helplessly back to her side.

"I went out jogging a couple of times, hoping I'd see you," she said, struggling to hold her voice steady.

His guarded look made her think of youngsters who had been abused. He had the same wariness in his eyes—signaling the same reluctance to trust anybody for fear of getting hurt. Well, she'd already figured that out.

"I've been wondering how you were doing, hoping everything was all right."

"Why?" He turned the question into a direct challenge.

"I didn't like what happened the other day. It wasn't what I intended when I came in to talk to you. Truly. And I've been worried that they might have hurt you."

He gave a little shrug that tugged at her insides. This time she couldn't stifle the impulse to reach out and lay a hand gently on his arm. Under her fingers, the muscles flexed. "What did the tranquilizer do to you?" she asked softly.

"My head hurt when I woke up. And my ribs. The ribs were from when they beat me."

She fought for control but found she couldn't prevent her eyes from filling with moisture. She felt a tear begin to run down her cheek.

He closed the distance between them and touched his knuckle to her face, stopping the downward flow of the droplet.

"You are crying," he said gruffly.

"Because I feel so helpless." Reaching up, she wrapped her fingers around his, feeling the warmth of his skin and the slight tremble of his hand as she clung to him. Her hand was trembling too. "I'm sorry about what happened. I didn't know that a security team was coming into the locker room."

He stiffened and pulled away. "Why should I believe that?" His voice was so low she could barely hear.

"Because it's the truth, Hunter." She saw him react to the name and added in a voice as low as his, "I'm not like everybody else around here."

He studied her face intently, his eyes darkening. She wanted to exchange confidences with him—about his life, and hers. Get him to tell her how he felt. Talk again about being friends. Clasp his large hand between her smaller ones.

But there were more important things she had to know—

things he might tell her if she asked. "We may not have much time," she said.

"Time for what?"

"Will you answer some questions?"

He gave no assurances, yet she proceeded as if she had his cooperation. "When William Emerson told me about Project Sandstorm, he said you were a—a convict who volunteered for a dangerous assignment. He claimed they used an experimental technique to—to wipe out the memory of your past life. Is that true?" Her pulse raced as she waited for an answer.

His eyes narrowed. "Colonel Emerson said that to you?"

"Yes."

"I have not heard it."

She kept her gaze steady. "If you aren't a convict, who are you?"

He shrugged.

"You don't remember your family. Your mother? Your father?"

Something flickered in the depths of his dark eyes, then he shook his head. "Things drift into my mind. The memory of picking up a coin. Crumpling a piece of paper in my hand. Smelling the wind coming off the sea. And..." He reached to touch her hair. "There is no one here with hair like yours, yet I keep thinking I remember it. I think I remember you. Stronger than the rest of the things." He stopped abruptly. "But that is not possible."

He had spoken earlier of remembering her, and she wanted to believe in it. Yet her own recollection was no help. "If we know each other, where did we meet?" she tried.

He didn't answer.

"What did we do?"

He shook his head. "I cannot answer your questions. All I know is that remembering you gives me...feelings. Like when a little of the music drifts into my mind."

"What kind of music?"

"With many instruments. Complex. Blending. Trumpets. Cellos. The music swells and dies down."

"A symphony?"

"Maybe."

She watched the play of emotions on his face as he stood very still, staring into space. "Before you came here, the music was the most vivid. But with you, it is even stronger."

She tried to imagine the deprivation of being cut off from her past—of snatching at bits of memory or making them up to fill a black void in her mind. Was he cursed with complete amnesia except for a few sensory memories? Or did he recall basic facts about history and other subjects?

"Who was president before John Kennedy?" she asked.

"Dwight Eisenhower. The first president was George Washington. The second was John Adams. The third—"

"You know all of them?"

"Yes."

Amazed, she came up with a more difficult question. "Can you name the countries on the continent of Africa?"

He began to tick them off, until she stopped him again. She didn't know many of the places he'd named.

She switched from geography to biology to math, and he answered all her questions brilliantly. Then she threw a personal one into the mix.

"Where were you born?" she asked.

He hesitated for several seconds, then shook his head.

"What's the first thing you remember about your life here?"

"Watching Swinton and Anderson in the research center." His face hardened, and he didn't elaborate.

She hated to get into deeper water, yet she wanted to

trigger recollections—and emotional responses. "When was the first time Beckton hit you?"

"He slapped my face on the rifle range. He was angry because I failed a qualification test. But I missed the target because somebody had bent the gunsight."

"Who would do that?"

"Someone who wants to stop Project Sandstorm."

"Who?"

He shrugged.

"How do you know?" she demanded.

"Things happen. Colonel Emerson gets angry and announces new procedures."

"What other things have happened?"

"A man was killed. The chief of security. His name was Fenton."

She drew in a sharp breath. "How was he killed?"

"I heard them talking about it. He fell off a roof. Winslow thought he was pushed. And McCourt took over."

So that was why a guy in his thirties had such an important position, she thought, struggling to take in the implications.

"Do you know anything else about it?"

When he shook his head, she sighed. He might not have any more information about the security chief, but his own life was a different matter. "The incident with the gun? When did it happen?"

"Time…I did not think about time at first," he answered slowly. "I think it was some months ago."

Her mind was starting to overload. She had wanted information about him, about this place. But his simple answers were providing more than she could handle.

Who was he? What was his background? How had he ended up at Stratford Creek? In her mind, she visualized him as he had looked when he first came out of the shower.

He was all lean muscle and sinew, and unblemished skin, except for the recent injuries. If he'd been a criminal before coming here, it didn't show.

"Your face looks strange. What thoughts are in your mind?" he asked.

She felt herself blush. "I was remembering how your body looked after your shower."

"Why does that make your face red?"

"Social conventions," she answered. "It's not exactly polite to think about another person with no clothes on— and admit it to him."

"I think about you that way."

"Oh." She flushed again and fumbled for another topic. "Tell me about your assignment."

He didn't answer.

"What are you supposed to do?" she asked, her hand tightening on his arm.

"I cannot talk about that."

"Why?"

His gaze slid away from hers, and she sensed that he didn't want to tell her the answer.

"You must go," he said suddenly. "You should not be with me. Alone. You will get into trouble."

"How do you know that?"

"The same way I knew about Major Fenton. I hear people talk. I listen to what they say. Granger and Winslow were laughing about your assignment checking personnel records. Winslow called it shoveling chicken guano."

She nodded. Probably they talked in front of him quite a bit without realizing how much he was taking in.

"Dr. Kolb will come back."

"Where is he?"

"He was called away. I was waiting for him. You came instead."

She wondered if someone had sent the doctor a note—like the one she had received.

"Go," Hunter said.

She raised her face toward his. "Do you want me to leave?"

A shadow crossed his eyes. "I made the mistake of wanting something from you before."

The look and the words made her heart clench. In this little room, she had created the illusion of privacy, just as she'd imagined they wouldn't be disturbed in the locker room.

But the same conditions prevailed as the last time they'd talked. Someone could come in at any time. And this time Hunter wouldn't be the only target. This time she'd get a reprimand—or worse—for disobeying Emerson's orders.

In the locker room, she had told Hunter she would help him. With all her heart, she longed to assure him that none of the unspeakable things they'd done to him would ever happen again. More than that, she wanted to tell him that she would help him get his memory back. That he would be whole again. Yet she'd come to realize that she couldn't say any of that. If she gave him assurances, they would be lies. And the worst thing she could do was lie to him.

"If you are my friend, Kathryn Kelley, please go away!" His voice was harsh.

She knew he was right, at least for now. Unable to look into his eyes, she turned and hurried across the little room, feeling his gaze burning into her back all the way to the door.

By the time she had left the building, she had made a decision. She was going to force a confrontation with Emerson. But half a block away, she pulled the car under the shade of a maple tree. It would be stupid to charge half-cocked into Emerson's office without first understanding her goals and thinking clearly about what she wanted to say. More importantly, she had to regain control of her emotions. When she reached into her pocket book for a tissue, she found the medical forms.

Stupid, she thought. Very stupid.

She returned to the medical center, and when the nurse at the front desk looked up inquiringly, she slapped the papers onto the desk. "I forgot these."

Thirty seconds later, she was out of the building again and looking up and down the sidewalk to see if anyone was watching. Luck seemed to be with her. What she wanted was to give Hunter back a normal life. However, she suspected Emerson didn't give a damn about that. He and the rest of the staff thought of Hunter as the subject of an experiment. They were training him for a dangerous assignment, and they wanted her to help make sure he completed it successfully. Somehow she had to make it seem as if her private agenda meshed with her official duties.

And maybe she had an ally, she thought, as she remembered the note. Someone who had been willing to give her the gift of a few minutes alone with Hunter. She considered the senior staff, pondering the possibilities, but could come up with no obvious candidates. Some of them seemed in favor of her working with Hunter. Some had voiced opposition. But she couldn't be absolutely sure which men were revealing their real feelings and which ones were secretly glad she'd been assigned to "shoveling chicken guano." The only thing she knew for sure was that whoever had left the note was afraid to come out into the open.

Which only reinforced the growing realization that both she and Hunter were in a precarious position. Every contact with him made her more sure that the story about his criminal background was a convenient fiction. If she operated on that premise, the logical way to help him was to bring back his buried memories by finding touchstones to his past and using them to trigger remembered responses. And if they'd made it impossible for him to remember his past life, at least teaching him about social norms would help him cope when he finally got out of this place.

The plan had a certain elegance, and she found herself with a genuine smile on her face for the first time since she'd arrived at Stratford Creek.

She took it as a good omen when she stepped into the anteroom to Emerson's office and saw that the tough-as-nails secretary was away from her desk.

"Sir?" she called, as she knocked on his door. "Mr. Emerson, I need to speak to you. And—"

The door flew open, and she found herself facing Chip McCourt.

Their gazes locked, and she thought for a moment that he was going to bar her way. Instead he stepped aside and ushered her into Emerson's office.

"Did you get my message?" the man behind the desk asked.

She came to a jerky stop two feet inside the room. Was Emerson the one who'd left the note on her car? As soon as the idea surfaced, she dismissed it as wishful thinking. If he'd wanted to contact her secretly, he'd hardly be talking about it in front of McCourt.

Without waiting for a reply, the chief of operations waved her toward one of the guest chairs. "I received an updated copy of your clearance this morning." He thumped a folder that sat in the middle of his desk blotter. "We've been trying to track you down so we could discuss your assignment."

"Good," she answered, striving for composure as she lowered herself into the seat. She'd come prepared to do battle. Now she needed to tone down her approach.

"You were supposed to be working on performance appraisals. Where were you?" McCourt asked.

She turned toward him, and made eye contact. "Dropping off my medical forms."

He nodded curtly, and she was sure he was going to check up on her. Thank God she'd remembered to leave the forms.

"The senior staff have been discussing how you might instill some of the social graces in...Hunter," Emerson said. "Dr. Kolb picked up on what you said at the meeting about most individuals learning to interact with other people in a home environment."

Kathryn tried to conceal her surprise. "Dr. Kolb?" she asked.

"He wondered if you'd be willing to take on that role with our subject."

"What role, exactly?" she asked cautiously.

"Providing a homelike atmosphere for him. I've been studying your professional background carefully, and I see you did an internship at an inner-city home for runaways."

"Yes."

"In many ways, Hunter is like an undisciplined teenager. At least in his emotional development. I think you could be very effective with him."

"I hope so," she responded, still trying to figure out where he was headed.

"What if we moved him into the guest cottage where you're already living? You could have access to him before and after the regular training day and when he has a break from other activities. Socialization lessons might fit naturally into that kind of arrangement."

She tried not to smile. Emerson was offering her more than she would have dared to ask for.

"That sounds highly unorthodox, but it might be a very

effective arrangement,'' she managed in a professional tone. ''I'd be able to teach social skills and reinforce them over an extended period.''

''Don't minimize the risk to yourself,'' McCourt interjected. ''We can give you a beeper to sound an alarm if you get into trouble. And we can have men stationed near the house. But we can't guarantee he won't fly off the handle.''

''Hunter won't hurt me,'' she said with conviction. She'd just given him the perfect opportunity to assault her, and he'd acted with a lot more civility than the security forces ''And if guards are looking over our shoulders, we won't make much progress.'' She thought for a moment, remembering the comments about the surveillance system in the locker room being disabled. ''And no microphones either.''

Emerson looked uncomfortable. ''Okay,'' he agreed in a flat voice.

McCourt gave her a wry look, but said nothing.

''Of course, I want to see some quantifiable progress,'' Emerson interjected. ''I want a report from you on my desk after the first week.''

''A week isn't much time,'' she countered.

''I insist on results. Or we try another approach.''

Beat socialization into him? Drown him until he saw things their way? She refrained from asking the sarcastic questions.

She wasn't sure if she'd won a major victory or stepped into a carefully constructed trap, but she allowed herself to be cautiously optimistic as the three of them discussed details. Still, she didn't relax. Perhaps Dr. Kolb had come up with the idea because he expected her to fail and get thrown off the project.

Afterward, when she left the building with McCourt, he

asked, "So are you going to function as his mommy or his wife in this little domestic drama?"

"His sister," she shot back.

"Ah."

"You don't think it's a good plan?"

"It's not my place to make that kind of judgment."

She wanted to say she was glad of that. Instead she tried a friendly, "I'll let you know how things go."

"Your report will make interesting reading."

"I hope so."

Back at the cottage, Kathryn inventoried the kitchen supplies, then drove to the small shopping center on the grounds to buy some groceries. Apparently Kolb had even suggested that she prepare meals for Hunter. Maybe he'd expected her to back down on menial work, but she didn't mind a little cooking.

As she circled the parking lot, she mentally reviewed the meeting in Emerson's office. Really, it was stupefying that he'd allowed her such unrestricted access to Hunter. Either he had enormous confidence in her. Or...

She deliberately shut off the disturbing speculations.

Inside the store, she showed the temporary card she'd been given to the woman checking IDs. Apparently her credentials hadn't been activated in the computer because the gatekeeper wouldn't let her enter.

"I'm afraid you'll have to step into the office," the woman said.

Kathryn tried to keep the annoyance out of her voice. "I'm in a hurry. I was told I could get some groceries here."

"We can't let you through without verification."

"What's your name?" Kathryn asked.

"Miss Collins."

"Well, Miss Collins, why don't you call William Emerson's office. I was just there."

"We don't call the chief of operations about a matter like this," the woman said firmly. "We check with personnel," the woman said firmly.

"Is there somewhere else I can shop?"

"I believe you're temporarily restricted to the facilities here."

She'd pushed that out of her mind. With a sigh of resignation, she took a seat in the small office. Half an hour later, she was impatiently tapping her foot when Miss Collins reappeared, all smiles.

"Sorry to hold you up," she said sweetly. "Go on in."

By the time Kathryn was finally allowed to make her purchases, she was fighting off the paranoid feeling that the delay was deliberate, although she couldn't imagine why.

When she arrived back at the cottage, it was four in the afternoon, yet it looked much later, she thought, as she eyed the dark clouds filling the sky.

Suspecting they were in for a thunderstorm, she quickly carried the groceries into the kitchen. She had just stuck a package of steak into the freezer when she thought she detected a noise from the back of the house. She strained her ears, trying to determine if she'd really heard anything or if her overactive imagination was playing tricks.

At first there was nothing more. Then a new sound drifted toward her, a scuffling noise followed by a loud thump like a body hitting the floor.

Was someone in the house?

She hurried through the dining room and toward the back rooms. It took only seconds to gain the unlit hall, where she was forced to come to a halt as she confronted the three closed doors. She'd left her bedroom door open; now it was shut.

Her hand froze as she heard a guttural exclamation from behind the door. Pulling it open, she saw the figure of a man standing in the middle of the darkened room, swaying on his feet as he faced the open sliding glass door.

Hearing her, he whirled, and she registered that it was him—dressed in the same clothes he'd been wearing earlier—even as he closed the distance between them in a few menacing strides.

She knew, then, that she'd been a fool not to fear him. He had put Beckton in the hospital. Now there was only coldness in his eyes as he looked at *her.*

He reached her before she could run and threw his weight roughly against her shoulder.

"Don't—" she managed as he backed her against the wall. She struck it with a thud that made the breath whoosh out of her lungs.

Chapter Five

In the moments before his hands closed around her flesh, he realized who she was. Stopping the forward motion of his body, he was able to keep from slamming her into the wall with the force he'd intended. Still, he heard the breath hiss painfully out of her lungs.

It was Kathryn Kelley. The woman with the soft voice and the kind eyes that promised too much. The woman who had come into the locker room and made him vulnerable so the security force could grab him.

In the medical center she'd said she was sorry and she'd made him believe her—again. Now here she was for the second time in the same day. And he'd come very close to killing her.

Perhaps his encounters with her were part of some new test, one more dangerous than all the others Swinton's and Beckton's staffs had devised.

Only seconds had passed as his hand shifted over Kathryn Kelley's mouth while he held her in place with the weight of his body against hers. But he had to make a decision quickly, he realized, as his eyes flicked to the sliding glass door.

Two minutes ago an intruder had come through that door. A man with a hood over his face, wearing black clothing and carrying a gun—which was now somewhere on the floor.

How did Kathryn Kelley fit into this particular scenario? Who had sent her? She said she wanted to help him. But it was dangerous to trust the words—or the look in her eyes. Or the vague memories of her from before Stratford Creek.

He could kill her easily, he knew, as he contemplated the slender column of her neck. Beckton and his team had taught him the skills he would need to kill with speed and efficiency—although they hadn't yet put him to the test. Perhaps they wanted to find out if he would do it now. Or perhaps it was part of a different plan. An unofficial plan. Like the time the trail markers had been switched in the woods, and he'd almost tumbled off a cliff.

He didn't know who had devised this scenario. He only knew the thought of killing Kathryn Kelley brought a wave of physical sickness. Was she a danger to him? Systematically he began to search along her body, feeling for the telltale bulge of a gun or the outline of a knife.

He heard her make a strangled sound as his hand paused to explore the rounded swell of a soft breast and the edge of her undergarment where she might have tucked a small weapon.

A routine search. But nothing with her had been routine. Not the things they'd talked about—or the strange surge of unexpected heat that coursed through him as his hands learned her shape. He had thought about her body, imagined it in vivid detail. He had wanted to touch her. Closing his eyes, he inhaled her scent and let it flow through him.

He blinked. What was wrong with him? Every time he encountered this woman, she reached him in strange, unexpected ways. And the images of her in his head—images from before Stratford Creek—grew more tantalizing. More real. He grimaced, torn between hopes and fears he had never known before.

With a jerky motion, he pulled his hips away from hers as his hand moved on, along her ribs, to her waist where he found a rectangle of plastic nestled against soft flesh. An alarm. With a growl, he yanked it free.

"No." She spoke the syllable against the fingers that pressed over her mouth, sending a vivid communication along his nerve endings.

Ignoring her protest and his physical reaction, he tossed the device onto the bed, where she couldn't reach it. Had Emerson issued it, or was she working for someone else?

He made an angry sound. He had told her someone wanted to stop Project Sandstorm. That had been a mistake. Would it also be a mistake to take his hand away from her mouth? Would she scream at the top of her lungs?

As his mind made rapid evaluations, his searching hand began to move again, continued down her body, lingering at the places where a weapon might be concealed and other places, too. Flare of hip, silky skin of thigh, delicate structure of knee. The touch of her flesh scalded his fingertips so that by the time he finished, his heart was pounding and he was struggling to breathe normally.

So was she. Did she feel what he did—the strange combination of weakness and strength that swirled within him when he touched her—or was she only afraid of what he might do to her?

What he or anybody else felt had never been of much concern to him. Tonight, feelings overwhelmed him. All his training urged caution. Yet there was no way of knowing where caution lay.

Kill her. Let her run to whoever had sent her. Or hold her within reach and ask his own questions—the way she had questioned him this afternoon.

He had never felt less sure. The right course of action escaped him, but he knew on some deep, instinctive level that he wanted to keep her close by his side. The scene in the locker room flashed into his mind again. Then her apology in the medical center. No one had ever made excuses to him for their behavior before.

But what did her words really mean? What would she say when he was the one in control?

Before he could change his mind, he dragged her toward the sliding glass doors. When she tried to struggle, he brought his lips close to her ear and growled, "If you do not want to get hurt, be still."

She obeyed at once, although he knew she could simply be waiting for a better opportunity to get away. Or to kill him. They had warned him women could be trained to kill. Perhaps she was only looking for the right opportunity to turn the tables.

Taking the chance, he lifted her over the threshold and carried her into the area behind the house, where tall trees had grown. Beeches, maples and wild cherries made a thick screen, hiding the two of them from view.

The branches were shivering in the wind, and dark clouds blocked out the sun, signaling the approach of a storm. If she screamed, the wind might hide the sound.

As soon as he was certain they were alone, he removed the hand from her mouth, tensing for her reaction.

Her eyes were wide and round as she focused all her attention on him. Her pale skin was as white as the chalk Beckton used on the blackboard. He watched her suck in a ragged breath and let it out slowly. Nervously, her hand went to her hair, pushing it away from her face, then patting it into place.

His breath was almost as uneven as hers as he waited, knowing he was taking the greatest risk of his life.

KATHRYN THOUGHT about running, but she forced herself to remain where she was, standing under the wind-tossed trees, facing the man who had slammed her against the wall, covered her mouth with his hand, searched her intimately. After each of their previous meetings, she'd convinced herself that she understood him—that he was a normal man forced into a diabolical experiment. As she cowered before him now, the criminal theory suddenly made a lot more sense. When she'd come into the bedroom, he had reacted with the instinctive ferocity of a cornered tiger. And she knew from the obdurate look in his eyes that if she made the wrong move, he was still poised for violence.

Yet as she faced him across three feet of dry leaves and the scraggly grass that grew under the trees, she could come up with an equally plausible theory. He had been normal and reasonable until Emerson and Swinton had wiped out his memory. Now he was simply reacting in the way he'd been trained. Unfortunately, that made the situation no less dangerous. She was still his captive, at his mercy.

"Why have you brought me out here?" she asked, trying to keep her tone even as she pressed her fingers against the rough bark of a tree trunk.

"So we can talk. There will be microphones or cameras in the house."

"Emerson promised we would have privacy."

"Do you believe everything he says?"

The only honest answer was, "No."

"He might think he's telling the truth. And someone else could be listening," Hunter suggested.

"Who?"

He answered with his own question. "Are you working with the man who tried to kill me?"

"Somebody tried to kill you? Who? When?"

"A few minutes ago. He came in through the sliding door in the bedroom. He thought I was asleep. He was wrong."

"Is that what I heard?" she managed. "You were fighting him off?"

"Yes. He dropped his gun on the floor. Are you working with him?" he repeated, watching her face carefully.

"No."

His eyes told her he wanted to believe her. They also told her he hadn't made up his mind.

"I wouldn't lie to you, Hunter," she said in as steady a voice as she could manage.

Once again, his face softened for a moment at the use of his name. Then his fierce expression was back in place, still challenging her. "Give me reasons to trust you. Why was I taken to the guest cottage and told to wait in the bedroom for further orders? What are you doing here with me?"

She couldn't hide her shock. "They didn't tell you anything else?"

When he shook his head, she hastened to explain. "Dr. Kolb thought that if you and I spent some time together, I could teach you things you need to know."

"What am I supposed to learn from you? Are you a weapons expert?"

She laughed, feeling a tiny glimmer of relief from her tension. "No. I'm a psychologist."

"Why do you keep coming to me?"

"I—" She swallowed. "I was hired to teach you socialization skills. Things you need to know to get along with other people. We would have started working together sooner, but some of the people here were against it."

He made a snorting sound. "They pretend they are all united, but they all have their own agendas."

She nodded, surprised by his perceptiveness. For a man with no memories, he was functioning on a very sophisticated level.

"You asked me to pick a name. Why do you care about that?" he suddenly asked.

"Everyone has a name. You need the same things other people need."

"Do I? What are those things?" he asked thoughtfully, as if he were considering the concept for the first time.

"People need to feel good about themselves. About their jobs. Their lives. They need to do things that make them happy. They need to love and be loved."

"I am good at my job. I do not need the rest of it," he answered, his tone blunt.

The denial—both the words and the staccato way he delivered them—tore at her. "What have they done to you?" she asked in a strangled voice.

He shrugged. She had come to hate that shrug.

But it wasn't as disturbing as his face, which looked as bleak as it had in the video—when he'd lain beside the water tank, half drowned. He'd reached out for help, and no one had come to him. Not this time. Gently, she laid her hand on his arm.

Around them, the wind roared, and she knew the storm would break any moment.

His muscles flexed, yet he didn't pull away. He'd said he never lied. Maybe not about facts. Yet despite his rough denial, she was utterly convinced that he needed the same things other people needed. She was equally sure he had long ago given up trying to ask for them.

She might have held him and rocked him the way a mother rocks a child. But he wasn't a child. He was a strong, dangerous man, trained in the craft of violence. And she needed to know more about him. Without breaking the physical contact, she went back to another topic he'd avoided earlier.

"Why won't you tell me about your assignment? About Project Sandstorm?"

"I cannot." He dragged in a deep breath and let it out in a rush as he looked at her. "There are questions you should not ask me."

"Why?"

"You said you are my friend. I want—" He stopped abruptly, and she understood that admitting he wanted anything from her was still too big a risk.

The knowledge made her throat ache. It seemed he had secrets, things that he didn't want her to know because he thought she would think less of him. But that was good, she silently added. It meant he wasn't as closed up as he pretended.

She wouldn't ask about his secrets. Not yet. Not until he trusted her enough. "It's not your fault," she whispered. "All the bad things they've done to you."

"It must be," he said in a strangled voice.

"No."

He turned his face away from her, and she sensed that he'd kept himself alive and sane in this place by hiding his doubts and fears, trusting no one. God, what an existence, she thought as she stared at the stiff, unyielding set of his shoulders.

"Don't."

"Don't what?" he asked, without looking at her.

There were no words to express all the things she wanted to tell him. Blindly she reached toward him, holding him close to her as if she could lock the horror of Stratford Creek away.

At first his body was rigid, then, as she ran her hands over the taut muscles of his back, he sighed and relaxed into the shelter of her arms.

She held him for long moments, feeling him let go of the wariness heartbeat by heartbeat. When he spoke, it was in a barely audible voice. "I saw two people like this. Outside, in the woods. A man and a woman holding each other, touching lips. It made me feel…strange to watch. I felt it again when I touched you."

He lifted his face and stared down at her, a deeply intense expression on his face. A millimeter at a time, he lowered his head and brushed his mouth softly, experimentally against hers.

She didn't move, couldn't move. She could only stand there feeling the gentle pressure of his warm lips on hers, enjoying the contact on a level that went beyond the physical. She had told herself that he needed her. It seemed that in this place of evil, she needed him as well.

He raised his face a fraction, looking down at her as if he couldn't believe she was embracing him.

She gave him a little smile.

"He touched her hair," he said, imitating the gesture, his fingers stroking through her tresses as he made a low sound of pleasure. "Your hair looks like fire. But it does not burn. It prickles. Not just on my fingers but other places."

Pull away from him, she told herself. Yet she couldn't let go.

She had taken a job at Stratford Creek because she thought she'd be safe on a secure government installation. Every moment here had added new levels of turmoil to the chaos of her life. And it seemed the only person who had touched her on a human level was this man, whom everyone else treated like an outcast.

His fingers skimmed her face, the column of her neck, gently, so gently. "You are not afraid of me." He said it in wonder.

"Should I be?"

"Yes."

"Why?"

"I could hurt you."

"But you've shown me that you won't," she said with absolute conviction.

His lips came back to hers, the pressure harder, more insistent. There was no finesse to the kiss, only an unschooled urgency that was strangely exciting.

She kissed him back, her own lips parting to capture the taste of him more fully.

She heard him make a rough sound in his throat as his fingertips traced along the line of her neck and over her collarbone.

"Good. That feels good," he said in a thick voice. "Like the memory of you."

Yes, the memory. She still didn't understand how she and this man who had named himself Hunter were tied together. Yet as they stood here touching and kissing, it was hard to doubt there was an unexplained link between them. Perhaps destiny had brought them together.

His lips captured hers again, made a bolder foray that set up little currents along her nerve endings. When the kiss ended, she moved her head against his shoulder. She was drifting, letting things happen, letting her response build because he was right, it felt good.

But when he let his hand drift lower to softly trace the rounded swell of her breast and brush across the hardened tip, her eyes snapped open. She had been lulled into a state of self-indulgence, and she had let this go far beyond the bounds of what was right. "No." The denial came out high and shaky.

He raised his head, his eyes questioning hers.

"We can't do that," she said, still unable to bring her voice under control.

"Why not?" he asked. "It feels good." He searched her face. "You said people should do things that make them feel happy." The word came from his mouth haltingly, as though he were speaking a foreign language.

"Yes. But there are limits—conventions." She felt trapped in a tangle of words.

"You didn't like it?"

She had promised not to lie to him. She wouldn't do it now. And she wouldn't lie to herself. "I liked it," she said in a whisper.

"Yes. I can see it. Your face has a wonderful color to it now. And your eyes are softer."

She felt more blood rush to the surface of her skin.

"It feels bad to stop," he said in a harsh voice. "We should do more."

She shook her head, trying to remember that she was supposed to be in control of this situation. "The man and woman you saw were lovers."

He thought about that for several seconds.

Then a look of comprehension dawned on his face. "They were going to join their bodies? Here?" He reached down and gestured toward the rigid flesh that swelled at the front of his sweatpants.

She nodded, trying not to feel the words in her center. "How do you know about that?"

"The On-Line Encyclopedia."

She made a strangled exclamation.

"And the men talk about sex. They boast about the women they have. I would never talk about you. Never," he added with strong conviction.

"I know."

"In the locker room, you said we were friends. Can friends do it?" he asked.

She shook her head. It was growing dark around them, yet she saw his eyes close and his face contort in disappointment.

How had all this happened so quickly, she wondered, reeling from an onslaught of emotions. He might have no memories of social interaction, but she should have had more sense than to allow such intimacy.

"I must not touch you now," he said before taking a step back.

He looked as if every bone and muscle of his body ached. She might have turned away to cut off her own sense of regret, instead she stared at him, still feeling the imprint of his touch on her body. She had to think, yet thinking had become almost impossible.

She was suddenly aware that the air had grown heavy with the smell of rain. Leaves had begun to fly through the air. Before she could figure out what to say, a crack of lightning pierced the darkness.

"It is not safe here," he said. "Lightning could strike one of the trees. We must go back."

CAMERON RANDOLPH paced to the window, then turned and started back across the room. Jo watched him, sharing his frustration. For the past few days they'd been trying to figure out a way to get a message to Kathryn. So far nothing had panned out.

They had never gotten through to her on the phone. She had answered no letters. And every chatty E-mail message to her old address had been rejected.

In desperation, they'd tried putting a short, coded message inside the label of a bottle of face cream, which they'd mailed to her with a selection of cosmetics she'd supposedly asked Jo to send. The innocent-looking package had been returned—with the contents damaged.

"Did you manage to talk to William Emerson?" Jo asked.

"Bill. He insists on Bill," Cameron replied. "Funny thing, the colonel asked me dozens of penetrating questions about Kathryn's qualifications and her background when he wanted to hire her. Today he spared me about sixty seconds."

"And?"

"He told me she's fitting right in with the research personnel."

"Glad to hear it." Jo pressed her hands against her hips. "Could you get him to tell you what she's doing?"

"No," Cam answered bluntly. He was wishing that he'd told Emerson that Kathryn's work was unsatisfactory when they'd talked the first time.

"Could we sneak into Stratford Creek with an assault team and bust her out of there?" Jo asked.

"Not a good idea. Raiding a top secret U.S. government research facility is an invitation to a hanging—or a media circus of a trial."

"I suppose you're right."

"All we can do is sit tight and wait for her to contact us."

Jo drew in a tight breath. "If she can."

TAKING KATHRYN'S HAND, Hunter tugged her across the backyard.

Although a few drops of rain had already started to fall, she stopped him when they reached the sliding glass door. He had told her the rooms might be bugged. Since she had to assume he was right, they'd better finish their conversation before they went inside.

The wind whipped at her hair, and lightning split the sky again. The storm was moving closer, judging by the almost instant crack of thunder.

Then, as if a sluice gate had opened, the rain began to fall. He looked at her questioningly.

"Wait," she said, grabbing his arm.

He turned his back to the storm, sheltering her between his body and the door. Yet his hands stayed at his sides. She wanted those arms around her, for warmth, for comfort. She was sure he wanted it, too. But she didn't ask him to hold her, because she understood that touching him now was playing with fire.

The water pelted down as she leaned toward him and brought her mouth close to his ear. "Before we go in I have to ask you a question. Can you and I keep secrets together, just the two of us?"

Lightning knifed through the sky. She had to wait through the sound of the thunder before he answered, "The staff give me orders, and I must obey. You are on the staff. If you give me an order, it is the same."

She clenched her fists. The more she heard about what they'd done to him, the more she wondered how she was going to cope with her anger. She didn't want to give him orders, but in this case it appeared to be necessary.

"All right," she said. "I order you to keep the things that have passed between us tonight confidential."

"I can do that."

Again she made herself think about what that meant— from his point of view. "I mean you should not tell anyone about the things we said tonight. Or that you and I are friends. Emerson and Swinton might not like it."

He nodded slowly. "I will keep the things between the two of us private. What we said to each other—and the kissing."

She managed a neutral nod. "Good."

"I do not want to share this with the others." His hand turned upward. "Even…even after they came with the tranquilizer gun, I wanted to believe you were my friend."

She closed her eyes for a moment, unable to speak without a hitch in her voice. Perhaps he didn't know it, but he had just given her what she wanted most—his trust. It took all her willpower not to reach for him again. Instead she took one last breath of the cold night air and stepped through the doorway.

He followed her inside, and when she turned she saw the dark hair plastered to his head and the strong lines of his body through the clinging fabric of his sweat clothes. He had kept her dry, but he was soaked.

"You should take a shower and put on dry clothes," she said.

His lips quirked. She wanted to see him smile, but she contented herself with what he could give.

"What are you thinking?" she asked.

"That I will not walk out of the bathroom naked."

"So I've already taught you something," she said, keeping her tone light.

"Yes. You should shower, too." He paused, thought for a moment. "You can go first."

"I'm all right. You protected me."

"It felt like the right thing to do." He shook his head. "I do not always know the right thing."

She brushed back a lock of wet hair that had fallen across his forehead. "You have good instincts." She wanted to tell him that he might be subconsciously remembering things from his past. Yet she was aware that what she said now might be overheard. She hadn't been hired to stir up his memories.

"What does that mean—good instincts?" he asked.

She drew her hand back. "It means you don't necessarily know in advance, but when the situation presents itself, you do the right thing."

"That sounds dangerous—not knowing in advance." He stopped short, and she wondered if he was thinking about the way he'd reacted when she first came into the room.

"Trust your instincts," she said.

To her surprise, he nodded. Then his face hardened. Pulling away from her, he knelt beside the bed. She watched as he began to search the floor. Reaching far under the bed, he pulled out an automatic pistol and held it up for her to see. The barrel was elongated, and she decided there must be a silencer attached, although she'd never seen one before except in a movie or on TV.

She'd forgotten he'd said his attacker had a gun. Now she reached out a hand to steady herself against the bureau as she wondered what they were going to do with the weapon.

He stood and reached for her free arm, holding her as he brought his lips close to her ear, the way she'd spoken outside. "My instincts tell me something...bad."

She waited, feeling the hold on her arm tighten.

"I thought the man who came into the house wanted to kill me," he whispered. "Perhaps I was mistaken about the target."

She wasn't following him. When she gave him a questioning look, he continued in a low, urgent voice. "In my training, we do scenarios."

Still mystified, she shrugged elaborately.

"Hypothetical situations," he murmured, so low she could barely catch the words and had to lean toward his mouth. "They put me into circumstances where I must respond to danger. Suppose the man who dropped the gun attacked me because he wanted to set up a scenario where he would escape and I would be on guard against attack—and kill the next person who came into the room. You."

Chapter Six

Kathryn felt an involuntary shiver go through her. He'd given her an elaborate theory—perhaps a combination of instinct, logic and recent experience, she thought, with as much detachment as she could muster. She wanted to dismiss the idea as far-fetched. Instead, she absorbed it with a kind of sick awareness. He could be right.

She saw he was watching her, watching her reaction.

"I am sorry," he said in a low voice. "I could be wrong. I should not have said it."

She shook her head. "You did the right thing. I need to understand the situation here."

He gave her a tight nod. After a little hesitation, he slipped his arm around her shoulder and held her to his side. Once again she needed his strength. When she relaxed against him, he touched her hair, and she allowed herself the luxury of closing her eyes.

"You should leave," he said. Again the words were barely audible.

"Leave the house?" she asked.

"Leave Stratford Creek, if they will let you."

Her eyes blinked open. "What?"

"The situation here is—it is not safe for you. I heard McCourt and Winslow talking about you. Using foul words. Beckton came in and told them to shut up. He was afraid someone might hear. They shut up, but they do not like having you interfering. They thought they were doing fine without you.''

She brought her mouth close to his ear. ''I'm not going to leave you.''

He turned his head, his eyes searching hers for confirmation, and she realized at that moment she had made a commitment.

Her lips skimmed his cheek. ''I mean it,'' she whispered.

His arms tightened on her. It was both an awkward and an intimate way to have a conversation. Holding each other close. Moving their heads so that they took turns feeling the other's warm breath against their ears.

''Why?'' he asked.

As she clung to him for support, she tried to think of what to say. ''We are friends. Friends help each other.''

''Yes. I will protect you—if I can.''

Again, he had spoken a simple truth, without censoring his words, and she realized he was making his own commitment.

''Friends,'' he murmured, as if savoring the idea. Yet there was a kind of sadness in his eyes, too. She was vividly aware that his lips were inches from hers, that he was staring at them with suppressed intensity. If she turned, if he turned, her breasts would be pressed against his chest and his mouth would touch hers. They both stood rigid as the moment stretched. Once again she wondered if they were feeling the tug of a mythical past neither of them could remember.

''I wish—'' he said, his voice hoarse.

''What?''

Without answering, he took a step back, breaking the contact.

She needed his warmth. More than that, she desperately needed to continue the discussion. There was so much to say. And so much to find out. But they could neither go out into the pelting rain to talk nor continue like this, because the heat building between them would reach flash point. After taking a little breath, she gave him a steady look, then raised her voice for the benefit of whoever might be listening. "Right now, we're going to get ready for supper."

"Supper? What is the difference between supper and dinner?" he asked, taking his cue from her without missing a beat.

She managed a strained laugh. "It's a subtle distinction. Supper is usually less elaborate." Turning she made a quick exit from the room, and after putting on dry clothes she went back to the kitchen. Unpacking the groceries gave her some sense of regaining control.

As she put the food away, she could hear Hunter showering. When she looked up a few minutes later, he had silently crossed the living room. He was dressed in dry jeans and another knit shirt, his hair still damp.

"Hi," she said.

"Hi." He stood very still, taking her in, and she suspected he'd been half thinking she would disappear while he was in the shower.

"I'm still here," she said, watching the color in his cheeks deepen.

He nodded, holding her eyes for several more seconds before taking in their surroundings. All at once he was like an archaeologist examining an ancient Roman city. He pondered the furniture, flipped the television off and on and studied the shelves along one wall that held books and a strange assortment of knickknacks. He picked up a small stuffed alligator, turning it one way and then the other in his hands.

"What is this for?" he asked.

"It might be a child's toy. Or a souvenir from a trip."

"But what is the use?"

"Some people like to stroke the fur. It makes them calm."

He nodded, his finger brushing the green plush. "It feels good, like—" He stopped, his gaze skimming over her hair. "It should be red."

She lowered her gaze to the box of pasta in her hand.

He moved farther into the room, testing the weight of a metal candlestick, touching the raised flower pattern on a lamp base.

Everything here was normal, ordinary. Nothing special. Yet the cottage was a novelty in his limited experience. It seemed Dr. Kolb had made a shrewd proposal. Simply taking Hunter out of his sterile environment was expanding his horizons.

She had impulsively bought a bouquet of pink and white carnations and set them on the dining-room table. Hunter studied them from several angles, touched the petals, bent closer.

"They're just to make the table look pretty." She anticipated his question. "Make the meal more festive."

He bent to smell them again. "On television, I have seen people living in houses like this. With flowers and the other things."

"Do you watch much television?"

"No. Colonel Emerson thinks it is a bad influence."

"Why do you call him 'Colonel'?" she asked, casually.

"I think of him that way—as a soldier. A lot of the men do, too."

Maybe they'd served with him, she thought. Or maybe he wasn't as retired as he'd claimed.

"Um. Well, he's probably right about TV," she said. "Except for a few good shows, it's superficial. Silly. It plays to people with low tastes."

"Like the men on the training staff."

She laughed. "You're perceptive."

He chewed on that for a while, then asked, "Where do you live?"

"In Baltimore."

He moved on to the kitchen, opening cabinets, taking out packages of food and examining them. After sticking his finger into a jar of mustard and stealing a taste, he gave her a guilty look.

"That is not polite, is it?" he asked.

"No."

Opening a bottle of vanilla, he contented himself with a deep sniff.

After carefully putting the bottle away, he reminded her that he wasn't simply on a sightseeing trip when he pulled the gun from the waistband of his jeans. Removing the silencer from the barrel, he tucked the weapon into an upper cabinet, in back of a bag of flour.

She wanted to ask why he didn't turn it in. She supposed he thought it might come in handy. And who was going to say it was missing, she asked herself. Not the intruder, unless he'd been acting on official orders.

Careful to hide her state of mind in case somebody was listening, she cleared her throat. "What do you want to eat?"

He turned to look at her, pulling at his earlobe the way he did when he was at a loss for words. "Nobody ever asked that before. They just brought food."

She gave him a quick little smile that was meant to mask the sudden tightness in her chest. "What do you like?"

He thought for a moment, then he answered in a flow of words. "Steak. Baked potato with sour cream. Peanut butter and grape jelly. Once Beckton let me have some potato chips. They were good. We have creamed chipped beef for breakfast sometimes. I like that better than eggs." His eyes took on a dreamy look, the hard planes of his face softened. "Once I had vanilla ice cream with chocolate syrup. Another time I had cherry pie." He stopped abruptly, then added wistfully, "You probably do not have any of those."

The way he said the last part made her eyes sting. "Well, as a matter of fact, I do have some. Most men like steak so I bought it."

"Steak," he repeated with enthusiasm.

Quickly she turned toward the refrigerator, "I have apple pie and vanilla ice cream. And popcorn. I should have gotten potato chips."

"You tried to think of things I would like?" he asked, his voice full of awe.

"Yes."

"Thank you."

"Friends try to please each other," she told him.

"Friends," he echoed.

"Yes. And I brought some music," she added brightly, crossing to the machine. There hadn't been much of a selection, but she'd found the *1812 Overture*. With its stirring themes and pounding rhythms, it should get some kind of response—particularly the cannons firing at the end.

He stood and listened intently for a minute.

"Do you recognize that?" she asked.

He shook his head. "No one here plays that kind of music."

"Do you like it?"

"Yes," he answered, his voice thick and deep.

"I'm glad."

He continued to listen, his face blissful. She might have stood there watching him for a long time. Instead she busied herself with the food preparations, working quickly to keep from weeping. He mustn't see her cry. Mustn't know that she was on the edge of breaking down as she discovered how deeply he responded to a little kindness, a little color in his bleak life.

Hunter moved around the house again, poking into the backs of shelves, looking at each object critically. When he wandered into the hall she lost track of him. Several minutes later he came back to the living room and switched off the music with an expression of grim triumph on his face.

"Don't you like it?"

"I will listen later," he said, and motioned her to follow him. After moving the pan off the burner, she followed him into the hall, where he had opened an access door that she had assumed held the circuit breakers. It did, but below the electrical panel was a niche hidden by a piece of plywood. Hunter removed the wood and gestured toward the interior. "I found another toy," he said.

Inside she saw a small tape recorder.

"What do you think of it?" As he spoke, the tape reels began to move.

"It's not as much fun as the alligator."

His lips quirked, but he didn't speak, and the tape stopped moving. Then he clapped his hands several times, making it move again.

"Understand how it works?" he asked.

She nodded. Apparently it was sound activated—to conserve tape. The spools only moved in response to speech or other noises.

Hunter rewound the tape so that their words would be erased, and replaced the panel. They silently returned to the kitchen. Now she understood that he hadn't simply been curious about the contents of the house. He'd been prospecting for microphones and recording devices—and he'd struck gold.

She hadn't wanted to believe that someone was listening to their every word. Now she felt a kind of sick anger that Emerson had lied to her. Or maybe Hunter was right; maybe it was the work of somebody else.

He cupped his hand around her shoulder, gave her a little squeeze.

She closed her eyes in frustration.

"Can I help you do anything?" he asked.

Her eyes blinked open. If he could function under battlefield conditions, so could she. Giving him a tiny smile, she stood up straighter and led the way back to the dining room. "Supper's almost ready," she said as she moved the laptop computer to the sideboard. "But you could set the table."

"What does that mean?" he asked.

God, she thought, what a mass of contradictions he was. One moment he was engaged in high-tech sleuthing, the next he was totally clueless. "It means laying out the dishes and cutlery."

"Okay."

She found the necessary items in two of the drawers and handed them to him.

He stood beside the table staring at the two place mats she'd put there earlier. For several moments he juggled the cutlery in his hands before starting to arrange the items—first in a line along one side of the table, then in various configurations, each of which he studied critically before beginning to move them around again.

"Is there a way it is supposed to be?" he finally asked.

She instructed him on the finer points of table setting, and he followed her directions.

"Perfect!" she approved. "Wash your hands, and we can eat."

He complied, while she brought their plates to the table.

When he came back, he sat down at once, picked up the hunk of meat off the plate, and began to chew on it.

In the middle of an enormous bite, he stopped and looked at her, watching the way she placed her napkin on her lap and cut off a piece of meat before forking it to her mouth.

"I am doing it wrong," he said in a tight voice. He picked up his knife and fork. "They like to make fun of the way I eat, so I give them a show. I am sorry."

"That's okay," she managed.

He cut off a piece of steak, then dug into the mashed potatoes. "This is…wonderful."

"Thank you." She took another bite, struggling to swallow around the lump in her throat. Everything that she learned about this man set off an emotional reaction.

"Will you tell me about your family?" he asked.

"Yes," she answered, glad of the distraction. "I have a younger sister. My mom's a part-time nurse. My dad retired after forty years as an auto worker. We lived in a suburb of Detroit, so I had a typical middle-American upbringing."

"Tell me the best parts," he whispered.

Her vision turning inward, she tried to capture the flavor of her childhood. She told him about dressing as a princess for Halloween, camping with her family in Canada, winning ribbons in swim meets, and curling up in bed with a purring kitten snuggled beside her.

He sighed. "It sounds like 'Father Knows Best.'"

"That's one of the shows you've watched?"

"Yes. I like it. The people are happy. And the parents help the children solve their problems."

"Well, nobody's life is quite that idyllic. But I guess I was pretty lucky."

"Do you have a husband?" he asked suddenly.

She swallowed. "No, I don't."

"Why not?" he probed, leaning forward across the table.

She thought about it for a minute, trying to give him an honest answer. "I've dated my share of men. But I haven't met anyone who would complete my life the way Mom and Dad did for each other."

He nodded solemnly.

"Maybe I'm asking for too much."

"No. You should have a man who cherishes you, a man who knows how lucky he is to have you for his life companion."

"Maybe some day." With a jerky motion, she picked up

her plate and carried it back to the kitchen. After several moments, he came after her and set his plate on the counter next to hers.

Then it was time for apple pie à la mode. The look on his face when he tasted was angelic, and his sigh of pleasure was almost gale force. "It is fantastic."

"I'm glad you like it."

"It is warm and cool in my mouth at the same time," he enumerated. "And crunchy and gooey and creamy and sweet."

She could only nod, thinking how easy it was to give him a great deal of pleasure.

"Thank you." He concentrated on the pie for several more bites, then looked up. "You have taught me many things today. Can you teach me how to talk like everyone else?"

"What do you mean?"

"My speech is...wrong."

"Not wrong, just a little stiff."

"I know that. I hear it, but I do not know how to correct it."

"It would help if you used contractions."

"What are they?"

"You say 'I do not.' Most people would say 'I don't.'"

"Tell me more of them so I can hear the difference."

She gave him other examples, and he listened intently. After sitting for a while with his brow wrinkled, he asked, "Do you know the rhyme about Peter Piper?"

"Uh-huh."

"Well, *I'm* sure Peter Piper *didn't* pick a peck of pickled peppers because he *hasn't* found the pepper picking pot *that's* lost. *It's* in the toolshed."

She laughed. "That's good!" Impulsively, she reached across the table and pressed her hand over his. He went very still, his eyes lifting to hers. For several heartbeats, he didn't move, then he shifted slightly so that his fingers were pressed to hers along their length.

She felt a strong current flowing between them, a current that increased in intensity as he experimentally stroked her with his fingertips. He wedged his fingers between hers, then inched them up, and she knew from her own reaction he was testing the heated sensations generated by the simple touch.

"Can friends do this?" he said in a thick voice.

She should say no but she couldn't force the syllable out of her mouth as he flattened her palm against the table and delicately stroked it.

Such light contact, really, his hand on hers. Nothing more.

His eyes were closed, his lips slightly parted as if to shut out everything else but the slender link of flesh to flesh. Her own lids fluttered closed as she sat across from him, feeling heat pooling in her body—heat generated simply by his touch on her hand.

Then a noise from the front of the house made them both jump. The front door, she realized with a start as he snatched his hand back and prepared to push himself away from the table. He was looking over her shoulder toward the cabinet where he'd hidden the gun, she realized.

"No," she ordered. "Stay here."

Sam Winslow strode into the room. "What are you doing? Where the hell is the security team that's supposed to be outside?"

Hunter's face went blank as he sat back down in his seat.

Kathryn lifted her face toward the man who had rudely interrupted their supper. "To answer your first question, we're having dessert. Would you like a piece of apple pie?"

Winslow ignored the offer. "Where are the men who are supposed to be stationed here?" he clipped out.

"Perhaps they went to their quarters for dry clothes. But as you can see, we're doing perfectly fine by ourselves."

His gaze shot to Hunter. "He isn't accustomed to these conditions. He could leave."

"I would not…wouldn't do that," Hunter answered.

"This is ludicrous," Winslow muttered. "Are you playing house?"

"We're not playing anything. I've already taught him how to set the table." She swallowed, hating to demean Hunter. "And we've been working on his table manners and his speech patterns. I'm sure you'll be pleased with the results."

"I'm moving a security detail to the porch," Winslow answered.

"Before you do, perhaps you can satisfy my curiosity about a matter of procedure."

He raised questioning eyebrows.

"When I arrived back home from buying groceries, I found Hunter already here. But no one had informed him that I'd be sharing the cottage with him. That led to a little misunderstanding between the two of us. Were you responsible for bringing him over without adequate preparation?"

"Certainly not," Winslow growled. "Informing him was supposed to be taken care of."

"But it slipped between the cracks?"

He gave a curt nod.

"Well, I appreciate your help," she said pleasantly.

"And I appreciate yours," he replied tightly. "Make sure he's ready for a field exercise at 0800 hours." Without waiting for an answer, he turned and strode from the room. Moments later, she heard the clump of heavy feet on the porch.

Hunter sat quietly for several moments. "You should not have asked him about that."

"I know. But I wanted to see his face when he answered."

"They do not...don't like to be caught making mistakes."

"I know," she said again.

He took a deep breath, then let it out before pushing back his chair and standing. "I would like to be alone," he said.

When she raised her eyes toward him, he avoided her gaze.

"Why don't you finish your dessert?" she asked.

"The pleasure of it is gone."

"Don't let him spoil tonight for you."

Her words fell into an empty silence as he turned away and walked down the hall. She heard water running, doors opened and closed. Then nothing more.

THE TWO MEN MET in the shadows behind the gym. One was young and in his prime, a real hothead, who chafed at the bit when the rules kept him out of the action.

The other was older, wearier, more cautious. Yet desperation made him willing to take risks. They had disliked each other on sight and been unspoken enemies since coming to work on Project Sandstorm. Now they found themselves united in pursuit of a common goal—eliminating Kathryn Kelley. One was convinced she spelled the kiss of death to his plans. The other bitterly resented her interference.

"What happened?" the older one asked.

"He damn near broke my arm," his junior partner answered. "I was lucky to get away." He prudently didn't mention the missing gun. Thank God it wasn't his service revolver, but he'd have to retrieve it.

"I mean—did he kill her, like we thought he would?"

"He didn't do it."

"Maybe he hid her body," the older man said hopefully.

"No. She was alive and well and eating apple pie a half hour ago."

The older man cursed. "You checked on that personally?"

"You don't need to know that."

"Listen, we're supposed to trust each other."

"Yeah," came the gruff response.

"Do you have a plan B?"

"I'm setting up another opportunity."

"Good. Make it work this time."

"I can't give you any guarantees." Before he had to listen to any more whining, he turned and stalked into the night.

HUNTER GOT INTO BED in his briefs, just like on all the nights he could remember since they'd trusted him to get ready for bed by himself.

But this wasn't like all the other nights, he thought, as he lay staring into the darkness, mulling over the way his life had suddenly changed.

The mere fact that he was thinking in such terms astonished him. For a long time he had followed orders without questioning how they made him feel. In the space of a few hours he had been bombarded with more feelings than he knew existed. Now he was angry. Not with Kathryn Kelley. Never her. His ire was directed at his attacker and at Winslow—who had spoiled dessert by stamping into the house as if he owned it.

Hunter sighed. Winslow had the right to question training methods. And tonight was supposed to be part of that. Yet it had been so much more. He felt a hollow place open in his chest. He should have stayed at the table and finished dessert so he could have kept talking to her, touching her.

But he wasn't supposed to touch, he reminded himself, even if she said it was okay. Because simply pressing his fingers against hers had made him want to do things that were forbidden.

He tried to switch his thoughts to weapons, clandestine communications, the art of covert operations. Anything but Kathryn Kelley.

But he couldn't drive her from his mind. Too much had happened since that moment he had almost run into her car.

He clenched his fists, unable to cope with the unaccustomed emotions seething inside him. He was a warrior, destined for a specific purpose. His life would be short. He had come to realize that essential fact months ago and had dismissed it as irrelevant. For the first time he felt a kind of sadness. Not for the end of his life—for leaving her.

He looked toward the door, remembering the sounds of her walking down the hall, getting undressed. Now he imagined her lying on the bed, naked, her creamy skin against the white sheets, her wonderful red hair against the pillowcase.

His body tightened as he pictured her holding out her hand to him the way she had reached across the table tonight.

Her hand on his. He hadn't imagined anything could feel that good. Or that intense. The feeling flooded back through him as he lay with his eyes closed, thinking about her, and he had to gather up a wad of bedding in each of his powerful hands to keep himself from getting up and striding into her room.

He tried to drive her out of his mind by remembering the taste of the warm apple pie with vanilla ice cream. In its own way, the taste was almost as good as the sensation of tasting her. Almost, but not quite. Her effect on his senses was beyond imagining. Yet it brought pain as well as pleasure.

Once he had had the flu. He'd had a high fever, and his body had ached. He felt a little like that now. Hot and achy. It was because his body wanted to join with hers. The sexual urge was a powerful force. He had read that somewhere. Now he understood what it meant.

In the darkness, he gave a little snort. He might want her, but he didn't know much about how to do it. He'd probably hash it up. Nonetheless he kept picturing himself leaning over her, closing his mouth around the crest of her breast. Tasting her. Stroking her with his tongue. Probably she would think he was disgusting if he did anything like that.

Don't think about it, he ordered himself. *She's your friend. That's enough.* Yet he knew he was lying to himself. It wasn't enough.

KATHRYN SLEPT FITFULLY, waking and thinking about the man lying in bed across the hall. So much had happened since she met him that her mind was in chaos. It seemed no one at Stratford Creek—no one but her—thought of Hunter as a human being with needs and rights. He was their test subject, who might go berserk if not handled correctly, who might escape if given the chance. But he was too honorable to run from them. That was one of the complexities of the personality they had tried to obliterate.

Now that she'd gotten a chance to interact with him, she couldn't for a moment imagine that he was a convict volunteer. She had studied enough criminals to characterize their basic behavior—and it was the opposite of what she'd learned about Hunter. He was fundamentally decent, honest, ready to protect her whether that was to his advantage or not. Those were the hallmarks of a good man whose innate integrity had survived Swinton's hellish experiment.

She supposed the best thing to hope for was that they hadn't had him long enough to damage him permanently. Or, she thought with a strangled sound that didn't quite make it as a laugh, that he'd watched enough *Father Knows Best* reruns to have some sense of life beyond the confines of Stratford Creek.

Talk about grasping at straws, she thought, sitting up in bed and swiping her hand through her hair. Life as a fifties sitcom. She could be the mom. And what would he be? Not her son. And not her brother. That had become pretty clear. Pulling up her knees, she sat with her chin in her hands, contemplating her relationship with Hunter.

Basically, she'd been hired to work with him, and it was highly unprofessional to be considering anything beyond that. Yet she couldn't help being drawn to him. Or responding to him physically, just as he responded to her. Every time they touched, she could feel the heat building between them. But that didn't make it a good idea. Really, she had to figure out a way to cool things down—which was going to be difficult with them sharing the same house.

She wasn't going to ask for a change of quarters, though. Being near him suited her purposes too well. She had promised herself she was going to help him and somewhere along the line, she'd come to understand that meant getting him away from Stratford Creek. The trouble was, she didn't have a clue about how.

But she vowed she'd find a way to do it. And when they were someplace safe, she could help him regain his memories, starting with the few things that seemed to have carried over from his former life. Which brought her to the topic she'd been avoiding, she silently admitted. He told her twice now that he remembered her. She was more convinced than ever that they'd never met. Yet she knew there was a kind of bonding between them. How else did you account for the instant physical response that was more potent than anything she'd ever experienced in her life?

She turned that around in her mind for a while, unable to come up with any answers. Around 6:00 a.m., knowing that she wasn't going back to sleep, she got up, showered and dressed in gray slacks and a turquoise knit shirt. Pulling aside the curtain, she saw two security men standing at the bottom of the front steps, close enough to come to her rescue if they heard a scream from inside. The thought made her laugh. Winslow had it the wrong way around. All her experiences here had taught her they were the threat, not Hunter.

When she came into the living room she found him sitting in front of the television set with the sound muted.

"What are you doing?" she asked.

"I didn't want to disturb you," he said, without looking up.

"But you can't hear anything."

"I can read their lips," he answered, his gaze flicking briefly to her before focusing on the screen again.

She nodded, no longer surprised by anything he told her.

He had barely looked at her, and instantly she felt the sting of his rejection—even as she reminded herself he had a perfect right to privacy. She should be grateful to him for putting some distance between them. Instead she felt hurt.

Very professional, Dr. Kelley. Annoyed at herself, she crossed to the kitchen and found a loaf of bread and some crumbs on the counter and a steak knife in the sink. On it were the dregs of some peanut butter. It appeared that he'd licked the knife. Another distinctive scent also lingered in the air. Peering into the trash, she found a banana skin and couldn't repress a grin. It looked like Hunter had fixed himself a breakfast sandwich.

She walked to the kitchen doorway. "You like peanut butter and banana?"

He shrugged. "Granger talked about it once. I wanted to see why he liked it so much."

"What did you think?"

"It was strange." He glanced briefly toward the counter. "I should have cleaned up better."

"I'll do it later."

When he turned back to the television. She pulled open

the nearest cupboard. "Did you leave room for some pan-cakes?"

That got his full attention. He focused on her with an undisguised look of naked hope. "Do we have any?"

"I bought a box of mix. Why don't you get out the syrup while I start making them."

He trotted into the kitchen and rummaged in the cabinet. "I can set the table again," he offered.

"Thank you. And you can make coffee."

"How?"

She handed him two of the packets next to the machine on the counter. "Read the directions."

He read quickly and followed instructions exactly, she noticed, as she mixed the batter.

"It takes a long time to make pancakes," he said, licking his lips.

"You can have the first two."

"No. You finish making all of them, then we can share."

"Why do you want to do that?"

He shrugged. "It seems like the right thing to do."

She smiled. "I told you you have good instincts."

He watched her work for a moment, then went back to the TV. As she often did when she cooked, she began to sing. She picked a folk song she'd learned long ago at camp, a song that took its words from the book of Ecclesiastes in the bible. *"To every thing there is a season and a time for every purpose under heaven."*

When the pancakes were cooked, she called him to the table.

"Are you angry at me?" she asked as she sat down.

"No," he denied.

"Why wouldn't you look at me this morning?"

"I—" He stopped. "I'm not used to conversation."

She knew that was part of the truth. She wouldn't press him for the rest. Silently, she watched him enjoy breakfast. Cooking for him on a regular basis would be very gratifying, she thought, then warned herself not to think in those terms.

After they carried their plates to the sink, she touched his arm and gestured down the hall toward the tape recorder. "Let's go outside so we can talk," she mouthed.

He nodded, and followed her into the yard.

Last night, she'd wondered about the wisdom of trusting him with her plans. This morning she'd decided that she needed his help. Yet she still didn't know how much she could tell him.

"What do you want to say?" he asked.

She ran a hand through her hair. "I need some background on the senior staff so I have a better idea of what's going on here."

"I can get that for you."

She stared at him. "How?"

"I have a computer session this afternoon. I can download personnel files onto a floppy disk to use in your laptop." He paused, considering. "Do not…don't transfer the files to your hard drive. Leave them on the floppy and erase the data when you are finished."

She grinned at him. "What other talents do you have that I don't know about?"

"I'm an expert mountain climber. I have a black belt in karate. I am qualified on many types of personal firearms and knives. I am certified as an emergency medical technician. I speak five languages fluently. I can drive a car. Once I heard Dr. Swinton say that I was a decathlon champion in one of my brilliant careers. Before I died that is."

Chapter Seven

"What?" Kathryn grabbed his arm. "What did you say?"

Patiently, he began again. "I am an expert—"

"No." She waved her hand for him to stop. "The last part. What did you hear Dr. Swinton say?"

"He said that—" he halted, his chest tightening as he realized what came next "—that I was a decathlon champion in one of my brilliant careers before I died."

"But you aren't dead!" she exclaimed with a combination of frustration and elation, her hands trying to shake him, the way Beckton sometimes tried to shake some sense into him. But her touch was very different.

"I—" He sucked in a deep breath and let it out in a rush as he considered the meaning of the words. His mind worked like that sometimes. He had information, yet he didn't know the significance. Holding up his right hand, he clenched and unclenched the fingers. "I feel alive."

"Of course you are! Are you sure that's what you heard? He used the word 'died?' He didn't say 'before his memory was erased?'"

"He said 'died.'"

Her palm flattened against his chest, feeling the beat of his heart.

"When did he say it?" she demanded. "When did Swinton say you were an athlete before you died?"

His eyes blinked open. "A long time ago, in the lab. He

was lecturing Beckton. He said to push me hard because I had been a decathlon champion.''

She stared at him, cleared her throat. "Only one of your brilliant careers!''

He shrugged. "I don't remember any careers.'' He had thought nothing came before waking up in Swinton's laboratory. Was it possible he was wrong?

"In your computer session, can you get onto the Web? Can you download me information on decathlon champions who died?''

He didn't let himself get excited about it. Hope could be dangerous, he had learned. "I can try.''

"We can find out who you are." She sounded breathless. Transformed.

This morning had been bad. He had been cold with her, thinking that pretending he wasn't aware of her every move would make life easier. But he had been wrong. The sad expression on her face had made him want to hold her close, tell her he was sorry for making her feel bad.

Now she was happy, and he allowed himself the luxury of enjoying her enthusiasm.

"On television there used to be a show about the 'Six Million Dollar Man,''' she went on in a rush. "He was nearly killed in an accident, and scientists repaired his body using bionic parts. Then they trained him and sent him out on important missions. It was just a story, but maybe they found a way to do it.''

He gave a casual shrug, sorry she had thought of it. "I have training,'' he said curtly. He didn't have to tell her the other things. That wasn't lying, he told himself firmly.

"I—'' She stopped.

"What?'' He waited, afraid that she was going to ask for information he didn't want to give.

"This is important for you.''

Her eyes were bright. Her skin flushed. Like when he'd kissed her.

"Don't hope too much," he said, in a voice that was harsher than he intended.

"Don't be afraid," she answered.

She didn't know his fears. He wouldn't voice them, but he would remind her to be careful. "Winslow was angry when he left us last night. He will ask me what we talked about. You must order me to keep this conversation confidential."

Her face took on a kind of resignation. "Yes. I order you not to discuss this conversation with anyone."

"I will keep this between us, too. But now I must go." Abruptly he started back to the house.

"Wait!"

He pivoted, worried by the sudden panic in her voice. "What is wrong?"

She looked embarrassed. "I didn't mean to startle you. I only want to know what you'd like for dinner."

"Oh." He thought about the things he liked. "Could we have cherry pie with vanilla ice cream?"

"I'll see if they have it at the grocery store."

"And more steak. With a baked potato and lots of butter."

"Yes."

He paused, wondering how much he could request. "And something else I had once. A doughnut. With a honey glaze."

"I'll try to get some."

He wanted to pull her close against him. Devour her mouth with his. He only said, "Thank you. For everything." Then he turned and left to go with the waiting security men.

HE WAS REASSEMBLING a sniper rifle when Granger planted himself a couple of feet away and looked around to see that nobody else was in the vicinity.

"Heard about your new living arrangement," he said in a conversational voice. "You're a lucky S.O.B."

Hunter went on with the job at hand.

"So did you get any last night?" Granger asked with a smirk on his face.

From the talk he'd heard among the men, he was pretty sure he knew what that meant. He chose to give him an innocent look. "Any what?"

"I guess if you don't know, the answer is negative." The comment was followed by a nasty laugh.

He bent over the rifle, as much to hide his expression as to finish with the weapon.

"She's one good-looking babe," Granger insisted. "If I was living with her, I'd get in her pants, all right."

It took all his willpower not to surge up off the bench and sock Granger in the jaw. But he knew that would be a bad move. He'd already taken out his feelings on Beckton. He couldn't afford any more mistakes. So he kept blandly working, pretending that he wasn't seething inside.

Was Granger the man who had attacked him last night? he wondered, surreptitiously examining the man's muscular build. The attacker had been strong enough to wrench himself away, and he'd been a skilled fighter. Granger was a possibility.

The man made a few more choice remarks about Kathryn Kelley's body. When that failed to get a reaction, he switched tactics.

"I see Beckton is keeping away from you."

He didn't answer.

"He's afraid of you now."

He shrugged, determined not to get in any more trouble, because now he knew his behavior could affect Kathryn. When Granger didn't get any reaction from his victim, he lost interest and drifted away.

AS SHE CLEANED UP the kitchen, Kathryn wondered what Hunter was doing. She had just finished washing the breakfast dishes when she heard a noise in the dining room and whirled. McCourt was standing by the table watching her.

"It's customary to knock before entering someone's home," she said.

"I did. I guess with the water running, you didn't hear me."

She was pretty sure he was lying, or he'd rapped so faintly that it would have been impossible for her to hear. She didn't waste her breath challenging him.

And he didn't waste any time getting to the point. "A sidearm is missing from the armory," he announced, watching her face for any reaction.

"And?" she asked, keeping her gaze steady, even as she felt her pulse speed up.

"I'd like to see if it turned up here."

"Are you asking permission to search the house?" she inquired.

"No. I'm just trying to show you I can be polite."

"Why should a missing weapon be in this cottage, of all places?"

"I'm checking various buildings. This one's on the list."

She forced herself to casually step aside and sweep her arm toward the kitchen. "Maybe it's under the sink," she said sweetly.

"Maybe."

Her mouth went as dry as sand when McCourt strode forward and opened several of the lower doors, moving aside cleaning supplies and loudly rattling pots and pans. When he straightened and started on the upper cabinets, she wanted to grab hold of the door frame to steady herself. Instead she only pressed her shoulder against the white-painted wood.

The gun was to the right of the sink. As if in a nightmare, she watched him open the cupboard and rummage inside. His fingers closed around the bag of flour, and she stopped breathing as she pictured him pulling it aside, revealing the weapon. It seemed eons passed before he removed his hand and slammed the cabinet.

"Are you doing this to harass me?" she asked in a voice that was almost steady.

"No. I'm doing it because I'm in charge of security, and if a weapon is missing, my neck is on the chopping block."

She managed a little nod as he strode past her and into the dining room, where he paused to open a few drawers. Then he marched down the hall and into Hunter's room.

Kathryn pulled a paperback from the bookcase in the living room and took a seat in one of the overstuffed chairs, pretending to read. McCourt was taking three times as long in Hunter's room as he had in the kitchen. Then he started on her room.

When he finally reentered the room, she looked up questioningly. "Find anything interesting—besides my preferred brand of toothpaste?"

"No," he snapped. Without another word, he crossed to the door and stamped onto the porch. She didn't relax until she heard a car drive away. Then she slumped in the chair. Her first instinct was to run to the kitchen and retrieve the gun. She stifled the impulse. McCourt hadn't found it, so it was safe for the moment.

HUNTER CAUGHT A FLASH of movement in the doorway. Keeping his head bent over the rifle, he slid his eyes to the right. It was Dr. Swinton. Why was he here today, when he hadn't come to the armory in weeks?

Although the research director stood watching him for several moments, Hunter didn't break his rhythm, even when he felt the man's gaze burning into the back of his neck. Then, thankfully, Beckton came over, and Swinton started asking low, brisk questions. Though Hunter couldn't hear, it was obvious from the expression on Beckton's face that he didn't like being quizzed. Still, he remained respectful as he showed Swinton some of the latest progress reports. Yet every so often threw a quick look over his shoulder, as if he were afraid someone would ask what he and Swinton were talking about.

If they had a secret, Swinton hid it better than Beckton. They finished talking and Swinton left. Beckton looked around nervously, then hurried out of the building.

Hunter finished with the rifle, completed a drill on the geography of Gravan—the country where he was going on his mission—and went outside to the paved area behind the building where a small truck was waiting. After studying a set of written instructions, he climbed into the driver's seat, started the engine and began to maneuver around an obstacle course that had been set up.

It was a normal day, yet everything had changed. He wasn't simply following orders anymore. He was noticing things around him, making assessments. He'd never tried to figure out if one of the men he worked with had killed Fenton, the ex-chief of security. Today he wondered if Fenton's death was connected to the attack last night.

When he came to no conclusions, he switched his thoughts back to the time with Kathryn Kelley—and found himself singing the song that she had sung. It was so different from the *1812 Overture*. He liked them both, but he liked this better—because she had sung it.

"To every thing there is a season and a time for every purpose under heaven."

Her voice was high and beautiful. His was a croak by comparison. But he sang anyway. What was his time? His season?

This morning he felt caught between two worlds. The old world where he did what he was told without question and without feeling. And the new world where his mind seethed with questions and emotions.

It was strange to admit that he took a kind of grim pleasure in Beckton's new fear of him. But he kept it well hidden, he hoped. He must not let them know how much he had changed since meeting Kathryn.

Kathryn. That was her first name. He didn't have to call her Kathryn Kelley, he suddenly decided. He could think of just the first name. The name her other friends would use.

If things were different, the two of them might—

He stopped the daydream before it could form. He would finish his instruction at Stratford Creek, then go on to his primary assignment, and that would be the end of it. But now he had another mission, as well. He must keep Kathryn safe while she was here. The problem was, he didn't know what would happen if he came to a juncture where the two aims clashed.

The worry made him lose his concentration, and he tapped the right front fender of the truck against a barrel. He had made a mistake, he thought as he forced his mind back to the obstacle course. He had taken this test before. He'd better not do worse than the last time or Colonel Emerson would ask questions.

LONG AFTER MCCOURT had left, Kathryn sat rigidly in the living room chair, afraid to trust her legs. She'd always been good about putting up a calm front. She hoped she'd fooled McCourt.

Ever since her arrival at Stratford Creek, she'd felt like a prisoner, but the security chief had just given her a vivid demonstration of his power over her. In a way he was worse than James Harrison. From Harrison she knew what to expect. She didn't know what to expect here anymore.

A glance at her watch, and she pushed herself out of the chair. She'd better pick up the groceries she'd promised Hunter. She started for the door, then stopped abruptly. Was it safe to leave the house, she wondered, looking uneasily toward the kitchen cabinet that held more than food. For a split second she thought about taking the gun. No, if she got caught with a gun tucked in her purse, she'd have some tough explaining to do.

HE'D BRAGGED to Kathryn that he could get personnel information. Now he realized that in his desire to please her, he had spoken too soon.

As he sat in front of the computer screen in a windowless basement room of the administration building, the chances of getting the files she wanted seemed slim.

Pushing the printer button, he half turned to look at the man sitting directly in back of him.

"You need some help?" the man asked. His name was Hertz. He was small and stoop-shouldered, and wore a baggy sweater in the chill of the basement office.

"No," Hunter answered, wishing that Hertz would leave the room. Apparently he'd been told to stay. In fact, he realized, someone was almost always watching him, except when he was being tested on a solo exercise. He'd never thought much about the lack of privacy. Today, however, he was vividly aware of the constant scrutiny—and a lot of other details of his life he'd never questioned.

He didn't know what Hertz had been told about him, except that he was preparing for a special assignment. Maybe Hertz had been told the same thing as Kathryn— that he was instructing a prisoner volunteer. They'd only worked together on a sporadic basis and always stuck strictly to business. Searching his memory, he decided that the man wasn't usually as conscientious as the regular instructors. Yet today he hovered nervously in the background like—

Like what? A fifth wheel? No, that was the wrong phrase. The wrong idiom.

Like a watchdog. That was better, he thought with a little grin. The grin vanished as he considered why the man was being so conscientious. Probably the incident with Beckton was being talked about around the compound.

Again he reproved himself for hitting the training chief. It was a mistake. But it was in the past, and he couldn't change it. He could only go forward, he thought as he booted up a government-restricted Internet search engine.

He had used the Net before and he had no problem locating a directory of the faculty in the physics department at the University of Stockholm and printing the biographies of selected department members. Then he went on to download and print out product specifications from an aircraft manufacturer in California.

But while he was doing the assigned work, part of his mind was on Kathryn's requests. She wanted Stratford Creek personnel records and a list of decathlon winners.

Perhaps he would have to make a choice between the two options. If he had time to get only one of the things, he would pick the personnel records. That was more important, he told himself. It would help her.

Finding out about dead athletes was another matter, he thought with a sudden prickle of fear at the back of his neck. He wasn't sure why he was afraid of putting a name to the face he saw every morning in the mirror when he shaved. He told himself that he didn't want to open a door that had always been closed.

After about forty-five minutes, he stood up. "I'm going to the men's room."

Hertz started to stand. "Okay."

"I know the way. I'll be right back." Without waiting for a reply, he walked into the hall. To his relief, the other man didn't follow him.

He hadn't been sure he could get out of the room alone. Making the most of the opportunity, he hurried down the corridor. After determining that no one was watching, he ducked into an empty office along the route and picked up a pack of matches and some cigarettes he'd seen lying on an otherwise empty desk.

The matches alone would probably work for what he had in mind, but if anyone checked to see what had happened, it was better to have a cigarette, as well.

He knew about smoking. He'd passed men clustered around exterior doors enthusiastically puffing on cigarettes when they were on their breaks. The smokers seemed to enjoy it. In fact, sometimes they sneaked into the men's room to smoke. Today he would find out how it tasted.

Locking himself into a stall, he struck a match, pressed the burning end to the cigarette, and dragged in a deep breath through the filter tip the way he'd seen guys do it.

The moment the stinging smoke hit the back of his throat, he started to gag. When it reached his lungs, he began to cough violently. It was as if he'd breathed in poison gas, he thought as he wiped the tears from his eyes, thankful that no one else was in the washroom. After gasping in several lungfuls of air, he tried again—this time a lot more cautiously. Instead of inhaling the smoke, he only pulled it into his mouth. When he was sure the lit end was burning nicely, he exited the stall and poked the cigarette into the paper-towel-filled trash bin.

By the time he finished washing his hands and rinsing the foul taste out of his mouth, the trash was already beginning to smolder. For good measure, he dragged over a wooden chair from the corner with a sweatshirt draped across the back and dangled the sleeve in the trash. Then he hurried back to the office where Hertz was still sitting and reading a magazine.

Only part of the next Internet search was completed when the fire alarm began to ring.

Hertz jumped up and went to the door. "Maybe it's a false alarm," he muttered.

Lifting his head from the screen, Hunter loudly sniffed the air. "I think I smell smoke."

Fearfully, Hertz took another breath. "Yeah. Let's get the hell out of here." He started for the door, then looked back in consternation. "Come on," he urged.

"I must exit the Windows program," Hunter said, making his voice loud and mechanical.

"It's okay to leave it. Come on!"

In the hall, several sets of feet rushed past as the workers assigned to the basement offices made for the exits.

"I am required to shut down the equipment properly," he answered, adding a stubborn note to the statement as he deliberately turned his back on the man and faced the console. His fingers were already moving over the keys. If Hertz approached, he'd discover that he wasn't shutting down the machine.

He felt the man hesitating behind him, apparently torn between escaping from a burning building and doing his job. The smoke wafting down the hall made the decision for him. After several seconds, he turned and dashed from the room.

Hunter bent over the keyboard, working rapidly. The smoke had begun to sting his eyes. Then he started to cough.

The spasm passed, and he peered at the screen through watery eyes. He had used the system many times. It was a simple matter for him to work his way into the personnel records. Quickly he typed in several names, along with records requests. As he waited for the information to download, he started to cough again.

Outside he could hear the wail of sirens. Fire trucks. He hoped everyone else had gotten out of the building all right.

He didn't have much time left, he thought, as he saved the personnel files onto a floppy disk. The smoke was getting thicker, and every breath made his lungs burn. It seemed like he was hardly getting any oxygen. He should leave now that he had the personnel information he had promised to bring. Yet something made him stay in front of the computer and switch back to the Internet search engine.

Long seconds passed during which he fought to not to pass out. Then he was into the Olympics web site. Trying not to breathe, he zeroed in on decathlon champions.

The smoke was so thick he could barely see the screen. Why was he doing this, he wondered. He didn't even want the information. Yet he stayed where he was, blinking to clear his vision as he downloaded the stats onto the disk. When he had them, he exited the Web site, then forced himself to shut down the program so that he'd have the right answer when they asked why he'd refused to leave a burning building.

He had stayed too long, he realized, as he ejected the floppy disk. Every breath he took now was agony, and his mind was enveloped in a gray haze, as if the cells of his brain were filling with smoke. With shaky hands, he stuffed the disk into his pocket, then dropped to his hands and knees to get below the smoke and dragged himself toward the door.

His trick had worked too well. The hall was filled with black, choking smoke that billowed from the direction of the men's room and made it impossible to see where he was going. Head bent, he lurched forward, hoping that he didn't crawl past the door at the bottom of the stairs.

Chapter Eight

Sirens shattered the afternoon quiet as Kathryn was on her way back from the shopping center. Two fire trucks and an ambulance sped past as she waited at the next cross street. Some sixth sense made her turn in the opposite direction from the guest cottage and follow the emergency vehicles.

When she caught up, they had pulled to a stop in front of the administration building. On the sidewalk and lawn, displaced office workers were milling around.

Craning her neck, she spotted Bill Emerson, who was conferring with an emergency medical technician. Another medic leaned over a man who lay on a stretcher on the ground. When the man moved, she felt a shiver cross her skin. It was Hunter—or her eyes were playing tricks on her. Her heart pounded as she tried to get a better view.

Then someone in the crowd blocked her line of sight. Unconsciously murmuring a little prayer under her breath, she maneuvered to the curb and leaped out of the car.

As she drew near the building, a fireman blocked her path.

"I'm sorry. You have to stay back," he said.

"I have to talk to Mr. Emerson." Ducking past the man, she made for the stretcher and saw with a sick feeling that she'd been correct. It was Hunter lying there, gray-faced, eyes closed. When she called his name in a high, strangled voice, he turned instantly toward the sound, his gaze searching for her in the crowd and zeroing in on her face.

She wanted to rush to his side, clutch his hand, hear his voice. She knew scores of eyes were watching her, so she remained standing where she was.

"What happened?" she asked, directing her question to one of the medics.

"Smoke inhalation," the man answered.

"Is he all right?"

"He crawled out of the building under his own power. But we're taking him to the hospital to check him out."

"I am fine," Hunter insisted. Although his voice was raspy, it sounded strong, and that reassured her.

He tried to sit up, but the medic put a hand on his shoulder.

Emerson came up behind her.

"How did this happen?" she asked.

"Some idiot started a fire in a trash can in the men's room," he clipped out. "Smoking. It's against regulations to light up inside. When I find out who it was, they're going to be damn sorry."

She noted the intensity with which Hunter took in the conversation. Near him, a stoop-shouldered little man in a gray sweater was also listening and looking sick.

"Who's that?" she asked in a low voice.

"Hertz. From computer support." Emerson made no attempt to hide his annoyance. "He was supposed to be in charge of Hunter. He was supposed to stay with him at all times. He came running out of the building alone."

"He wouldn't leave the computer," the man said. "I wasn't going to stay in there and get turned into toast."

"The computer?" Kathryn asked, her gaze shooting back to Hunter.

"I had to shut down the program properly," he said in a flat voice, avoiding direct eye contact with her. She was pretty sure that it wasn't the whole story.

"What was I supposed to do, carry him?" Hertz whined.

"I made him go without me," Hunter wheezed.

"That was foolish," the chief of operations growled.

"I could not disobey orders."

"Your orders." Emerson nodded. "Yes, I understand."

Hunter's eyes flicked to Hertz. "I do not wish to cause trouble for him. He is a good computer instructor...he did his job every moment until the smoke began to fill the room."

The man looked relieved, and bobbed his head vigorously in agreement.

A fireman came up to Emerson, and they conferred briefly. Then the chief of operations raised his voice and spoke to the group of people who had turned toward him. "The fire's out," he announced. "And the damage is confined to the men's room where the blaze started and the hall immediately outside."

The crowd gave the firemen a round of applause. When they finished, the medics moved into position on either side of the stretcher, raised it to waist height, and began to roll it toward the ambulance. Kathryn wanted to follow. She wanted to ride with Hunter and stay with him. Yet she understood that showing too much concern wasn't prudent.

"I'll wait back at the house," she said.

"Good idea."

The last observation was made by Chip McCourt, who had come out of the crowd.

She gave him a little nod.

"We've been going along for months just fine." McCourt walked beside her as she left the crowd and headed toward her car. "Then you show up and our incident rate suddenly goes through the roof."

"Don't you mean *off* the roof?" she muttered under her breath, thinking about Fenton.

"What?"

"What incident rate?" she said more loudly.

"A fight in the gym. A missing weapon. Now we have a mysterious fire."

"Well, I think there are a number of witnesses who will swear that I was at the commissary when somebody tried to burn up the men's room."

"You think it was deliberate?" McCourt asked.

"I have no idea."

"It's interesting that you showed up so quickly."

"I heard the sirens. I was curious."

"I'll bet."

She raised her chin, gave him a direct look. "What are you getting at?"

To his credit, he kept his gaze steady. "Nothing."

"Good." Turning on her heel, she left, feeling several sets of eyes drilling into her back.

THE MOMENT KATHRYN walked into the dining room of the guest cottage, she knew something was wrong. Some of the knickknacks in the shelves had been moved, and the sweater she'd left on a chair was on the floor. A feeling of dread overwhelmed her.

Was the gun still in the kitchen?

She had to assume the tape recorder was still waiting to pick up sounds from its place behind the access panel. Suppose it was sensitive enough to tell the listeners that she'd made a beeline for the kitchen cabinet where the weapon was hidden?

She'd never had a devious mind. Now she forced herself to take a breath and consider how she would really act if she came in and thought her house had been searched.

Probably she'd check her personal belongings. With a grimace, she started down the hall to the bedrooms. Drawers had been opened and the contents moved about. Someone had poked through her and Hunter's things and hadn't bothered to hide the search. With shaky steps, she returned to the kitchen, opened the cabinet to the right of the sink and moved the bag of flour. She wasn't surprised that the gun and silencer had both vanished. Had McCourt waited for her to leave and come back for a more thorough search? Or had someone else done it? She couldn't discuss the possibilities with anyone but Hunter. And she wouldn't be discussing them with him, either, she reminded herself, barely managing to suppress anguish. He was in the hospital, and she didn't know when he was coming back. When he did they couldn't have a normal conversation because the house was bugged.

In an attempt to regain composure she began putting away the groceries. More time passed. The house remained quiet except for the sound of her own breathing. She ached to call the hospital and make sure Hunter was all right. She told herself firmly that he was, and that he'd come home when they released him.

Yet what if they didn't let him come back to the guest cottage? What if Emerson had changed his mind about the living arrangements? Fighting the clogged feeling in her throat, she sprinted across the room toward the telephone, but didn't make the call. In her present state she'd never be able to hide her feelings, and if Emerson knew she'd lost her objectivity, that would be the end of her access to Hunter.

She would have to wait for official word, she told herself firmly. Still, as the minutes turned into hours, she thought she would go crazy. Crazy with frustration. Crazy with worry.

Dragging herself into the bedroom, she slipped off her shoes and flopped down in her clothes, prepared to jump up the minute she heard the front door open.

It didn't, and she lay rigid, staring into the growing darkness, telling herself over and over that Hunter would surely be back soon and everything would be all right. But nothing could stop her mind from churning.

Finally, desperate, she staggered into the bathroom and

splashed cold water on her face, trying to shock herself into steadiness. Feeling a little more in control, she called the medical facility. The woman who answered didn't know who Hunter was. When Kathryn switched to his old name—John Doe—she was told the information was classified. Now more upset than ever, she stood rocking back and forth with her arms wrapped tightly around her waist. Maybe Hunter was already out of the hospital, she told herself. Maybe he was already back in his old quarters. Maybe McCourt was supposed to give her the news, and he'd conveniently forgotten. A mirthless sound bubbled up in her throat. That would give him the last laugh, all right.

Only the sound of the front door opening saved her from hysteria. Her heart skipped a beat, then hammered into overtime as she barreled down the hall.

Relief flooded her when she saw Hunter standing there in clean clothes, the effects of the fire scrubbed away. Yet she came to an abrupt halt in the face of the two security guards flanking him. One was the guy named Reid—who probably didn't like her any better than she liked him.

"Here's your wayward boy," he said with a touch of sarcasm in his voice.

A sharp retort leaped to her lips. She bit it back and managed a simple "Thank you."

"Do you want us to stay?"

"No. I'd like the arrangement to be the same as last night," she answered in a cool, dismissive voice.

Reid nodded and the duo departed, leaving Hunter standing in the hall staring at her with his arms stiffly at his sides and a strained expression on his face.

She felt almost dizzy as she faced him. "Are you all right?" she gasped.

He gave a little nod.

"Thank God." Seeing him after the long hours of worry was like getting struck by a tidal wave. Struck from the back, so that she was propelled toward him. With a little cry, she flung herself across the space between them.

He took the impact of her weight, his arms coming up to catch her as she held on to him for dear life. Her hands slid possessively across his broad shoulders, up and down his back, as she assured herself that he was well and whole.

"I wanted to go to the hospital with you," she choked out. "I wanted to be there. It was hard to come back here and wait."

"They wouldn't have let you be with me there. But I'm here now."

"Yes." She reached up, tunneling her fingers though his dark hair so that she could bring his face within reach.

"Oh," was all he had time to exclaim before his mouth melted against hers. She sobbed as her lips moved frantically against his. There was so much she wanted to say to him. So much she couldn't say with the tape recorder ruling their lives.

But she could show him what she was feeling. Closing her eyes, she shut out everything but him, the taste of him, the feel of him. Each thing registered separately on her senses—the slightly coarse texture of his hair, the hard muscles of his shoulders as her hands came back to them, the clean smell of soap and water.

"Kathryn." Her name sighed out of him like a plea—like a prayer of thanks.

"I'm here," she answered. "Right here."

His mouth opened, perhaps in surprise, as she eased his lips apart so that she could taste him more fully. And as she drank from him, she taught him the ways that two people could express their deepest feelings to each other without words. Soon his mouth was moving hungrily over hers, tasting, sipping, nibbling at her tender flesh until she was shaking with the strength of her response.

His strong hands were under her blouse, burning the skin

of her back, and then her front where he cupped her breasts through the sheer fabric of her bra.

He made a rough sound, half pleasure, half frustration. "This thing is in the way," he said thickly.

"Yes." Reaching around, she unhooked the catch, and he pushed the fabric up, taking her breasts in his hands.

She heard him suck in a strangled breath, as he moved his fingers over her heated flesh.

"So soft." The words were almost a moan.

She was just as inarticulate. She could only gasp at the pleasure of his unschooled touch, a touch that made up in ardor and tenderness what it lacked in sophistication.

His hips moved against hers, instinctively, insistently. "I want to…" The sentence ended with a choking sound in his throat. In the next moment, he wrenched himself away from her, his hands balled into fists in front of him, his chest heaving.

She reached for him, but he stepped farther away.

"No," he ordered, his eyes fierce.

They both stood sucking in drafts of air.

"Friends can't do—" He stopped abruptly, looking over her shoulder.

She wanted to say he was wrong. Then with a start, she realized he was looking toward the tape recorder.

Oh God, how bad did his homecoming sound?

All she could do was shake her head in despair. What she had told him about the two of them was wrong. What she felt for him was a lot more powerful than friendship. She had tried to deny her feelings, but denial had become impossible when she'd seen him lying on the stretcher and then during the long anguished hours while she'd waited for him to come home.

When she felt a little more in control, she turned away and rehooked her bra.

She waited for the heat to fade a little from her cheeks

before reaching for his hand and leading him into the dining room where the light was better.

The stark look on his face made it difficult not to clasp him to her again. That would only make things worse. After several shaky breaths, she touched her finger to her mouth. His eyes followed.

"Can you understand what I'm saying?" she asked, moving her lips slowly.

He nodded.

"You and I are more than friends," she said silently, knowing that she wasn't exactly helping the situation. But she'd vowed not to lie to him. And what had just happened between them had certainly passed beyond the bounds of friendship.

"What are we?" he spoke, but in a barely audible whisper.

"A man and woman who care deeply about each other," she told him silently.

When his face contorted, she realized she could only speak for herself. "At least I do," she said, forgetting not to vocalize the words.

"I—" He reached for her hand, drew her closer so that he could fold her fingers around his and bring her knuckles to his lips. Eyes closed, he kissed her hand tenderly, then carried it to his heart. Her vision clouded with moisture. She had never been so affected by a gesture, so affected by another human being. Silently, taking small steps, she moved closer so that she was standing with her cheek against his shoulder.

One of his large hands came up to stroke her hair, the other clasped her shoulder, and she stood with him, fighting tears. God, what a mess. They could hardly talk, and there was so much she wanted to say, so much she needed to tell him, she realized suddenly. Personal things. But the personal part would have to wait.

She brushed her lips against his cheek. "I have to tell you things that happened," she mouthed.

He nodded.

After giving him a flicker of a smile, she cleared her throat.

"Did you have dinner?" she asked in an almost normal voice.

"They gave me a turkey sandwich. It was dry and—" He stopped. "It doesn't matter."

"Well, you can have dessert. Cherry pie with vanilla ice cream."

His eyes lit up.

"Come into the kitchen and give me a hand."

He followed her toward the cabinets. Turning, she glanced at him, then opened the door where the gun had been and showed him the empty place behind the bag of flour.

His face took on a questioning look.

She turned her palms up and shrugged. "McCourt was here—officially," she mouthed slowly. "Looking for a gun from the armory. He didn't find it."

Hunter nodded his understanding.

"When I got back after the fire, the house had been searched again."

His eyes narrowed but he said nothing.

Turning she opened the box of pie she'd bought and warmed a slice in the microwave before topping it with ice cream.

"You have some, too," Hunter said when she handed him the plate.

Dutifully, she cut herself a small slice, although she had almost no appetite. She started to say some more about McCourt's visit, then caught herself. The strain of remembering not to speak was getting to her.

After a few bites, she gave up the effort and simply watched Hunter enjoy his dessert. He looked like a little boy who couldn't believe he deserved such a wonderful treat.

She was too keyed up to do more than nibble at her food. When she couldn't stifle a yawn, he nodded. "You...we... should sleep," he amended.

"Yes."

Standing, she started to carry the dishes to the kitchen, but he stopped her. "I'll do it."

"Thank you."

"Go to bed."

She shouldn't lie down, she told herself. But what good would it do the two of them to sit and stare at each other? Leaning over, she gave Hunter a small kiss on the cheek. She had intended it to be brief, but she clung for a moment, needing to hold him, touch him before she let him out of her sight again. Finally she headed down the hall to her bedroom.

HE PROWLED through the kitchen and felt a shiver of gratitude when he found the box of doughnuts she had bought. Slowly he ate two, savoring the sweet taste. He thought about finishing the box, then elected to save some for breakfast. He would eat them and drink coffee with a lot of milk and sugar, he decided as he licked his fingers.

He had never chosen what to eat. When to eat. What to do. It made him feel strange as he washed the dishes. Turning he looked toward the stereo, thinking he would like to hear the *1812 Overture* again if he couldn't hear Kathryn singing. But he didn't want to wake her up, so he hummed the song she'd sung.

"A time for every purpose under heaven."

He wished it were true.

He knew it was a lie for him. He had only one purpose. The song died in his throat as he began to prowl the house, checking to make sure no additional sensors were monitoring their activities. There were only the tiny microphones he'd found before and the tape recorder. At least he hoped.

They were hard-wired, meaning that the system had not been updated to state-of-the-art technology. He had lain in his hospital bed thinking about what to do. If they could listen to the tape, so could he. Now he opened the utility panel, rewound the tape and fast-forwarded, stopping every minute to listen. He heard the sound of someone searching the house. Then the broken words and phrases from the frantic time in the hall when he had come home to her. He had to clench his teeth to get through that part. Methodically, he erased everything that had been said since he got home. The listeners wouldn't know how much was on the tape, because they wouldn't know exactly when it had been activated by speech or other noises.

After turning off the machine, he started down the hall. He and Kathryn had to talk. Now they could do it in privacy—at least for a few hours.

Quietly he pushed open her door and stood looking down at her in the shaft of light that came from behind him in the hallway.

She had fallen asleep on her back, with her flaming hair spilling across the pillow. The way he had imagined her.

Well, not quite the way he had imagined. The covers had slipped down to her waist, and he saw she was wearing a T-shirt. Yet as he moved quietly closer and waited for his eyes to adjust to the dark, he could see the outlines of her beautiful breasts against the fabric and the darker centers that had made his body tighten when he touched them.

He pressed his hands to his sides to keep from reaching for her.

"Kathryn?" he called out quietly.

She stirred a little on the bed.

"Kathryn?"

Her eyes fluttered open. When she saw him looming over her, she gasped and tried to climb out of his reach.

The terror in her eyes made him afraid she would scream and bring the security men. Flinging himself on top of her, he clamped his hand over her mouth.

She kicked at his legs and struggled to tear herself from his grasp. All he could do was try and hold her still as he told her over and over, "I didn't come to hurt you. I came to talk to you."

At first it seemed she didn't hear him, didn't even see him, for her eyes were glazed and her frantic struggles continued.

Then, all at once, she focused on him. In the next moment, she went very still, except for the sobs that began to rack her body.

"I came to talk to you," he repeated.

She nodded against his shoulder but kept sobbing. When she clung to him, pulling him down beside her, he gathered her close and held her gently, wishing he knew what to do to make her feel better. He had frightened her badly, and sadness descended upon him. He had thought…well, it didn't matter what he had thought.

In that unguarded moment when she had wakened, he had discovered her true feelings.

He felt her struggling to get control of herself. When she fumbled for a tissue on the bedside table and blew her nose, he eased away from her and sat up, moving to the side of the bed.

"We can't talk," she whispered.

"Yes, we can. I turned off the recording machine," he explained. "Since it's voice-activated, they will think we are sleeping now."

She tipped her head toward him. "Are you sure?"

"Yes." He swallowed painfully, looking down so she wouldn't see his face. "I'm sorry. I shouldn't have come in. I frightened you."

She sat up and put her hand on his arm. "It wasn't you I was afraid of," she said quickly.

"Who?" he asked, hardly daring to hope he had been wrong about her terror.

She sucked in a deep breath and let it out in a rush. "I took the job Emerson offered me because I wanted to hide out from a man named James Harrison. He tried to kill me a couple of weeks ago," she said in a shaky voice. Moving her hand to his, she held on tight.

"Why would someone try to kill you?"

Her grip was almost painful, yet he didn't loosen her fingers.

"One of my jobs is testifying in court—in trials—as an expert witness. Three years ago, I gave an evaluation of Harrison. He lived at home with his mother because he couldn't sustain a relationship with a woman. He'd been fired from his job as a computer programmer, and he was depressed. His mother had a lot of money, and he wanted to get his hands on it. So he was holding her captive—starving her, hoping she would die."

"A person would do that to his mother?" he asked, hardly able to believe it.

"Not usually. He was sick—mentally sick. The mother didn't die, so he wasn't charged with murder. And she wouldn't press charges against him. I testified that he was a danger to society. Because of my testimony and another psychologist's, he was confined to a mental institution."

He listened intently, not sure he understood everything, but getting the gist of it.

"He escaped, but the authorities thought he was dead. He came to the apartment building where I live. He tried to kill me. I got away from him, but the police haven't found him yet. And sometimes I dream about him. I dream he's coming after me again," she ended with a little gulp that made his heart melt.

"Come here." He held out his arms to her.

She came into them without hesitation, and he felt a

wave of warmth and protectiveness sweep over him as she nestled her head against his chest.

On a deep sigh, he cupped his hands around her shoulders. He liked it so much when she gave herself into his care. It made him feel strong. Good. Able to protect her, although he didn't know if he really could.

"I thought I'd be safe at Stratford Creek. I didn't know I was jumping from the frying pan into the fire."

He repeated the phrase. He'd never heard it before, but he understood what she meant.

She burrowed closer to him. "It wasn't you I was afraid of," she said again, her warm breath seeping through his shirt to heat his skin. "I saw your shape in the doorway— a man's shape—but I couldn't see your face."

He stroked her hair. He had told himself he wouldn't touch her when he came to her room to talk. Still, it was impossible to deny himself the pleasure of running the silky strands through his fingers. He could feel his body getting hot and tight again. It was a strange combination of pain and pleasure that compelled him to seek more.

Remembering the kiss in the hallway, he turned his head. She opened her mouth for him, and he gave a sigh of gratification at the soft touch of her lips and the sweet taste of her. Some part of his mind knew this was the wrong thing to do. He shouldn't have come to her bedroom. Perhaps he had been fooling himself about his reasons.

The pressure of his lips on hers made him dizzy, hot, achy. His fingers shook as they stroked the tender line where her hair met her cheek. When she made a little sound of wanting in her throat, he answered with a growl of satisfaction.

Helpless to stop himself, he cupped one of her breasts and stroked his fingers over the tip.

It was hard. Touching it made him harden in response as if her body were giving a signal to his. The fabric between his hand and her flesh frustrated him. He wanted to pull the shirt over her head and push her down to the surface of the bed.

He wanted to make love with her.

He knew nothing of lovemaking, yet the image was very vivid in his mind—his body joined to hers so that it would be impossible to tell where one of them stopped and the other began.

He pulled her down, gathered her as close as he could with their clothing in the way. The tight, swollen part of him fit perfectly into the cleft between her legs. She must know it too, he thought, drunk with sensation as they rocked together on the bed. Blood surged through him in a roaring torrent. Need built, like a hot, raging river sweeping away sanity in its path.

He was caught and held in a spinning whirlpool of hunger—held by the soft sounds she made, the woman scent of her, the frantic little movements of her hips against his.

In a few moments he knew he would be unable to deny himself, unable to think beyond physical need. He would have to give himself over to the blinding, deafening desire for her.

But he couldn't let that happen. He had come here for another purpose. He must talk to her. Find out about the gun. Protect her.

That thought gave him strength he hadn't known he possessed. With a strangled sound deep in his throat, he lifted his mouth from hers, moved a few inches away so that his aching body was no longer pressed tight to hers. Still, it was impossible to let go of her completely. His hand stayed clasped on hers as he spoke in a voice so thick that the words were barely articulate.

"We can't," he said, then more strongly, as he sat up and moved to the side of the bed. "We can't."

Her eyes were dazed, her face flushed. The color deepened as she focused on him.

"We have work to do," he rasped, knowing that if she

held out her arms to him, he would go into them. "We must look at the disk—with the personnel files."

KATHRYN BLINKED, sucking in a shaky breath as she struggled to remember where they were, and why they couldn't do what both of them wanted so much. Sitting up, she ran an unsteady hand through her hair, pushing it back from her face, buying a few moments to collect herself. He was right, she thought as she forced her mind to start functioning again.

"The disk? You have it?"

He nodded and pulled it out of his pocket. "I brought it out of the administration building. In the hospital, I folded it into my clothes when they had me get undressed."

"Did you set the fire?" she asked, her fingers digging into his hand.

He kept his gaze steady. "Why would I do that?"

"You said you'd get me information from the computer. Then you realized it was going to be impossible. But you did it for me, anyway, didn't you?"

A flush crept up his cheeks. "How did you know that?"

"It was a guess. Hunter, you shouldn't have taken a chance like that!"

He shrugged. "It was like a field exercise."

She made a low sound of distress, and her fingers tightened on his.

"It was all right."

"You could have gotten killed."

"But I didn't."

Before she could lecture him on taking unnecessary risks, he changed the subject.

"McCourt was here? Tell me about that. And about the gun."

"He came in the morning after you left and said a gun was missing from the armory. He looked for it, but he didn't find anything. Then when I got back after the fire, I could tell that someone else had searched the house. The gun and the silencer were both gone.''

"He could have come back.''

"Or it could have been someone else.''

"I heard the sounds of searching on the tape.''

She nodded tightly.

"The gun may have come from the armory, but not the silencer.''

"I—''

"We must make the most of our time,'' he interrupted. "You must read the computer disk and then erase the data. It's dangerous to keep the evidence if the house can be searched at any time.''

She gave him a tight nod. Yes, the house could be searched. And men like Winslow and McCourt could burst in. Yet that didn't negate a basic fact that kept nagging at her. Why had she been given such unprecedented access to Hunter?

He must have seen the question on her face. "What?''

"The more I think about being left alone with you, the more I wonder why it's been arranged this way.''

"I heard Dr. Kolb and Dr. Swinton talking about it when I was in the hospital.''

"They were talking in front of you?''

"They were in the hall. I heard them. Dr. Kolb said this is the best field trial he could think of. If I pass this test, I'm ready to go off into enemy territory. Dr. Swinton thanked him. He said that he had thought Dr. Kolb was fighting him. But now they were working like a team.''

"Enemy territory? Where?'' she asked, hoping the answer might slip out.

"A country where Americans aren't welcome,'' he answered evasively. "A country where one man might be able to slip in.''

"Who is funding Project Sandstorm?'' she tried.

"The Department of Defense.''

She kept her voice neutral. "And does the Department of Defense own Stratford Creek?"

"Yes."

When she tried to ask another question about his mission, he stopped her with a quick shake of his head.

"I can't tell you any more about it."

"I want to understand."

"You have to read the computer data tonight," he reminded her.

She knew he was right. They didn't have much time.

"What are you going to do?"

"Check the security at the motor pool," he said.

"Why?"

"Don't ask me that either." He made a quick exit from the room, and she stared after him. If he was checking the security of the motor pool, he must be thinking about leaving the base.

Could that really be true? Was he preparing to go against his training, after he'd told Winslow he wouldn't run away?

She couldn't answer the question, and she knew she was wasting time speculating. Taking the laptop off the dresser, she brought it to the bed where she propped up the pillows so she could sit comfortably. On the disk were two files. One was labeled "pers." The other "Olympics."

She ached to go right to the second file. But she knew the first one was more urgent. She had to see what she could find out about the men she was dealing with here.

An hour later, her head was swimming with information—information that didn't come entirely from reading dry personnel entries. Apparently Bill Emerson liked keeping track of his staff's peccadilloes and record the information in memos he'd attached to each man's record. Kind of like the J. Edgar Hoover method of personnel control, Kathryn thought with a shudder. If your employees knew you had something on them, they were likely to stay in line.

Among other things, she'd learned that Lieutenant Chip McCourt had a violent streak. He'd been thrown in the brig on several occasions. And he'd almost gotten himself court-martialed for assaulting a civilian worker on a tour in Germany. That time, Emerson had personally stepped in to get him off the hook. The lieutenant was allowed to leave the army with an honorable discharge, and he'd come straight to Stratford Creek to help set up Project Sandstorm.

Also enlightening were the confidential notes on Dr. Jules Kolb. According to Emerson, Kolb was an alcoholic who had badly mishandled a score of patients at a V. A. Hospital in Virginia, causing the deaths of several. The scandal had been covered up, and Kolb had been ordered into an alcoholic rehab program.

Reid, the man who had brought Hunter home this evening, had been jailed for selling supplies stolen from military bases. And then there was the brilliant Dr. Avery Swinton. His early reputation had been damaged by a scandal involving the fudging of test results in a scientific paper he'd published in the *Journal of Biological Sciences*. Still, he'd gone on to win a research grant at Berkeley—and then been dismissed for illegally experimenting with human fetal tissue.

Well, now she knew why she'd instinctively disliked most of the staff, she thought with a grimace. They were lawless and ruthless. And she had the data to prove it.

Was there some way she could use the information to her advantage? She didn't know yet. But maybe a plan would come to her. Closing the file, she switched to the information on decathlon winners.

At first she was disappointed because she didn't find anyone who could be the right man. None of the recent champions was dead, she saw as she went down the list. The first deceased medal winner she came to was a man named Ben Lancaster who had taken the gold seventeen years ago—when he was twenty-five, she noted, her brow wrinkling. That would make him forty-two, if he were still alive. And there was no way Hunter could be anywhere near that old. If she had to guess, she would say he was in his late twenties.

Still, Lancaster was the only one who fit the prime criterion—death. So she accessed the additional information Hunter had downloaded and found herself confronting the image of the man.

The hairs on the top of her head prickled as she stared at the picture. It was Hunter, but a different Hunter. The man she was looking at was at least fifteen years older than the man she knew.

Chapter Nine

Impossible. Nobody turned back the hands of time. The clock ran in only one direction. Plastic surgery? It might take years off your face, but it couldn't give a forty-two year old the body of somebody in his twenties. Could it?

Feeling strangely light-headed, Kathryn studied the man who could be Hunter's older twin, trying to dredge up some feeling of connection to him. But she could generate no emotions but shock at the remarkable resemblance. Perhaps if she read the information, she thought as her eyes began to scan the text. Lancaster had been a track and field superstar at the University of California at Berkeley in the early eighties before going on to the Olympics. He had given up his sports career, gone back to graduate school and ended up as a research physicist at the Sandia National Lab, of all places, working on cold fusion.

He had married a high school teacher, she read with a sharp pang. She had wanted Hunter to have a life before he lost his memory. She hadn't bargained for discovering a wife. But she should have been prepared, she told herself with a little inward stab.

However, two years ago, the Lancasters had been killed on a New Mexico highway when a tractor-trailer had come around a mountain curve on the wrong side of the road. So the wife was dead, she thought, caught between relief and guilt.

And so was Lancaster…

She studied the picture and reread the short bio, trying to make sense of the startling new information. Ben Lancaster had been an athlete and a scientist—an unusual mixture that could account for the combination of multiple talents and high intelligence in Hunter. But he was much too young to be the same person. Could Lancaster have had a secret child—who had somehow fallen into Emerson's clutches? The possibility seemed remote. And it didn't explain the cryptic remark about previous careers.

A feeling that she was being observed made her look up to find Hunter standing in the doorway watching her. He'd slipped back into the house so quietly that she'd never even heard him.

"How long have you been standing there?" she asked.

"Two minutes."

"I've found something," she told him.

"I know. From the look on your face." His own face had hardened into a look of resignation as he watched her gesture toward the computer.

THE TWO MEN HAD ARRANGED another meeting—this time well past midnight in the woods behind the research center. The older one was angry—angry with himself for being reduced to working with morons. Angry with the way things were falling out. He usually hid his frustration well. Tonight, he took out his fury on his companion.

"Your dumb idea backfired. They're still cozied up in that house like newlyweds."

The answer came as a sharp retort. "You thought it was a great idea at the time. All you have to do is sit back and let me take the chances."

"I'm paying you well enough."

"You're paying me peanuts, considering the risk. Maybe I'll quit."

"The hell you will. We have an agreement."

The younger man cursed. He'd wanted to get back at Kelley. Now he wished he'd thought before he hooked up with this nut.

"Relax. I've got an idea that will do the trick."

"Oh, yeah?"

The more intelligent of the two began to outline his plan. When he finished, the other one nodded.

"It might work—if we have the time. Deployment has been moved up."

"Are you sure?"

"I heard Emerson talking to Beckton. By the end of the week, John Doe is on his way to Gravan. And you can take credit for a job well done."

In the darkness, the other man's fists clenched. "And what about Dr. Kelley?" he asked.

"Come on. Do you really think Emerson is going to let her leave?"

The younger one smiled to himself in the darkness, thinking he'd imparted good news. The older one hid his look of alarm. It appeared he was going to have to speed up his own timetable, and he wasn't sure if he could pull that off.

HUNTER MADE no comment as Kathryn stood between him and the computer screen.

"I read some of the personnel files. Then I accessed the information on the decathlon champions," she said.

As she took in the tension in his face and body, she understood why he hadn't wanted to be the one to read the disks. He was afraid to unlock the secrets of his past. Well, she could help him deal with that. Stepping aside, she revealed the picture of Ben Lancaster, watching Hunter's expression as he scanned the image. He stared into the mirror over the dresser, then flicked his gaze back to the sports figure.

"He looks like me," he said. "But...he's older."

"Yes. He died at the age of forty-two in an automobile accident. He was a star athlete. Then he went back to school and got a Ph.D. in physics."

"He must have been smart."

"Yes. Like you."

"Am I?"

"Yes. You're very smart."

While he chewed on that, she took advantage of the light from the bedside lamp to examine his well-honed muscles, supple body and thick head of almost black hair. His face was almost unlined, and his skin was smooth and young-looking. There was no way he could be over thirty, even if he had kept himself in excellent shape.

She reached for one of his hands, turning it over and examining the pads of fingers. They belonged to a young man.

"You can't be him," she said. "But does the picture make you remember anything?"

He stared at the man on the screen for a long time. "No. I'm sorry."

"Why?"

"You want to know who I am."

"You don't?"

He swallowed. "You ask me too many questions. In some ways it was better before you came."

She turned her palms upward, unsure of how to answer.

"I was peaceful. I followed orders. I didn't get angry."

"McCourt warned me you attacked some of the instructors."

"Yes." He opened his hands in a helpless gesture. "In the early practice sessions, I didn't know when to stop fighting. I had to learn that."

She nodded, understanding.

"You stir up questions in my mind. I can't answer the questions, and they make my chest feel tight."

"Everyone has scary things they're afraid to face," she whispered, reaching for him.

"Everyone?"

"Yes. Even me. Like James Harrison."

She gathered him into her embrace, glad when his arms tightened around her. She drew strength from him, even as she gave him comfort.

His hands moved on her back, in her hair. "Feeling things is…" he paused for a moment, searching for the right word, "inconvenient."

"Yes, sometimes feelings are hard to deal with," she answered, "but that's part of being human."

He gave a low, mirthless laugh. "You are the only person here who thinks of me as human."

Her vision blurred, and she fought to keep from coming undone. "Because they can't let themselves!" she said vehemently, cradling him more tightly in her arms. "It's a defense mechanism. They know they've done things to you that are morally and ethically wrong. The only way they can protect themselves is by making you the enemy."

"I didn't think about it like that." A shiver went through him. "I thought it was something wrong with me."

"No!"

"But there *is* something wrong with me," he persisted. "You must know I'm not like other people. I have no history before I woke up in the research facility at Stratford Creek. I know how to be a fighter. I don't know the rest."

"That's not true. You know more than you think," she insisted, her lips skimming his cheek. "Take my word for it."

He moved back, his eyes bright as they searched hers. "What do you like about me?" he demanded.

She raised her face, met his worried gaze. "I like your

kindness. Your discipline. Your honesty. I like the way you haven't given up."

"Maybe I did give up—before you came."

She felt her heart squeeze painfully. "Then I'm glad I'm here."

"You—" He stopped, swallowed hard. "I think I have learned more from you than any of the rest of them."

"I hope so. But I think we're learning from each other."

"Like what?" he asked incredulously.

She gave a little laugh. "Well, I didn't know much about turning off hidden recording systems until I met you."

"Beckton could teach you that," he said dismissively.

"I'm not interested in interacting with Beckton. But seeing things through your eyes gives me a fresh view of the world." When his dark gaze continued to challenge her, she went on quickly. "You remind me how much enjoyment there is in simple things. Like music. Or cherry pie with ice cream. Or—" she stopped short, flushing as she realized what she had been about to say.

The flush gave her away. Hunter found her hand, stroked his fingers against hers, sending familiar currents of heat licking at her nerve endings. Her breath hitched as she stared at him.

"When I kiss you and touch you, what do you feel?" he asked with an urgency that turned the heat up several notches.

"The same thing you feel, I think," she answered softly.

His face was a study in stunned disbelief. "You want to...to make love with me?"

Dangerous ground. They were treading on very dangerous ground, yet she had vowed not to duck his questions. "Yes. I want to make love with you," she said, raising her face until their gazes were locked.

She saw him swallow hard. Another man would have reached for her then. Pulled her against him, fast and hard. Taken up where they'd left off in her bedroom. But he only stood with his whole body tight and stiff, fighting primal needs, proving once again that he had more strength of character than any other man she'd ever met.

She could be the one to do the reaching. She could be the one to do things that would break through his iron discipline. It was tempting to make it happen. For a little while they could blot out the intrigue swirling around them. But it would only be a temporary reprieve. And in the morning, their situation would be worse. Every hour they spent in this place made it worse.

"I should read some more of the personnel files," she whispered.

"Yes." He agreed, yet neither one of them moved.

When he spoke again, it wasn't of personnel files. "None of the men call it making love," he said in a thick voice. "They say having sex or—" He stopped, flushed. "They make it sound—dirty. But I can tell they are embarrassed, too. Why is that?"

"Because it's the most intimate thing two people can do together," she said, moistening her dry lips with her tongue. "It can be an expression of strong feelings—of love and commitment. Or it can be done as casually as scratching an itch. Men who don't value its deeper meaning generally make it sound cheap and dirty."

He took in the explanation, then spoke in a rush of words. "I don't know enough about making love to do it right."

His cheeks were bright, his eyes averted.

She inhaled slowly, knowing that few men would have the guts to make that confession. They always thought they were great lovers. "You're worried about that?"

He nodded.

"You're already good at it. Can't you tell I like the things you do?" she said softly.

"We have not done much." As he looked down, his gaze found the front of her shirt.

Her nipples had hardened while they talked. It seemed he didn't need to touch her to heighten her response.

"I can see the centers of your breasts—standing out against the fabric," he said thickly.

His slow, husky sigh of frustration almost undid her. The temptation to press his hand against her aching breasts was almost unbearable.

When she didn't move, he dropped his hands to his sides. "I should not have asked you about...making love. We do not have much time left now for the computer files."

She closed her eyes for a moment and pressed her forehead against his shoulder. "It's not your fault," she whispered. "I keep letting my priorities get twisted up. I keep wishing we could be alone together, like two people who have nothing more pressing to do than get to know each other better."

"Yes," he said without hesitation. "If it were daylight, I could take you to the place in the woods where the stream makes a little waterfall. There are young spruce trees to make it private, and flat rocks where we could sit and talk—or do anything we wanted."

"You've thought about taking me there?"

"Yes. I found it once, when I was doing survival training. If you sit very still, you can see deer come down to the stream to drink."

"I'd like to go there with you."

"Sometime," he said in wistful voice.

"Sometime."

"But not now."

She nodded, turned back to the computer, forcing her mind to business. "I want to ask you a question about these files."

"What?"

"Most of the men's duty assignments are listed on their personnel records. Dr. Kolb works at the medical center. Beckton and Winslow are at the training facility. McCourt is at the administration building. And there's a summary of their duties. But the only thing it says about Dr. Swinton is that he works in the research center and Building 22. It also mentions that the building is off-limits to everyone but the research staff.''

"And?'' Hunter asked carefully.

She had learned how to read him, and she knew he wanted to drop the subject.

"Maybe that's where Swinton keeps his records. Maybe I can figure out a way to check it out. Do you know where I can find that building?''

His gaze turned inward. It was several seconds before he answered, "Yes. But I don't think you should go there.''

The way he said it made her even more sure that he knew something about the place, something he didn't want to discuss. And she preferred not to press him. Instead she said, "I'd appreciate it if you could draw me a map.''

He gave her a long look, then picked up pencil and paper and began to work rapidly.

Building 22 was an annex to the research facility. When he handed her the paper, she saw his face was pale. All at once, she felt a sudden stab of guilt. He had been in the hospital this afternoon, and now she had kept him up half the night.

"I'm sorry. I wasn't thinking. You should be in bed— not up working half the night. I can finish with the files on my own.''

"I'm all right.''

"No. You need to get some sleep.''

He considered the advice, then nodded. "First I must turn on the recorder.''

"Yes.'' She followed him down the hall and watched him open the access panel that hid the listening device.

After he reactivated it, they returned to the back of the house.

He hesitated outside his door, his gaze dark and intense. That look was enough to make her blood turn molten.

Before temptation overwhelmed her, she gave his hand a quick squeeze and went back to work. But she found she was still thinking about Hunter. She had never met a man like him—such a potent combination of competence and naiveté. Strength and wonderment. A man with no memories because they had been taken away from him.

At least that was what William Emerson had told her when he described Dr. Swinton's research. At the time, it had sounded illegal and immoral. But what if it was actually worse than she imagined?

A terrible thought had been rattling around in her head since she had read the information on Ben Lancaster and seen his picture. Hunter was like a younger version of Lancaster. A younger identical twin.

Eyes narrowed, she went back to Swinton's file. He had earned a medical degree from George Washington University. After a residency in neurology at Johns Hopkins, he had gone back to school at Hopkins to get a Ph.D. in physiology. Then he had won a prestigious appointment to the National Institutes of Health where he had specialized in cutting-edge research in genetics. Next, he had taken a research post at Berkeley, but he had been dismissed for illegal work on human fetuses.

After that, he had switched to animal research at a remote, privately funded laboratory in the Colorado Desert. Not so far from Los Alamos, where Ben Lancaster had been working, she realized with a sudden start.

The lab had produced some notable successes in the cloning of animals.

Cloning.

She felt a wave of cold fear sweep over her as the force of the word hit her. Swinton had cloned animals. Would he dare to try it with human beings?

God, was she really thinking such things? Kathryn asked

herself, her mind boggling as she tried to come to grips with the implications. It couldn't be true! She didn't want it to be true. Yet she'd always been a logical person, and against her will, logic forced her mind to move on to the next step.

Cloning was the only way she knew to produce identical twins of different ages. And to clone Lancaster, Swinton wouldn't have needed the whole body, simply a few cells. That she had progressed so far in her thinking in so short a time shocked her to the core. Her assumptions would make Swinton a lawless monster.

Silently, she got up and pulled on black sweatpants, T-shirt and running shoes. Before the sun came up in a few hours, she was going to check out Building 22. Maybe it would turn out to be like Area 51 in Roswell, New Mexico, she told herself, the place where the Air Force was supposed to be hiding a UFO. But she wanted to see for herself.

She took out the computer disk and held it in her hand. Hunter had told her to erase it. But the information she'd just read on Swinton was electrifying, and she hated to give up the chance to find out more about the other key players—particularly since Hunter had almost gotten himself killed bringing her the files.

The thought made her struggle for composure.

God, she must be the only person on this whole damn place who understood his basic humanity, his basic goodness.

Her vision clouded. Emerson must have been struggling not to laugh in her face when she told him she wanted to give Hunter the experience of a normal life. Emerson didn't give a hoot about his welfare. Neither did any of the rest of them.

Her lips pressed into a grim line, she took another few minutes to carefully open a small hole in the seam of her pillow, stuff the disk into the middle of the foam rubber layers, and sew up the seam with the mending kit from her suitcase. Then, for good measure, she turned the pillow around in its case.

Satisfied with the hiding place, she took a small flashlight from her emergency kit and stole out through the sliding glass doors into the wooded area where she and Hunter had stood the night before.

The night was cool, and she shivered as she oriented herself to the map Hunter had drawn. Though she'd been to the research center before, she knew that things would look different in the dark. At least there was a gibbous moon, making it easier to pick her way through the woods. She came out onto a field about a block from the house and began to jog toward the research center. If anyone spotted her, she'd say she couldn't sleep and had decided to see if exercise would help. Still, when she saw the lights of a car coming down the road, she faded into the shadows under the trees.

It was a patrol car, she noted with a little shiver as it passed. Apparently the security force patrolled the grounds at night.

Staying away from the road as much as she could, she wound through the complex, stopping once more when she saw another vehicle approaching. With the two interruptions, it took her ten minutes to make it to the research building.

Building 22 was in back. The night patrol had made her careful, and she stood in the shadows of some oak trees, watching for activity, before cautiously moving forward and making a partial circle of the building. It was only one story, with a flat roof and metal doors on two sides. The moonlight did nothing to soften its stark lines, or the general impression that the exterior was in even worse repair then the rest of the facilities.

Now that she was here, she wished she had worked out a brilliant plan of assault. Probably it would be better to scope out the place tonight and come back tomorrow. That approach was sound, though she suspected that it had as much to do with a failure of nerve as anything else. She didn't want to prove her shocking theory. Yet she had to know one way or the other. So, after a nervous fifteen minutes during which she saw no sign of activity, she stepped cautiously forward.

She half expected the nearest door to be locked. But the knob turned easily. As she pushed the door open, she started worrying about a silent alarm. But why would Stratford Creek need one, since she was the only spy?

And not a very cool spy, she acknowledged, feeling her pulse race as she tiptoed down a tile corridor with painted cinder-block walls illuminated by dim lights. Deep inside the building, she could hear air-conditioning or other similar equipment running. After listening to the background noise for several moments, she crept ahead, feeling more and more vulnerable the farther she progressed into the interior.

The dim, empty corridor was like the set of a slasher movie. Ordinary—but filled with hidden danger around the next bend.

The intersection of the two hallways loomed directly ahead. Stopping a couple of feet short of the juncture, she paused and listened intently, but heard only the sound of the unseen machinery. When she cautiously peered around the bend, she saw a desk that might have been a guard station. At this hour in the morning, it was empty.

Making a quick decision, she proceeded to her right. Along the new route, she found several doors, the first of which was locked. The second was open. When she shone her light inside, she saw a small office with another desk and a chair. But the surface of the desk was bare, and the space looked unused.

Maybe the research center had been moved to another

building, she speculated, ordering herself to chill out. The advice only raised goose bumps on her arms.

What if she got trapped inside this place, she wondered, as she continued down the hall, then tried to cancel the frightening thought. Moments later, she realized the worry wasn't pure speculation. It had been triggered by a tiny sound coming to her above the whine of the machinery.

Voices. Someone talking in an angry tone. Someone answering. They were coming the way she had come. And they were getting closer.

She had only seconds to make a decision. Another door was several feet in front of her, but it might be locked. Going back toward whoever was coming along the hallway was terrifying, yet it was the best choice she could make. In a frantic dash, she turned and sprinted toward the oncoming sound, yanked the office door open, and leaped inside. The moment she was hidden from view, her knees turned to jelly, and she pressed herself against the wall to keep from melting to the floor.

Heart thumping against her ribs, she looked around the little room. There was no other exit, not even a window. If whoever was coming down the hall opened the door, she would be caught like a rat in a trap.

The voices came closer, and with a chill that went all the way to her bones, she realized that the angry person was Dr. Swinton.

"I don't understand why we're having this problem!" he growled. "We should be getting a much better success rate. But another one is going bad."

"I'm sorry, sir," the other speaker replied. "Perhaps, you've…uh…pushed the growth rate a little high. A few more weeks to maturity shouldn't hold up the project too much, and it might make the difference…."

She recognized this man, too. It was Swinton's assistant, Roger Anderson.

An ominous silence followed Anderson's reasonable-sounding suggestion. Then Swinton asked, his voice so sharp that Kathryn felt the words were piercing her flesh, "Are you sure you followed procedures exactly?"

"Yes, sir. It's not the fault of the life support system. It's the inherent problems with keeping genetic material viable."

The voices were receding now, and she dared to let out the breath she was holding.

"The genetic material is perfect!" Swinton growled.

"Yes, sir. But there are always problems. If you read the literature—" She didn't catch the rest of the response because the man's placating voice was now too far away. But she still heard Swinton loud and clear.

"I don't need to read the damn literature. I know more than anybody else working in the field. And I don't want to hear any excuses. You will prepare for a new trial. We will start on the next shift."

She stood silently in the dark, thinking about the conversation and the strained relationship between the two men. Things weren't going the way Swinton expected, and he was blaming his subordinate. But what type of experiments was he conducting?

After ten minutes without any further interruption, she decided it was safe to open the door. When she peeked cautiously out, the corridor was empty. Though the temptation to run for the nearest exit was overwhelming, she considered her options, finally deciding to retrace Swinton and Anderson's route in hopes that she might find out what they'd been doing.

Turning in the direction from which she'd come, she headed for the place where the hallways crossed. This time, she went left and found herself in a section of the building where the temperature was even colder than before. The only sound she heard was the constant whine of the machinery, which seemed to be coming from behind a door about ten feet along the corridor. She could see the red glow of a night-light shining along the bottom of the jamb. Somehow it made her think of fire seeping up from the depths of hell, and she had the sudden conviction that she didn't want to find out what was in that room.

Yet she kept moving forward until she could wrap her fingers around the door handle. In the back of her mind, she hoped it would be locked. Instead, it turned noiselessly, and she stepped inside. In the red light she could see several large tanks with glass walls. For a moment, she wondered if this was an aquarium. Then she saw what was floating in the rectangular containers, and a scream of mingled horror and protest rose in her throat.

Chapter Ten

Somehow she managed to stifle the scream so that it came out as a kind of helpless sob. She wanted to back out of the room and run headlong down the corridor, but her legs quite literally refused to move. Rooted to the spot, she stood in frozen horror, her eyes fixed on the closest tank. Inside, a naked man floated, a man lying on his side, with his knees pulled toward his chest and his eyes closed.

In the eerie red light, she could see tubes attached to his wrists and his mouth. For feeding and oxygen? Some detached part of her brain asked the questions, as she observed him. The rest of her fought horror at what she was seeing.

She stood breathing in gasps of the chilly air, trying not to pass out. The crazy thought ran through her head that she was watching a scene from a horror movie, except that special effects masters had not created this experimental laboratory.

It was an invention from the diabolic mind of Dr. Swinton. Aided by Anderson and Emerson and the rest of them.

Revulsion engulfed her, and it took every ounce of fortitude she possessed to keep standing in the doorway. But she had to know more, so she managed not to turn and run.

Stay calm, she ordered herself. *You have to stay calm.*

Taking a few steps into the room, she eyed the machinery

attached to the tanks. There was monitoring equipment that looked like the kind used in intensive care units. Only this was no hospital.

Her eyes darted to the other containers ranked around the laboratory. Two were empty. Two others held men who looked like twins. The remaining four tanks held boys—or rather, what looked like the same boy—at different stages of development, ranging in age from a few years to a young teenager.

Clones? Started at different times. And growing at a much more rapid rate than any normal human child, she speculated, as she remembered the conversation in the hall.

Logic had forced her to consider the possibility that Swinton had progressed to cloning humans. The reality was more than she could cope with.

"No," she gasped as she backed away, out of the room, into the blessed solitude of the hall. Then she was running for the exit and freedom.

She was barely thinking, barely functioning at anything approaching a normal level. All she knew was that she had to get away from that place. Blind to caution, she staggered down the corridor. If Swinton or Anderson had still been in the building, they would surely have caught her.

Reaching the door through which she'd entered, she twisted the knob. For a few dreadful seconds it wouldn't open. Then the catch moved, and she stumbled out into the night. Moments later she found herself standing under the oak trees sucking in great gasps of air.

It was still dark, she saw with shock, since it felt as if she'd been in that terrible room for centuries. When she looked at her watch, she discovered that only half an hour had elapsed since she'd first entered the building.

Breath wheezing in and out of her lungs, she made for the cottage. Too late, she realized she had forgotten to pay attention to her surroundings. About a hundred yards from the cottage, a cruiser came gliding up behind her and gave her a blast from the siren, almost making her jump out of her skin.

She thought about fleeing, then imagined a bullet plowing into her back. Trying to wipe any expression from her face, she stood dragging in air as two security men got out of the vehicle and came toward her. She didn't recognize them, but they seemed to know who *she* was.

"Dr. Kelley?" the taller one asked.

"Yes."

"Do you mind telling us what you're doing out here at this hour of the morning."

"Running."

"You weren't moving very fast."

"I know." For a terrible moment her mind went completely blank. Then she raised her chin. "I had a stitch in my side. I've been walking for the last half mile, I think." As soon as she said it, she wondered if they'd been quietly following her. And how far?

"What was your route?" the one who seemed to be in charge asked.

"I don't know the compound all that well. I assume it's perfectly safe to be out at night," she said, pretending that the man's chief concern was for her safety.

"Of course," he agreed.

"Well, I probably should get home now. Thank you for stopping."

The guard looked at her consideringly.

As if she assumed the interview was over, she turned her back and walked toward the house. Then she remembered that the front door was locked. She'd have to go in the sliding door, the way she'd come out. Hoping they wouldn't wonder why she was disappearing around back, she hurried into the shadows under the trees.

It had taken every ounce of concentration to focus on the conversation with the security guards. Every ounce of concentration to sound sane and rational.

She was reaching for the door handle when Hunter appeared, slid the glass panel to the side, and stepped into the backyard. After her experience in the laboratory, seeing him was a shock. She made a muffled sound and stepped back.

"I frightened you," he said. "I'm sorry."

Her lips moved, but no words came out.

"I heard the siren," he said in a strained voice. "I looked out the window and saw you with the security guards. I didn't know what they were going to do. I thought I should protect you from them. Then I thought I would make things worse if they saw me."

"I'm fine," she said, although she knew she had broken her rule about lying. All at once, it was impossible to keep herself from shaking.

Hunter reached for her and wrapped his hands around the cold skin of her arms, rubbing the gooseflesh. "You're not fine," he said. "You're cold and shivering."

She tried to deny it, but gave up the attempt.

"Where were you?" he demanded.

Building 22, her mind screamed, as all the horror of the place came rushing back over her, swamping her, choking her, making it impossible to speak.

Hunter gave her a critical look. When she didn't say anything, he continued in a flat voice, "You asked me how to get to Building 22. Then you went there."

When she managed the barest of nods, his hands dropped away from her arms. "You saw the tanks."

Slowly she raised her head, hoping against hope that she had heard him wrong. "How do you know about that?"

"I've seen them. I tried not to think about it." When she continued to stare at him, he explained. "I—I guess I knew what they meant."

An involuntary shudder racked her.

"I hoped you wouldn't go there. I knew you would feel differently about me if you saw that place." When she didn't answer, he continued in the same strained voice, "I can see the horror in your eyes. Now you are like the rest of them. You know I'm not a real person."

She was still in shock, unable to think clearly. Her mouth was dry, so that her words came out rough and sharp. "You told me you never lie. Why didn't you tell me about Dr. Frankenstein's laboratory?"

He turned his face away from her and spoke rapidly. "Last night, when the storm came and we talked, you asked if I remembered my mother or my father. I said I didn't. That was a true statement. But I didn't want to tell you I remembered waking up in the lab. Lying on a table, cold and naked and confused."

She sucked in a strangled breath. Her knees threatened to give way, and she locked them to keep standing. "Hunter—" She tried to speak, even when she didn't know what to say. But the memory of that nightmare place was too vivid. She had seen things that could drive a sane person to madness.

He closed his eyes for a moment, then focused on her face. "The time with you was good," he whispered. "Like nothing else in my life—before or after. You were my friend—and more." She saw his hands clench and unclench. "I will remember all of the things that happened between us. The alligator toy. The steak. The sound of you singing." His voice hitched. "Holding you. It was all good. But I understand that you will no longer have anything to do with me." He reached toward her, then his arm fell back to his side. "For a little while, with you, I had the things you said people need. But at least now it will be easier to go on my mission."

"No," she whispered, unsure of what she meant. Yet after the shock of Swinton's lab, it was impossible for her to respond in any kind of normal fashion. She had been stunned past her capacity to function, and she truly didn't know what she felt.

"I can't—"

"I know," he answered. "It's all right. I understand. I've been waiting for you to change." With that, he turned toward the house and in moments he disappeared from view.

On legs that barely supported her weight, she tottered forward and gripped the door handle, somehow finding the strength to pull herself inside and slide the heavy glass panels shut behind her.

The ten feet to the bed might have been ten miles, but she made it across the vast distance and collapsed. As soon as her legs no longer had to carry her weight, her shoulders began to shake uncontrollably. The shaking turned to sobs, and she pressed her face into the pillow to muffle the sound.

HE GOT UP at the usual time, dressed and neatly made his bed the way the orderly had taught him. Outside Kathryn's door Hunter stopped and imagined he could hear the sound of her breathing. She had been crying last night, now she was sleeping. He was glad, because he didn't want to see her now—see the look of fear and disgust in her eyes. He wanted to remember the relief and joy on her face when he came back from the hospital, but the scene kept slipping out of his mind.

Quietly he walked down the hall to the kitchen. He warmed a little of yesterday's coffee in the microwave and drank it as he eyed the box of doughnuts on the counter. He could eat more of them. As many as he wanted. Instead, he picked up the box and pitched it into the trash.

Moisture blurred his vision. Like when Beckton had slapped him. But this pain was different—not physical, but worse.

He had thought he could deaden himself, the way he had been dead before Kathryn. But banishing the anguish churning inside him was impossible. He had told himself he didn't care what she thought of him, just the way he didn't care what any of them thought. With them it was true, but with Kathryn, it was a lie.

Quietly he walked back to his room and packed the clothes he had brought from his quarters. He had never asked Beckton or anyone else to do him a favor. He would ask for something now.

In the living room, he hesitated in front of the bookshelves. The green alligator was where he had left it. Before he could stop himself, he snatched it up and stuffed it in his bag.

When the security men came to pick him up fifteen minutes later, they eyed the duffel bag slung over his shoulder.

"Hey, what are you doing?" the senior one asked.

"I am going back to my quarters."

"You don't make those kind of decisions."

"Living here is interfering with my work. I will tell that to Major Beckton."

"Oh, yeah?" The man laughed. "I guess Dr. Kelley would interfere with my concentration, too."

Hunter kept his expression blank. He would not talk about the things he and Kathryn had done. That was a private memory he would lock away in his heart for the rest of his short life.

He climbed into the car, and set the duffel bag on the seat beside him. The driver started the engine, and they rode to the training center. But leaving the house didn't help. The pain rode with him.

It wouldn't go away. He had invested too much of himself in the feeling of being connected with her. In the talks, and the sharing, and the touching and kissing, and all the little things.

The song she had been singing while she worked in the kitchen began to run through his mind. He liked the song. It had words that talked about life.

He had thought that he and Kathryn might have a little more time together before he fulfilled his purpose.

He had been wrong. But he knew his duty, and he hoped now that they would deploy him soon. He could go off and assassinate General Kassan, the dictator of Gravan. Kassan was evil. Colonel Emerson had explained many times that the man was destroying the lives of everyone in his country. Killing him would be a good deed. But nobody could get close enough to kill the general and escape. So the clone Swinton had made was going off on what Colonel Emerson called a kamikaze mission. Like the Japanese airplane pilots in World War II who dive-bombed American ships and sacrificed their lives for the glory of the empire. He would be killed, too. But that was good, because then the pain would stop.

KATHRYN FOUGHT against waking, fought against the need to face reality. But once awareness returned, it was impossible to slip back into the blessed oblivion of sleep. The images from the night before came back like demons sent to carry her off to hell.

With a small sound of protest, she tried to push them out of her mind. But the pictures were too vivid. Over the course of her career, she had seen shocking things, like the miserable conditions that could prevail in a state mental hospital. But nothing had prepared her for the laboratory in Building 22.

Who had given the approval for the research here, she wondered. Did the President know Dr. Swinton was growing men in tanks? Or had permission come from some madman in the Pentagon?

She shuddered, then thought of Hunter. Oh, God, Hunter. He'd been worried when he'd heard the siren and come out to meet her. Then he'd seen the horror on her face, and she'd been too upset to talk to him coherently.

She'd been in shock, and much of the scene between

.them was now a blur. But she could remember some of the things. His words. Her totally inadequate responses.

Leaping out of bed, she rushed to his bedroom. It was empty, with the bed neatly made. A drawer was slightly open. He never left anything out of place, she thought, as she crossed the room and looked inside. The drawer was empty.

With a feeling of dread, she ran down the hall. The front of the house was also deserted.

Hunter was gone.

Eyes stinging, she sank into a chair, thinking about what she'd done to him. For the first time in his life, someone—she—had reached out to him on a human level. At first he'd been wary. But she'd worked hard to make him understand she cared, and finally he'd let himself trust the warmth and sharing growing between them. Last night she had shattered that trust, destroyed the private world she and Hunter had built.

She felt her heart being ripped from her chest as his words came back to her. He had said that he would always remember the things that had happened between them.

Oh, God. What have I done?

He seemed so strong in many ways. Yet he didn't know what to expect from himself, she realized, as she remembered the way he kept checking his reactions with her—checking to see if he was normal. And he certainly didn't know what to expect from her.

Trying to block out the look on his face, she covered her face with her hands, her body rocking back and forth. But she couldn't hold back the tears welling up inside her. They leaked from between her fingers and ran down her cheeks as her shoulders began to shake.

BECKTON CALLED Emerson. Thirty minutes later, they had a staff meeting in the little office off the training area. Emerson, Beckton, Swinton, Anderson, and Kolb.

While the five of them argued, Hunter was sent off to clean his spotless automatic weapon. But he could hear the loud discussion. Kolb wanted him to move back into the cottage. Beckton and Winslow had always thought it was a stupid idea. Emerson said that Hunter had changed—his request to leave the guest quarters proved it.

They called him in and asked questions about what Kathryn Kelley had taught him. They watched to see if he could eat a sandwich neatly. They made him pretend he was sitting in an airport waiting area, then asked what he would do if someone accidentally bumped against him.

He said, "Excuse me."

They asked him to talk about other things. He remembered to use the contractions. They asked why he wanted to change the living arrangements. He told them he wanted to concentrate on his assignment.

He was pretty sure that he did everything right. He showed them he had learned a lot of important socialization skills. Really, he had known many of the things already. He simply hadn't thought of them as important—because nobody had made them important before Kathryn. Now he demonstrated that he could pass for human. He hoped he had convinced them he was ready for his assignment.

They let him put his clothing back in his quarters. He unpacked everything and softly touched the green fur of the alligator before shoving it into the back of a drawer. If anyone asked, he would say it was a souvenir.

That night he would sleep in the narrow bed where he had slept since he had left Swinton's laboratory—except for the two nights he had lived with Kathryn. Only two nights. It seemed like longer. His whole life. The meaningful part of his life. He clamped his teeth together, trying to hold back any sound. But he couldn't hold back the feeling of emptiness inside.

KATHRYN COULDN'T GET an appointment with the chief of operations until well into the afternoon. She entered his office braced to argue that she could still be of help in Hunter's training.

To her surprise, Emerson concurred immediately. "You've done a tremendous job with him in a very short time," he complimented her.

"Thank you."

"I was hoping you'd stay at Stratford Creek in case we need some further assistance."

"I'd certainly be willing to do that," she agreed, both relieved and elated that she wasn't being dismissed.

"And I'd like to see the report on the sessions you had with him," Emerson added. "Could you start writing it up?"

She nodded, wondering exactly what she was going to say. Some double-talk or other. But at least making it up would give her something to do.

When she left the office, she almost ran into Dr. Kolb, who was pacing back and forth in the waiting room.

He looked up when he saw her, his face gray-tinged, his upper lip beaded with perspiration. "Are you leaving us?" he asked.

"No. Mr. Emerson wants me to stay."

He relaxed a fraction. "I was hoping we would get a chance to talk."

"Uh, yes," she said, unsure of what they had to say to each other.

"Maybe we—" He stopped and glanced at the secretary, then ushered Kathryn into the hall.

She eyed him questioningly.

"I was wondering if we could meet somewhere private."

"Where?"

"You jog. What about the woods at the end of East Road?"

She thought about rendezvousing with this man she didn't trust in an isolated patch of woods. Too dangerous.

Before she could politely decline, Emerson's voice rang out. "Kolb, where the hell are you? We have an appointment."

The doctor went rigid. Giving Kathryn an unreadable look, he squared his shoulders and marched into the outer office, leaving Kathryn staring at his back.

THE NIGHT WAS THE WORST, Hunter thought. He missed being with Kathryn. Missed her smile, the little jokes she made, sharing food with her, the warm looks she gave him. He had said he would lock those things away, that they could no longer be part of him.

But as he lay alone in his narrow bed, he found he needed them. In his mind, he brought them out, one by one, like jewels from a treasure chest.

She had sung while she had made the pancakes. When he came home from the hospital, she had leaped into his arms. Later, they had talked about making love. They would never do it now, but he had held her close in her bed—kissed her, felt her body rocking against his. That had felt so good—even the tight aching part of it. Better than anything he could imagine.

In the darkness, he could relive the moments with her, pretend they were happening again. In the daylight, as he ate runny eggs and drank cooling black coffee, he knew he was only fooling himself.

But it helped a little to focus on the training sessions, and to remember that he wouldn't have to stay here for long.

Reid came to get him after weapons drill and took him down to the lake to practice setting plastic explosives. Usually Reid was in security, but it seemed he had also been an explosives expert, so he was on the instructional team today.

It was odd for Reid to be working with him alone, he

thought. But he didn't ask questions. He simply followed orders.

"Have you detonated these before?" Reid asked, holding up two plastic bricks.

"Yes."

"What is the explosive power?"

He recited the specs, until Reid stopped him with another question. "What do you think about using a transmitter instead of fuses to blow up the cabin at the end of the pier?" He pointed to a weathered house that sat about fifty feet from the shore.

"No problem," he answered, thinking this was like a test, only he wasn't sure that Reid knew the answers.

KATHRYN SAT with her laptop computer at the dining-room table, working on the report Emerson had asked her to write, trying to make it sound as if she and Hunter had focused exclusively on business.

But her mind kept wandering. She wondered where Hunter was, what he was doing, whether he was thinking about her as much as she was thinking about him. But probably that wouldn't be good for him, she decided with a pang as she pictured the tortured look on his face two nights ago.

She clenched her fists, trying to wipe away that scene. She had messed up badly. But it was Swinton's fault, damn him. Swinton and his Frankenstein lab. And as she contemplated his research, she couldn't stop her mind from starting to form a terrible hypothesis—a hypothesis based on what she already knew and what she could guess.

This was a secret DOD research center, and they must have invested millions of dollars in a project to develop clones and train them for special assignments. Why?

Well, suppose you had a human test subject, she thought. But you didn't think of him as a man, because you'd grown him in a laboratory, so you could send him off on a dangerous mission. Would you care about bringing him home when he finished the job? Or would you figure that you didn't need him anymore, because you could always produce another one to fit your specifications?

Maybe you didn't even care if he succeeded in his assignment, because you could always try again with an equally expendable subject.

She almost gagged, then thought of something equally sinister—something that helped confirm her hypothesis. You didn't have to kill a man to clone him. If you had his cooperation, you could ask him for cell samples. There were lots of guys at Stratford Creek Swinton and Emerson could have used. But they had wanted a particular blend of brains and physique—combined in the person of an ex-athlete and physicist named Ben Lancaster. She'd bet they hadn't asked him for cell samples. Or maybe they had, and he'd refused. Then they'd been afraid he'd blow the whistle on the project, and they'd murdered him. Maybe that so-called accident that took his life was anything but.

Unfortunately, Lancaster wasn't going tell her what had happened, because he was dead. And now they had Hunter to send off on a one-way trip. The whole theory made a kind of awful sense, once you added up all the other factors.

She told herself there was still time to wreck their plans, but how?

Feeling trapped and helpless, she got up and paced restlessly around the house. It had become impossible for her to work on the report, so she wandered back to the bedroom and picked up her pillow with the disk sewn inside. She might as well get it out and read about the pack of criminals who ran this place.

To her relief, the pillow was still stitched the way she'd left it. After ripping the seam, she pulled out the disk and brought it back to the dining room where she inserted it into the floppy drive.

She had planned to go over the personnel records. Instead she was drawn back to the biographical information on Ben Lancaster, avidly reading the details of his life and his career. He had been a strong, capable man. Like Hunter, she thought with a pang. So many athletes never went on to achieve anything noteworthy after their early successes. Lancaster was different. He'd been one of the outstanding researchers at the Sandia Lab, and he had traveled widely. Maybe his personality was part of Hunter. Maybe in some unaccountable way, some of his memories had also come through.

But at least they'd picked the right candidate for cloning, she thought with bitter irony. A man with a superb body and an IQ to match. Her thoughts switched easily from Lancaster to Hunter. She had to figure out how to get to him as soon as possible, how to regain his trust, and how to get him out of Stratford Creek. Small stuff, she thought with an edgy laugh.

If she had more specific information on Lancaster, maybe that would help her figure out how to approach Hunter. She knew she was grasping at straws, but it was better to have some constructive focus for her thoughts than to simply sit and worry.

Perhaps she could get what she wanted from Dr. Kolb. He had proposed a meeting. What if she could use that to her advantage?

She was about to call him when the phone rang, making her jump.

A man with a stuffed-up nose said, "Dr. Kelley?"

"Yes?"

"This is Bob Perry calling about Hunter."

As he started to speak again, she'd thought she recognized the voice that was muffled by the nasal congestion. But she'd never talked to a Bob Perry, as far as she could remember.

"What can I do for you?" she asked, waffling between hope and caution.

"There's been a change in plans. Mr. Emerson wants to

know if you would you be able to work in a session with Hunter at noontime.''

She tried to hide her burst of elation as she answered, ''No problem.''

''He's on a field exercise at one of the cabins down by the lake. He'll be having a lunch break in forty minutes. Would that be convenient for you?''

''Of course.''

''The cabin is a little unusual. It's on the end of a pier that juts out into the water. You should recognize it right away.''

''I'll need directions.'' Opening the drawer under the phone, she found a notepad and a pen.

''It's about a ten-minute drive,'' the caller said, then went on to give her precise directions.

He was more civil than most of the other staff members she'd had contact with, she thought, as she replaced the receiver and headed for her bedroom. She needed a shower and clean clothes.

As she hurried to get ready, she started worrying. Did Hunter know she was coming? It wouldn't be good to take him by surprise.

Praying that they'd let her talk with him alone, she got into the car and headed toward the woods. When she'd jogged down here, the road had had a security barrier blocking off traffic. Now the gate was open, and she drove through, into an area she'd never seen before. There were no buildings, only virgin forest and then a lake sparkling in the sunshine at the base of the hill.

Another quarter mile and she came to the parking lot Perry had indicated. There was only one other vehicle in the lot, a jeep sitting at the far end. She pulled in next to it and scanned the woods. Several paths led downhill— presumably toward the lake. She took the middle one and came out facing a stretch of pristine beach. No one was in sight, and the only sign of habitation was the weathered pier with the cabin Perry had described.

"Hunter?" she called, but the noise of a jet overhead blocked the sound of her voice. If he was there, he couldn't hear her, she thought as she stepped onto the worn boards and started toward the cabin.

The footing was uneven, and she picked her way, hoping she wouldn't step through rotten wood.

OVER THE NOISE of the jet, Hunter thought he heard Kathryn call his name and looked up in surprise. He and Reid had set the explosives on the underside of the shack at the end of the pier. Then Reid had gone off to do something, leaving him alone to wait for additional instructions.

He'd been sitting with his back against a tree, holding a flower by its stem and stroking the petals against his mouth, remembering the wonderful softness of her Kathryn's lips against his. If he closed his eyes, he could imagine she was with him, and they were in the place where the deer came to drink from the stream.

Now he heard the sound of her voice. Was she really here?

He saw her step onto the dock and start walking tentatively toward the doomed little house. The charges were in place, expertly positioned to blow the structure into oblivion. All somebody had to do was press the buttons on the detonator.

"Get back," he shouted at Kathryn above the drone of the jet. She didn't hear him, and he started running, calling more loudly and frantically waving his arms.

She stopped at the sound of his voice and tipped her head to the side, but she was looking in the wrong direction and didn't see him. After a moment, she started moving again, along the pier toward the enclosure with its deadly charges.

At the same time, from the corner of his eye, he saw Reid running down one of the other paths from the parking lot. He broke into the clearing along the shoreline and dashed toward the spot several hundred yards away where they'd set up the detonators.

Hunter's eyes narrowed. "What are you doing?" he called.

The man didn't answer. Instead he kept moving toward the firing mechanism. If he'd wanted to get Kathryn Kelley out of danger, Hunter reasoned, he would be running in the other direction—shouting at her to get away from the pier.

Instead, he was hurrying to set off the charges!

Reid was farther away than Kathryn. There was no chance of intercepting him before he could get to the detonators. All Hunter could do was dash toward Kathryn, sprinting with every ounce of power he possessed, knowing that he had little chance of getting to her in time.

Chapter Eleven

Kathryn reached the cabin and stooped to peer in a broken window, but there was no one inside.

"Hunter?" she called, turning away in perplexity from the dilapidated building.

Had Perry been mistaken?

Then she saw Hunter dashing madly toward her and heard him shouting, "Get away from the house. Get away."

He came toward her at full tilt. Behind him she saw a man running toward a little stand of trees. It was Reid, she realized. The security guard who had cursed Hunter in the locker room.

At that moment, Hunter gained the end of the pier, leaped onto the worn boards and came straight at her. He plowed ahead like a freight train speeding down a mountain, and she knew that when he hit her, the impact would be painful. Cowering back, she stiffened her body against the inevitable crash.

She screamed as he struck her with the weight of his muscular frame, screamed again as he took her over the side of the flimsy railing and into space.

They fell toward the lake, her body under his. And she had time for only a partial gasp of air before they hit the cold water.

As they splashed down, she heard an explosion like a dozen thunderclaps coming together in the air above them. Then they plummeted below the surface, and she felt a shock wave hit the water.

Hunter held her down, at the same time kicking strongly and towing her away from the spot where they'd gone over the side. She hadn't taken in much air, and she felt as if her lungs would burst. Then suddenly he tugged her to the surface, where she dragged in grateful drafts of air.

"Breathe. We must go down again," he gasped.

Pieces of wood were raining down around them in the water. One hit her shoulder and she winced as Hunter dragged her under again, pulling her parallel to the shoreline and into a stand of water grass that swayed wildly in a sudden pounding of waves.

They surfaced among the quaking stalks, and she sucked in oxygen, shivering in the cold water.

Hunter put his arm around her. "Stay low."

She ducked into the greenery, lifting her head only enough so that she could breathe.

"Did I hurt you?" he asked urgently, his hand gliding along her arm. "I saw you on the dock, and I didn't know what else to do."

"I'm okay," she assured him as she swung around and stared at the spot where she'd been standing moments ago. It no longer existed. In fact, only the first quarter of the dock was still visible, listing at a steep angle toward the water. As she watched, it fell sideways and hit the surface of the lake with a large splash, adding to the fury of the churning waves.

Wide-eyed, she gaped at the scene, her mind trying to make sense of the destruction.

"What happened?" she asked in a strangled voice.

"He waited until you were out on the pier. Then he set off the explosives. Why were you here?"

"A man named Bob Perry called me. He told me to meet

you here. He described the location. But just now, I saw Reid.''

"When did this Bob Perry call you?"

"Around eleven-thirty."

"That was one of the times when Reid left me alone."

She nodded tightly, remembering that she had thought the voice was familiar. It might have been Reid.

As they watched, the man in question moved along the beach near the ruined pier, shading his eyes and scanning the wreckage.

"We must get away from here," Hunter said. "When he doesn't see our bodies, he'll look for us farther from the explosion."

She made a small sound of agreement, gripped his arm. The last time they'd met, she had been too shocked to speak coherently. This morning she'd come prepared with explanations and apologies. The words still raged inside her. She wanted desperately to make him understand what was in her heart, but it would have to wait.

"Follow me," he said, "and stay down."

Her legs felt shaky, but she managed to keep up with him as they moved farther from the site of the devastation.

She imitated his crouched posture as they moved through the reeds. When a small black snake slithered past, she gasped.

Hunter turned and looked at the creature. "It won't hurt you. There are no poisonous snakes in this lake."

"Glad to hear it."

"But watch for snapping turtles."

Right. She didn't tell him she wasn't an expert at turtle identification. She simply kept following him, her teeth chattering both from the cold water and from reaction.

"It will take longer if we climb out of the water," Hunter told her. "And you will be colder in the air."

"I'm fine," she lied.

Hunter paused, then gestured toward a point of land in the distance. "Can you swim that far?"

She eyed the peninsula, telling herself it was well within her range. Never mind that she'd never been in worse shape for a long swim.

"I can make it." To prove the assertion, she pushed off and started stroking. Hunter came after her, caught up, and kept pace easily as they crossed the open water.

She was a good swimmer, but not today. By the time she was three-quarters of the way across, she was breathing hard, and her arms were aching.

"Are you all right?" Hunter asked.

She nodded and kept moving, then finally she reached a point where her limbs simply wouldn't work.

"I—" She started to slip below the surface but he grabbed her around the chest and pulled her up.

"It is only a little farther. Rest for a minute."

She let herself go limp, holding on to his arm, relying on his strength to keep her afloat. She thought she felt his lips brush her cheek. "You are very brave," he whispered. "Very determined."

"I've tried to be," she answered, then gulped, her vision blurring as his murmured praise rekindled the deep feelings of guilt that had haunted her since he'd fled the guest cottage. All at once it was impossible to hold back the unspoken words pressing on her heart. "Hunter, the other night…I was too shocked and frightened to act normally. I hurt you. I'm so sorry. I don't feel the way you think I do."

His grip on her stiffened, but he said nothing. When she tried to twist around so she could see his face, he held her fast.

His reaction made her take a gasping breath so that she could keep talking, force him to understand. "When I got up the next morning and found that you had left, I felt so awful. I wanted a chance to explain what happened—that

I'd been frightened. And upset. But not with you. Then Reid called, and I was so glad I was going to see you again…"

"We cannot stay in the water," was all he said, sounding as if he hadn't heard anything she'd tried to tell him.

"Hunter, please."

"This is a dangerous place for a discussion." Stroking strongly with his free arm, he began to tow her toward shore. She wanted to dig her fingers into his flesh and force him to listen, but she knew he was right. She also understood that he wasn't prepared to let her hurt him again.

"I can swim," she managed.

"I'll do it," he said in a gruff voice.

Though pride made her want to insist, she knew it was better to save her strength for walking when they got out of the water. So she let him tow her.

Finally, she realized he must be standing on the bottom. After climbing out onto a flat boulder, he pulled her from the water. In the chilly air, she began to shiver again.

His look of concern made her clamp her teeth to try and stop their chattering.

"We can't stay here," he said. Taking her arm, he guided her toward a stand of pines.

While she propped herself against a rock outcropping, he went back to scatter pine needles over their trail.

She watched him numbly. When he came back, he took her hand and led her farther along the rocks, searching the edge of the cliff.

His face took on a look of satisfaction as he pointed to a spot where a narrow trail wound upward.

"I thought this was the right place."

He helped her up the rocky trail to a low door hidden in a crevice. The door looked like it was secured with a padlock, but it wasn't really locked. Hunter twisted the hasp open, then helped her through the doorway. They crawled about ten feet down a dark tunnel.

"Where are we?"

"I think this is what they used to call an atomic bomb shelter," he said, switching on a powerful portable light. "It must be from the time when Stratford Creek was a military base."

In the shaft of light, she could see a small room cut into the side of the mountain. Various supplies were ranged on metal shelves around the wall.

Too worn-out to stand under her own power, she leaned against the wall, breathing hard and making little pools on the plastic floor where the water dripped off her clothing.

"Are we safe here?"

"Yes. I discovered this place when I was on a survival mission. I come here sometimes, when I am supposed to be hiding in enemy territory. Nobody has ever found me here. I brought some lights and emergency rations." He switched on another large flashlight, then swung the door shut, dropping a stout metal bar in place to seal the entrance.

"Is the air all right with the door closed?" she asked.

"There are ventilators," he said.

After turning a crank in the wall, he eyed her critically in the dim light. "You are cold. You must get warm and dry." Briskly he crossed to the wooden boxes on the shelves and rummaged through them until he found blankets. Then he turned back to her and began to unbutton her shirt, his fingers a bit clumsy as they struggled with the wet buttonholes. Where he touched her chilled flesh, he left a trail of heat.

He finally got the buttons open, then slipped the shirt off her shoulders and down her arms.

A moment ago she had been wilting with fatigue and aching with the knowledge that he didn't want to hear her explanations. Now she felt a new burst of energy and hope. Although he hadn't listened when she'd tried to tell how she felt, perhaps a more basic approach would get through to him.

"Maybe we'd better make a comfortable place to sit down," she suggested.

"Yes." He spread blankets on the floor before turning back to her and tackling the snap at the waistband of her slacks. Then he worked the zipper open so that he could kneel and skim the wet pants down her legs. When she stepped out of them, she was wearing only panties and a bra and feeling a good deal warmer than she had when she'd come into the shelter.

He stayed on his knees for a moment, his warm breath fanning her belly. She lifted her hands as she gazed down at his dark head, wanted to tunnel her fingers though his hair and press his face against her. But she bided her time, letting him stand and drape her soggy clothing over the edge of a box.

"You're as wet as I am," she said, trying to sound objective.

He looked down at his clinging knit shirt and chino pants, then tugged the shirt over his head. Unselfconsciously, he unzipped the pants and stepped out of them.

He was still wearing his wet briefs, but the knit fabric left little to the imagination. As she regarded him through half-closed lids, she wondered when it would dawn on him that there was more than one way to get warm.

"We should dry my hair," she said in a thick voice.

He searched the storage boxes again and found a thin towel, which she took from him. Briskly she began to rub the long strands of her hair between her towel-covered hands, observing him through heavy-lidded eyes. He was watching her intently.

"My arms are tired from swimming," she said, in a languorous voice. "Could you help me?"

He took the towel from her and began to work on her

hair, rubbing the way she'd demonstrated. With a deep sigh, she let her head drop to his naked shoulder.

Her eyes were downcast, not with modesty but with interest. He might be a whirlwind of activity, but the clinging briefs gave him away.

His hands became a bit shaky, but he kept at the drying until she made a small sound in her throat.

"Am I hurting you?" he asked anxiously.

"No," she answered, silently admitting she enjoyed shredding his composure. "But I'd like to get out of this wet bra." Reaching around, she opened the catch and pulled the garment away from her body. Straightening, she tossed it in the general direction of the boxes.

She could hear the uneven breath rushing in and out of his lungs as he stared at her breasts.

Her nipples were already hard. They tightened further under the heat of his scorching gaze. Silently, she lifted the towel from his hands, dropped it onto the floor, and took a step closer, so that her naked breasts touched the hard wall of his chest.

His strangled exclamation was as gratifying as the feel of his flesh against hers. For long seconds he seemed too stunned to move.

"Touch me," she whispered. "Please touch me."

In slow motion, his hands came up to cradle her breasts. When his fingers began to knead and stroke, she made a high sound of pleasure as she arched into his caress.

Silently she raised her hands to his chest, combing through the crisp mat of hair and finding his nipples, drawing a sharp gasp from him as she showed him ways to touch—ways that he might imitate.

He did just that, to her delight.

"I don't think I can stand up much longer," she murmured.

His hands stilled. His breath drew in sharply. "I should stop doing this to you."

"Not this time."

"Kathryn, when you came back from Swinton's lab, you...had changed. I saw the look on your face." His eyes were bleak as he put distance between them.

"Hunter." She grabbed his arm and held tight. "I saw things there that upset me. And I was in shock."

"Yes. You saw. You know."

The look on his face made her eyes sting. "Please believe me. It hasn't changed the way I feel about you."

"It must." His lips hardened. "Emerson told you I was a man who had lost his memory. When I heard it, I wanted it to be true, but I knew that was just a fantasy. I knew that you would find out the truth."

"I did, and I was angry with Swinton. Angry with Emerson and Beckton and all the rest of them. But I wasn't angry with you, Hunter. I wasn't frightened of you. Or...or offended."

The doubt in his eyes made her hurry on. "My feelings for you are the same as they were when we were talking about making love, both of us wanting it so badly we ached. The other night, we both knew we couldn't give in to that wanting. But now we're alone. And safe. And I think I can show you how I feel better than I can tell you." She prevented further discussion by pressing her mouth to his, using her lips in ways that would stop him from thinking.

She knew to the heartbeat when she had won. For several seconds he remained absolutely still, then his lips began to move against hers with a hunger she felt in every cell of her body.

He made a low sound in his throat as her tongue entered his mouth, sliding over strong teeth and sensitive tissue before withdrawing slowly, inviting him to try out the same technique.

When he raised his head, he was shaking. But she suspected he still wasn't quite convinced.

She skimmed her hand along his ribs, down to his hips,

drawing him against her, as she found his eyes with hers, held his gaze. "I want the same thing you do. Please. If we don't make love now, I think my body is going to self-destruct."

"You feel that way, too? Like a volcano about to explode?"

She managed a little laugh. "Oh, yes." Taking his hand, she tugged him down to lie beside her on the blanket, then rolled so that she was facing him as she held out her arms.

He stared at her with a kind of wonder, touching her face, her shoulder, her breasts, as if he couldn't quite believe they were finally together like this, both aching with desire.

"I want to do the right things," he said in a thick voice.

She moved her lips lightly against his. "Anything we do together will be wonderful. It's already wonderful."

"Yes. Everything with you is perfect for me." Tenderly, he stroked his thumb against her lips, tracing their outline. "But I think that's because you know how to make it that way. I want to do the same for you, but you must tell me what I need to know."

His eyes were so serious that she took his face in her hands and gave him a soft kiss. Again she marveled at his candor. His caring.

"You only need to know one thing," she told him gently between tiny kisses. "Men are ready for joining more quickly than women. But a woman needs a little more time if she's going to reach sexual climax. She needs to be kissed and touched first."

"Sexual climax?"

"The burst of pleasure that comes at the end."

She didn't know whether he understood all of that yet, but she had no doubt that he would. "So kiss me. And touch me," she whispered, kissing the warm place where his neck joined his shoulder as her hands stroked his cheek, his neck, his chest, down the flat plane of his stomach, over his thighs, and finally to the rigid flesh straining behind his briefs.

He drew in a quick, sharp breath when she cupped her hand around him, and she permitted herself only a few brief caresses, knowing that she could bring this to completion too quickly.

Instead, she tugged off her panties so she would be completely open to him. With a little smile of reassurance, she lay back on the blanket, her arms bent upward, her body and soul open and vulnerable to him.

"You are perfect," he said with awe. He stroked the hair on her head, then touched the triangle of red hair below.

"It's the same beautiful color against your creamy skin." He rose over her, kissing her mouth, then moving his lips to her shoulders and then to the tops of her breasts.

"Can I?" he asking in a thick voice, his lips hovering above one taut nipple.

"I was hoping you would," she told him, curling her hand around his head and bringing his lips down to her breast. His mouth opened around her nipple, and she melted under the exquisite tugging sensation as he drew on her.

"That's good," he said, raising his head to look at her in wonder. "I was afraid you wouldn't want me to do it."

"I told you. I want the same things you do," she whispered.

And perhaps that gave Hunter confidence, because he set out on a journey of exploration that left her aching with arousal. No one had ever focused on her like this. No one had ever devoted himself so completely, so unselfishly to pleasing her. Each thing he did brought her delight, and that delight was multiplied by the light in his eyes as he learned the secrets of her body.

"Here. I need to feel you here," she told him, taking his hand and guiding it to the hidden warmth between her thighs.

He watched her face again as he stroked her, learning what she liked best.

Still, his touch quickly became shaky and his breath ragged, and she knew that she'd better end the preliminaries.

"There are lots of ways to manage the last part," she whispered. "This time, let me do most of the work."

She asked him to lie back, then dragged his briefs off and straddled him, her eyes locked with his.

His face was a study in awe as his hard flesh touched her softness, as she brought him inside her.

"That is—" He seemed to have no words to finish the sentence.

Then she began to move, finding a rhythm that captivated them both. She saw his features tighten as his body trembled in its climb, heard his shout of surprise and gratification, felt him spasm within her. Then she was driving for her own completion, moving in a frantic rhythm that brought her to heights she had never reached. She called his name, feeling her whole body convulsing above him in tremors of raw pleasure that went on and on.

Afterwards, she lay on top of him, her skin slick with perspiration, her body boneless as she felt him stroke her hair and shoulders.

"Thank you for that," he whispered.

She moved to lie beside him, snuggling against him, and he held her close.

"The thanks are mutual," she answered.

His fingers skimmed her lips. "You're a good teacher."

She laughed. "Well, you forgot one thing I tried to teach you."

His eyes clouded in alarm. "What?"

"Didn't I warn you not to get undressed in front of a woman?"

His cheeks colored. "This was different. We were wet and cold. I was trying to get us warm."

She gave a little laugh. "Well, you did that, all right."

"I guess I did. Very warm," he said, his lips breaking into a grin.

She smiled back.

"I like this," he said.

"So do I. I like making you happy." Finding his hand, she stroked her fingers against his. "I like being happy with you."

He didn't answer, and she suspected he was still afraid to trust anything good coming into his life. She would teach him differently, and teach him how much a man and a woman could mean to each other.

But for the moment, she was exhausted.

"How long can we stay here?" she murmured, her lids fluttering closed.

"Until dark."

"Good."

"Then I will get you away from Stratford Creek."

Her eyes opened, searched his. "And you'll stay with me, get me to—to a place of safety," she clarified.

"Yes."

Perfect. If he could get them off the grounds, she would make sure Emerson and Swinton never got their hands on him again.

She wanted to talk about escape plans, ask when he had made the decision. But emotional turmoil and lack of sleep had finally taken its toll. For the time being, it was enough to know she was safe with him and that he would take her away from Stratford Creek. She closed her eyes, snuggled close to him, and drifted off to sleep.

DR. JULES KOLB'S face was set in hard lines as he slipped through the trees in back of the guest cottage. His breath coming in painful gasps, he waited under the shade of the branches, watching the house. He was too old and used-up for this. And he knew it would be disastrous for him to be caught inside, but he was going to take the chance. Because there was no better time than now, with every available security patrol out searching the grounds.

News of the explosion had taken him by surprise when he'd been writing up notes on a patient's records. He'd heard two of the nurses babbling excitedly and was about to yell at them to keep it down so he could work. Then he'd caught the name "John Doe." Slamming his pen down on the desk, he'd run out into the hall to find out what in the name of Sam Hill was going on.

Everybody was talking about it. But nobody was sure what had actually happened. A team had gone out to the site of the explosion, but they hadn't found anything. Now they were searching farther along the lake and in the woods.

He couldn't repress a high laugh as he wondered whether he should be excited or upset. It all depended on whether Reid was telling the truth. He'd told Emerson that the clone had set explosive charges on the cabin at the end of the pier in order to kill Kathryn Kelley. Reid had tried to stop him, but he'd been too late. How many people had believed that absurd story?

The staff meeting had been a zoo, he thought, with everyone pointing fingers. Swinton was angry that Kelley had ever been brought into the project and Anderson kept saying that the fault was in the basic specifications of the program. That was one of the little bastard's constant themes. Luckily, that had turned Swinton's wrath on his subordinate. Emerson had tried to quiet things down. But it was obvious he'd lost control of the meeting.

Kolb sighed. At least no one had turned on him. But now Emerson would go back through the records. And that was bad news.

He had to press his hands against his sides to keep them from shaking. Muttering under his breath, he began to move toward the sliding glass door in one of the bedrooms. Weeks ago, he'd discovered the defect in the doors. One of them had a faulty locking mechanism. All you had to do was lift the glass panel upward, and you could disengage the latch.

Grasping the handle with shaky fingers, he pulled upward, straining with the effort, uttering an explosive curse when the panel refused to come free. Then it suddenly gave, and he almost hit his damn hands against his chin.

Yanking the door open, he stepped inside. Quickly he checked the bedroom. Finding nothing of interest, he made his way down the hall and spotted the computer sitting on the dining-room table. When he saw what was on the screen, he sucked in a sharp breath. So she'd found out about Ben Lancaster! With a shaky hand he reached out and closed the file, then removed the disk from the machine.

WHEN KATHRYN OPENED her eyes again, she sensed that time had passed. Turning her head, she looked at Hunter. He had covered them with an extra blanket and lay with his arm possessively around her.

"Hi," she said.

"Hi," he answered, reaching to touch her cheek.

"Did you sleep?"

"A little. Then I got up and went out to set alarms. I want to know if someone comes near this place."

"I would have worried if I'd woken up and found you gone," she murmured.

"You were very tired—after the explosion. And the swim." He swallowed hard. "And making love."

She nodded.

"You didn't wake up even when I got back under the covers and held you," he said, his voice full of tenderness and a kind of wonder. "I watched your face. It was peaceful. And your breathing was even. You felt safe here with me."

"Of course," she answered, kissing his chest, snuggling

against him. She looked around the small room. It was dark and bleak, and the bed was only a couple of blankets on the floor, yet she was more content than if she'd spent the night in the world's most sumptuous honeymoon suite.

His hands drifted over her. "I was thinking about the time we lay together on a blanket in the desert," he said. "With the sunset making everything glow."

"That sounds like a nice idea," she said dreamily.

"It isn't an idea. I mean, it is one of the memories in my mind. I can bring it back. The way I can bring back the look on your face when I came back from the hospital."

She turned her head toward him. "Ben Lancaster lived in New Mexico. Maybe he did that. Maybe it's his memory."

"You are part of it. I see your face. Your hair."

"It can't be me. I would be too young for him. And he had a wife."

He nodded.

She stroked the side of her hand along his beard-stubbled cheek. "We need to know more about him," she said. "And about how you can remember things he did. Maybe you have a stronger connection to his life than you think. Maybe it helped you survive in this place."

He looked as if he didn't think it was possible, and she didn't want to spoil this time together by making him worry. So she changed the subject. "Did you say you brought field rations here?"

"Yes." He slipped out of bed, and she saw he'd dressed in sweat pants. He opened a canvas pack. "They're not very good."

"I'll manage. And while you're at it, maybe you can find me something to wear."

"I like looking at you the way you are."

She blushed and pulled the covers over her breasts as she sat up.

"I like to see your face get warm, too."

"You'll see a lot more of that unless you find me some clothes. I'm not used to lounging around like this."

He got up, looked through the boxes, and handed her a T-shirt, which she pulled over her head. When he rejoined her on the bed, he brought protein bars and bottled water.

They ate sitting with their backs propped against the wall.

"While you were asleep, I was thinking."

"About escape plans?"

"Yes. And about Reid. He could be the same man who came into the cottage that first night. But I don't think he could have made elaborate plans by himself." He hesitated. "I think he was supposed to kill me after the explosion. Otherwise I could tell what happened."

She gave an unwilling little nod.

"Someone wanted us both dead," he continued.

She struggled to think objectively. "Not Swinton. At least I don't think so. This project is important to him. On the other hand, he didn't want me working with you in the first place. I guess he thought I would make you start asking questions and refuse your assignment."

"That's possible," he conceded.

When he stared into the distance without saying more, she touched his arm. "What are you thinking?"

"About living in the guest cottage with you. I think they wouldn't have let me do it if they were planning to let you leave afterward."

A shudder swept across her skin.

"I shouldn't have said that," he muttered.

"No. It's best to be honest about the danger."

"Staying is more dangerous to you than trying to escape. But—"

"It's not going to be easy," she finished for him. "But if anybody can get me out of here, you can." She couldn't hold back another laugh. "Because Beckton and his team taught you everything they know."

"Damn right!"

She raised her face toward him. "I've never heard you use that kind of language."

"I'm experimenting."

"You're loosening up."

"Is that good?"

"Yes."

He bent toward her, his free hand gently stroking her arm, her shoulder. "There's only a little time before we have to leave, but I want to talk about so many things."

"You'll have to make a choice," she said, wondering what he would decide.

"Can I ask you questions?"

"Of course. I like answering your questions."

He reached for a lock of her hair, wrapping it gently around his finger, playing with it. "Is making love always that good?" he asked.

So he had been thinking about their lovemaking. "I don't think so," she answered. "Only when a man and a woman—" she stopped. "Well, I can only speak for myself. For me, it was wonderful because my feelings for you are very strong."

After the easy give-and-take of a few moments earlier, his reaction wasn't quite what she'd expected. She'd thought he'd be pleased. Instead, he looked sad.

Raising her head, she searched his face, knowing she should say what she really meant. "Why do you think I can't love you?" she asked.

"Love," he said softly. "You should not love me. I'm not a real person."

"Of course you are!" She grabbed his arm. "Don't say things like that. Genetically, you are a man named Ben Lancaster. Maybe you even have some of his memories."

He made a dismissive sound. "It's not that simple. What about the other men Dr. Swinton is growing in his tanks?"

She shivered at the memory, then watched as his face took on a sad, angry look.

"I am like them," he said with sudden vehemence. "And none of us has a soul."

Chapter Twelve

Hunter's words brought a strangled feeling to her throat. "Where did you get that idea?" she managed.

"Dr. Swinton said it."

"The bastard!" she hissed. "He knows that raising men in laboratory tanks in order to send them off on dangerous assignments is morally wrong. He's frightened by the consequences of what he's done so he's shifting the blame to the victims."

"Yes, I come from his laboratory, and I'm not a human being," Hunter said.

She cupped her hands over his naked shoulders, feeling the flesh and muscle and bone. "You're a better human being than Dr. Swinton," she said with conviction. "When you saw me standing on the dock, and you knew Reid was going to set off the explosives, you could have moved out of danger. Instead you came running toward me. So why did you do it?"

"I—" His features took on a look of remembered pain. "I saw you standing there, and I—I couldn't let him kill you. What happened to me didn't matter. I had to save you if I could."

She folded back his hand and brought it to her mouth, stroking his flesh with her lips. "You put my welfare before your own. If you had no soul, you wouldn't have done that.''

He raised his face toward hers, his expression achingly hopeful, and she knew that he wanted to believe her.

''Swinton may be expert at illegal biological experiments,'' she said, ''but I have a lot more experience with people. I've worked with all kinds. I know what kind of man you are. You are good. Moral, honest, intelligent, giving. All the things I value.''

''That can't be true.''

''It is. Or I wouldn't have wanted to make love with you.'' She kissed his fingertips.

Emerson and his men had done their best to damage Hunter. Yet there was a deep well of strength and of resilience within him. She knew it was true, or they wouldn't be sitting here talking so intimately.

''Who do you believe?'' she asked softly. ''Swinton or me?''

After a long time, he answered, ''I want to believe you, more than anything, but—''

She lifted her face to his, found his mouth. At first he held himself like a man turned to stone. Then with a strangled sound of wanting, he began to respond. She gave him a long, desperate kiss, her hands moving over his naked chest and shoulders.

''Hunter, never doubt yourself. Never doubt that you are a good man. A normal man, and an extraordinary man, too. Very few people could have survived what they did to you. But you have. And from now on, everything will be better for you. For us.''

There was still uncertainty in the depths of his dark eyes.

She pulled his mouth back to hers, and her hands began to move urgently over him again, trying to show him the truth of her words. Trying to show him how much she cared.

A sigh of gratification went through her when she felt him surrender to his need for her.

"Yes. Make love with me," she murmured.

This time there was no way either of them could go slowly. This time was hot and sharp and full of the desperation of two people caught in a trap that might destroy them both.

A RUMBLING VIBRATION made her raise her head and look anxiously around.

Beside her, Hunter sat up, his gaze fixing on the door.

"What is it?" she asked. "What's happening?"

"One of the alarms I set out while you were sleeping. We must leave here quickly." He pulled the cover from a screen that sat on a low shelf and stared at what looked like a round green target with a series of concentric circles. At the bottom left, several small blips moved toward the central area.

"Four men," he said, watching the screen. "They are heading straight in our direction. Maybe somebody dug into the old records and found out about this place."

She felt a shiver go through. After they'd made love again, Hunter had urged her to get ready to leave. She was dressed, except for her shoes, which weren't quite dry. Now she pulled them on.

"We must assume they are looking for us," he said as he checked the packs of supplies he'd gathered earlier.

Handing her the lighter one, he silently moved the bar away from the door.

"We can't use a flashlight. Someone might see," he whispered. "So stay close to me."

"You can count on it," she murmured, following him down the tunnel and waiting while he scanned the immediate area before they both slipped outside into the cool evening air. He closed the door and used another lock he'd found inside to reseal the entrance.

She looked around her in the gathering darkness, half expecting an attack from someone poised on the rocks above their heads, but she saw no one.

Quickly and silently, he led her down the path they'd taken earlier. There were large rocks and tree roots under foot, and she would have fallen several times if he hadn't been gripping her arm.

It was hard to keep up with the pace he was setting, but she didn't voice a complaint. About halfway down the trail, she heard footsteps, then a gruff voice.

Hunter went stock-still, his fingers digging into her arm as he brought her to an abrupt halt.

"This must be the place," a man said.

"Anyone home?"

"The door's locked," the first speaker answered, and she knew he was talking about the shelter they'd vacated only minutes earlier.

"I guess this is another dead end."

"Maybe they were here. I'd like to look for footprints, but it's too dark to see much."

"All right, we've got another couple of hours before we can report back to the chief of operations. Let's head back toward the lake," another voice ordered. "See if we can spot anything along the shoreline."

The feet started down the path, directly toward them. Kathryn went rigid as she stared at the rock walls hemming them in. Now what? Run for it? They'd never make it. At least, she wouldn't, she silently amended. Hunter could probably get away if he didn't have to wait for her. But she knew with absolute certainty that he would never leave her. He had vowed to get her to safety, and he would do everything in his power to keep his promise.

He tugged on her hand, and she came out of her trance, following him around a boulder. He pulled her into a crevasse on the far side, shielding her body with his and pressing her into the shadows. She buried her face in the front of his shirt, breathing in his familiar scent, trying to match his apparent calm, though her heart threatened to pound its way through the wall of her chest as the search team moved closer and closer.

To her vast relief, they didn't leave the trail, didn't stop as they descended to the lake.

In a few minutes, Hunter tugged at her hand again and whispered, "We will go the other way."

They retraced their steps up the hill. Before they reached the shelter, Hunter led her down a branching path. In the fading light, it was even slower going than before.

When they reached the bottom of the hill, she stood dragging in air.

"We can't stay here long," he said in a barely audible voice. "But we can take a shortcut through the woods," he added as he scanned the area and began to edge forward into the forest.

He moved with caution, stopping to listen every few minutes, but they met no more patrols. She was starting to relax when she saw flashlight beams cutting through the gloom.

Hunter swiftly pulled her behind the trunk of a tree as the lights and the sound of moving feet drew closer. Swallowing a little moan, she melted against him, resisting the urge to close her eyes. Unable to look away from the lights, she watched them approach, feeling like an animal being stalked.

She felt Hunter's muscles tense as he prepared for a confrontation. But at the last moment the men passed a few feet to their left and moved into the distance.

The air frozen in her lungs hissed out. Stratford Creek might not be a military base anymore, but it looked like Colonel Emerson commanded a small army. "That was close," she said, when she dared to speak.

"Yes. Lucky for us none of them have night scopes."

He made a low sound. "I should have made a better evaluation of the situation. We have less time than I thought."

Before she could answer, he started off again, moving faster, but watching to see if she could keep up. When he heard her breath coming in little gasps, he slowed his pace. "I'm sorry. This is hard for you."

"I'll manage."

"You can rest here for a little while," he said, gesturing toward a dark hulking building just visible against the night sky. Cautiously, he led her to a high window. "I need something in here. I can get it if you boost me up to the window."

She eyed the building. "What is this place?"

"The garage where they store auto parts, and vehicles that need repair. There is no guard."

We hope, she silently added. After their two close calls, she wanted to beg him not to go inside, not to leave her alone. But she knew her best option was relying on his judgment, so she made a cradle with her hands and boosted him up to the window frame. She watched him open the window, then disappear into the darkness beyond. Straining her ears, she thought she heard him drop to the floor inside, but she wasn't even sure of that.

After standing and staring into the opening for several moments, she decided it was foolish not to take his advice and get as much rest as she could. Sinking to the ground, she pressed her back against the cold metal wall and tried to relax.

But all her senses were on red alert.

A dry twig cracked in the underbrush, and she went rigid. Then the sound of movement through the woods receded, and she figured that some nocturnal animal was as wary of her as she was of it.

Minutes dragged by, and she felt her tension mount. Then she saw the figure of a man running toward her. For an awful moment her heart blocked her windpipe, until she recognized Hunter's shape and realized he had probably exited through a door she couldn't see. As he drew closer, she saw he was holding a set of license plates.

"We will put these on the car we take," he said. "That will make it harder for anyone to figure out which one we have stolen."

"How did you think of that?"

He gave a low laugh. "*They* taught me to be devious—to use tricks to hide myself."

"Good."

"Now we must go to the motor pool, where the working vehicles are kept." He hesitated. "We could circle around the main buildings, but we'll lose time. It would be faster to go straight across the compound."

"Won't there be people?" she questioned.

"Yes. But they won't be looking for us there. And they won't recognize us." He pulled two jackets and caps from his pack and handed one set to her. "Put these on. In the dark we will look like men who work here. Walk as if we have somewhere to go—but not as if we are afraid of being discovered."

She nodded as she donned the jacket and twisted her hair into a knot before pushing it under the cap. Hunter looked at her critically, then reached to tuck in several wayward strands that had escaped her attention.

He stroked his finger against her cheek, and she turned her face to brush her lips against his hand.

"We will be away from Stratford Creek soon," he said in a gruff voice.

"Good. I don't like it here. The only good thing about it was meeting you."

His face contorted, and he gave her a quick, rough embrace. "It's the same for me."

Before she could say more, he turned and started toward the end of the garage. Her eyes widened as they rounded the corner. She hadn't known how close they were to the center of the action. Now she saw they were only fifty yards from several low buildings where lights shone through the windows.

Hunter started off at a purposeful pace. Trying to imitate his masculine gait, she strode along the road, swinging her arms briskly and keeping her eyes straight ahead.

They came to a sidewalk, and he stepped onto the pavement. She followed, feeling exposed and vulnerable. When a man emerged from one of the low structures and stood at the top of the steps staring into the darkness, she imagined he was looking directly at them. She wanted to dart around the side of a building, but she realized that would be a fatal error, so she forced herself to keep pace with Hunter. To her relief, they walked on past the watcher without being challenged. But before she could relax, she saw two men coming directly toward them on the sidewalk. And each step closer seemed to increase her heart rate.

She barely heard Hunter over the roaring in her ears.

"This way." He gave a little tug on her arm. Stopping short, she followed him onto a side road, fighting not to turn and look over her shoulder to see if they were being followed. Several minutes later, she spotted a parking area ahead of them, surrounded by a chain-link fence with razor wire at the top. Moving onto the grass, Hunter stopped under the shadows of some trees and ran his hand over her arm. "You did perfectly."

She let her body relax against his. "I'm scared spitless. How can you act so calm?"

"I was trained for espionage."

"But even trained agents have nerves."

"What happens to me is not important," he said dismissively.

She turned him toward her, clasped his shoulders, wished she could see him better in the darkness. "It is to me."

He didn't answer and she added, "You're going to have to adjust your thinking."

"Right now, I have to get you away from Stratford Creek." He paused, and she heard him swallow. "If anything happens to me, you must try to escape. This time *I* am giving *you* an order."

"I—"

"Do not go to Colonel Emerson," he clipped out. "Do not trust him."

"I don't."

"Kathryn," he said in a thick voice, folding her close. "What I feel for you is very strong. If it's possible for a man created the way I was created to love, then I love you."

"Hunter," she whispered, holding on to him for dear life.

"This isn't a good time to speak of my feelings. But I want you to know. In case I don't get another chance to tell you."

"You will," she vowed.

"You make me want to believe that." For several heartbeats he clasped her tighter, then eased away from her.

She shivered as the warmth of his body left her. When she saw him watching her closely, she stood up straighter, determined to show him she wasn't going to fall apart.

"Wait here. I will put the plates on a car and come back for you."

She gave a tight little nod and watched him walk toward the parking lot. As he drew abreast of the gate, a guard stepped out of a small building.

A guard. She hadn't even been thinking about that, she realized. But she was sure Hunter had grasped the situation when he'd checked the motor pool earlier. She couldn't hear what the man was saying, but she heard the note of challenge in his tone.

Kathryn held her breath.

"I have orders to report to the administration building with a sedan," Hunter said, reaching inside his jacket. Instead of pulling out a piece of paper, he brought his hand out in a lightning-quick stroke that connected with the guard's neck.

The man gasped, yet he also was well trained. At the last second, he moved a fraction of an inch, deflecting the worst of the blow. Then he spun around, coming back at Hunter with his own martial-arts move.

As they circled each other, Kathryn wondered if somehow she could tip the odds in Hunter's favor. What if she caused a distraction, she thought, starting forward. Before she had taken two steps, another man materialized silently out of the shadows. She bit back a tiny sound as he raised a gun and landed a hard chop on the guard's head. Confused, she tried to figure out what was happening.

Before the combatant hit the ground, the newcomer took a quick step back and pointed the gun squarely at Hunter. Until that moment, she hadn't gotten a clear view of his face. When he raised his head, she saw it was Reid, the security man who had lured her down to the cabin, then set the fuses and tried to blow her up.

Hunter started forward.

"Don't come any closer." Reid gestured with the gun. "Just pick him up nice and easy and dump him behind a car."

When Hunter hesitated, he gestured with the gun. "Do it. Then turn around slowly."

Hunter complied.

"Don't move a muscle except to put your hands up," Reid hissed.

Slowly, Hunter raised his hands. He was facing in her direction, but he didn't once look at her, and she knew he was doing it to protect her hiding place.

"Where's the Kelley woman?" Reid demanded.

"You wanted to kill her," Hunter said in a flat voice. "You did an excellent job of setting the explosives."

"You'd better not be lying to me."

"I never lie," Hunter said in the same unemotional tone.

And he wasn't, Kathryn realized. But he had done a masterful job of twisting the truth to make it sound like she was dead. Yet even as she admired his resourcefulness, she watched in sick horror as Reid held the gun leveled at his chest.

God, what was she going to do now?

"I bet my pension you'd come here and try to get a car," he said in a voice that rang with triumph.

"Yes, you are clever," Hunter complimented him without a trace of admiration.

"That's right. Like when I told everyone you set off the explosives that killed the broad. That puts me in the clear. It's all the fault of the clone run amok."

"Why did you lure Kathryn Kelley to the shack?" Hunter asked.

"I was well paid. And I'm going to do even better when I bring you in."

"In where? To Colonel Emerson?"

"Hardly."

"Swinton? Beckton?"

"Stop asking questions," Reid growled. "Get moving. And don't try any sudden moves. I know all the defensive gambits they taught you in those fancy martial arts classes."

Hunter's jaw was tight.

"Move. Down the sidewalk along the fence," Reid clipped out. "I'll be right behind you. And hope we don't meet up with one of those search parties out beating the bushes for you. Because if I have to, I'll shoot you in self-defense."

Kathryn fought to stand unmoving and silent. Still not glancing in her direction, Hunter followed orders. She watched him and Reid head along the edge of the parking area.

When she tried to take a steadying breath, it rattled in

her throat. Hunter had told her to leave Stratford Creek if something happened to him. But she couldn't do it by herself. More importantly, she wasn't going to leave him in Reid's clutches. She had to follow, and find out where the security man was taking him.

When captive and captor turned the corner, she leaped from her hiding place. Sprinting along the fence, she prayed they wouldn't disappear from view before she reached the end of the parking lot.

Panic roared in her ears when she thought she was too late. Then she spotted them in the shadows at the edge of an unkempt field that bordered the research center.

Hunter had wondered if Reid was working for Swinton. He must be right, she decided as she followed behind the pair, darting from shadow to shadow.

She was about to step into the light again, when Reid suddenly stopped at the edge of the lawn and spun around, scanning the open area behind him. Kathryn froze in midstride. Thank God he hadn't waited a few seconds longer, she thought as she pressed herself against the wall of the building, hardly daring to breathe.

She sagged back against the wall when Reid issued a gruff command to Hunter and started moving again. They were skirting the front door of the research center, aiming for another destination. Building 22, she realized, feeling the blood drain out of her face. *Please, not Building 22.* But her guess was confirmed as they made directly for the low structure, with Hunter in the lead and Reid right behind him with the gun.

As she watched in horror, Hunter pushed open the same door where she'd previously entered, and stepped inside. Reid followed, pulling the door closed behind them.

For long moments she was rooted to the spot where she stood, fighting the urge to scream. Her first trip inside that building had been the most terrifying experience of her life.

And she'd silently vowed never to go back. Now here she was again.

About thirty yards back, she had passed a telephone box on a utility pole. It wasn't an outside line, she knew. It was only connected to the base phone system. Uncertainly, she turned and stared at it. She could call for help, and a security team would come on the double. Yet she didn't need Hunter to tell her she couldn't trust Emerson. Worse, if Reid was telling the truth, everyone now thought Hunter was a killer. Maybe they had orders to shoot him on sight. For all she knew, they had orders to shoot her, too.

She was on her own. If she couldn't save Hunter, they were both doomed. Clenching her teeth, she forced her legs to carry her toward the building. But when she reached the door and tried the knob, she discovered it wouldn't turn. The entrance was locked. Reid had shut her out.

For endless moments she stood making little sounds of distress in her throat as she tried to force the knob. Finally, with a sob, she gave up the futile effort. Stifling the impulse to pound her fist against the door, she straightened and started along the perimeter of the lab, searching for another entrance.

She had almost made a circle of the entire building when she heard the sound of someone muttering in a low, angry voice. Freezing in place, she looked wildly around, but there was nowhere to hide.

The voice sounded frustrated, but it grew no louder. Realizing that the speaker was hidden from view around the corner of the building, she crept cautiously forward and peered around the wall. A man was standing hunched over, trying to insert a key into the lock of another door. When he met with no success, he cursed, then switched to another key on the same ring.

The man was a disheveled Dr. Kolb, she saw. Apparently he too was trying to get inside and having little success.

Emerson must have tightened security all over the base and ordered doors locked.

What was Kolb doing here? she wondered as she peeked around the corner. Hunter had told her Reid wasn't capable of carrying out elaborate plans. Maybe the security man was supposed to deliver Hunter to Kolb, and maybe the physician had accidentally gotten locked out of the building. He looked like he was coming unglued, Kathryn thought as she watched him try several more keys. His fumbling hands dropped them on the grass. Cursing furiously, he went down on his knees and scrabbled frantically until he found them again.

With a groan, he heaved himself up. Squaring his shoulders, he attacked the lock again, still muttering to himself. It seemed to Kathryn that he was taking half the night to accomplish a relatively simple task—if the ring he'd brought held the right key.

Finally he let out a growl of satisfaction, pulled open the door, and stepped inside.

The hinges were cushioned by air cylinders. Praying that she wouldn't be too late, Kathryn sprinted forward and caught the edge of the metal just in time to give her fingers a sharp pinch. Repressing a gasp of pain, she pushed her shoulder through the opening and saw Kolb scurrying down a hallway.

If he glanced over his shoulder, he'd spot her. But he appeared too preoccupied to check his surroundings. She mouthed a little prayer of thanks when she realized he was heading away from the room with the tanks. At least she wouldn't have to see that awful sight again.

About thirty paces down the hall, he stopped and stepped through a door. As silently as she could, she crept forward. Pausing to listen, she heard muffled voices. When she cautiously stuck her head around the corner, she found she was staring into a vestibule that led to three more doorways. Kolb had stepped through the one on the right.

In his hand was a gun, pointed at a man whose face she couldn't see. But she could tell he was standing in what looked like a medical supply room and was wearing a white lab coat.

Afraid to approach any closer, Kathryn strained her ears as she tried to figure out what was going on. The guy in the lab coat wasn't tall enough to be Swinton. When he turned to face Kolb, she saw with a little jolt that it was the research director's assistant, Roger Anderson, the man who had let her look at the videotapes of Hunter.

Anderson drew himself up to his full five feet eight inches. "What's the meaning of this intrusion?" he growled. "You're not supposed to be in this building unless you have direct orders."

"I'm not going to let you and Swinton go any further with this," the doctor said, his voice quavering, the gun shaking in his hand.

"Any further with what?" Anderson demanded.

"With your diabolical experiments."

"Then we're on the same side," Anderson said in an even tone. "I've been trying to stop Dr. Swinton ever since he began growing human cells in a petri dish."

"It will be a cold day in hell before I believe that," Kolb said, moving farther into the room so that Kathryn had a better view of the interior of the lab.

Chapter Thirteen

Hunter was slumped in a chair, his elbows resting on a narrow table in front of him and his head cradled in his hands. From the tension in his arms and body, Kathryn judged that he was in considerable pain.

Kolb and Anderson were too absorbed in their little drama to look at him, or to be aware that she was on the scene. But as she stood in the shadows beyond the doorway, Hunter slowly raised his head. As if some sixth sense told him she was behind the doctor, he raised his face and stared in her direction. When his gaze focused on her, his face contorted into an expression of such anguish that she had to press her fist against her mouth to keep from crying out. Then a pleading look came into his eyes.

"Go away," he mouthed.

She gave a small but emphatic shake of her head.

He kept his gaze on her for several more heartbeats. But it was clear that keeping his head up was too much of a struggle. With a grimace, he dropped his face back into his hands.

It was almost impossible to contain her anger as she took in his appalling condition. He had been through so much. Now what torture had they devised for him? Her own hands clenched into tight fists. It was all she could do to stop herself from rushing to his side. But she forced herself to stay where she was. All she'd accomplish by going to him would be to get them both caught.

In desperation, she glanced around the anteroom, looking for some sort of weapon. A long metal pole leaning against the wall. Not even sure of how she could use it, she began to move across the room.

"At first I thought you were on my side," Kolb was saying. "Like Fenton, when he was chief of security. He had the guts to complain to Emerson about this hellhole."

"Look where it got him," Anderson growled. "Somebody pushed him off a roof."

"Probably McCourt." Kolb's voice rose an octave. "I thought after that that you were afraid to speak up, even though you wanted to close down this obscene project. But I kept my eye on you. Finally, I realized you didn't give a damn about the subjects of the experiment. You were only trying to discredit Swinton so you could take his place. You don't like playing second fiddle. You want the glory for yourself."

"That's right," Anderson answered mildly. "I hate doing the dirty work of a pompous ass who thinks he has all the answers. I can do a lot more for this project than he ever could—if I just get the chance to prove the flaws in his methods."

The physician made a noise of disgust.

"If you think cloning human beings is obscene," Anderson asked in a conversational tone, "why are you part of the jolly little team at Stratford Creek?"

"Not by choice. That bastard Emerson's got something on me, just like he's probably got something on you. That's his specialty, digging up garbage and using it to his advantage. I wanted to atone for my sins, but he forced me to come here. Now the joke's on him. It turns out I'm not going to live long enough to enjoy my retirement. So I don't have to do his dirty work anymore. I'm taking Hunter out of here. I thought Dr. Kelley could turn him around. If she's gone, I'll have to do it myself in the time I have left."

As she heard her name mentioned, Kathryn stopped in the act of reaching for the pole.

"You had her killed, didn't you?" the doctor demanded. "And you wanted it to look like Hunter did it."

Anderson shrugged. "That was my plan," he said, laughing, as if he were enjoying a private joke.

"What did you have against her?"

"Nothing personal," Anderson shot back. "But she gave me the perfect opportunity to prove that Swinton's methods produced unstable subjects unsuitable for secret missions. You need to use more brain-altering drugs to control their reactions."

Kolb answered with a low curse.

"While we're discussing Dr. Kelley," Anderson said, "would you mind telling me why you moved heaven and earth to get her on the team here? And why you arranged to have her shacked up with our friend in that nice cozy cottage?"

"Because I thought if anybody could get through to him on a human level, she could. She looks a lot like Ben Lancaster's wife."

"Oh, really?"

Hunter's head jerked up, and his unsteady gaze fixed on the doctor.

"Yes," Kolb said. "I was willing to do anything to get her. Even—" He stopped short.

Kathryn felt a trail of shivers travel across her skin. She looked like Ben Lancaster's wife? Kolb had done *what* to get her here?

Anderson sneered and glanced at Hunter. "So what was the big deal? Hunter doesn't have any of Lancaster's memories. Or do you think he's genetically disposed to get the hots for blue-eyed redheads?"

"You're wrong about his memories," the doctor shot back. "You may remember Lancaster wasn't dead when he arrived here. I was able to save some of his brain cells; I transferred them to Hunter."

"What?" Anderson practically shouted. "How dare you!"

"Maybe you should thank me. You haven't exactly had a tremendous success rate bringing your subjects to maturity. Maybe the brain cells were crucial to his survival. Maybe they're the reason he's the only one of your Lancaster clones to make it."

Anderson started toward Kolb, his hands balled into fists. "You've invalidated our tests."

"I don't give a damn about your precious tests, you moron. I care about the dignity of human life."

Anderson made a low sound and raised his fist.

"Stay where you are," Kolb ordered as he moved toward Hunter. "I'm taking him with me."

"I don't think so," Anderson answered in a voice that had turned surprisingly mild.

To the doctor's right, a door that had been cracked an inch quietly opened to admit Reid, holding a gun. It appeared he'd been there most of the time, waiting for a signal from Anderson.

In the space of a few heartbeats the whole situation changed.

"To your right!" Kathryn shouted.

The doctor whirled, saw Reid and fired. But the security man had also pulled the trigger. The noise of two sidearms being fired reverberated in the close confines of the room even as both men collapsed to the floor.

The shots seemed to reverberate through Hunter as well. He had been sitting at the table as if he were no longer capable of free movement. The gunfire released him from the paralysis. He sprang to his feet, leaped across the space that separated him from Anderson, and struck the researcher on the back of the neck with the side of his hand.

Anderson crumpled, and Kathryn found herself moving toward Hunter across a room where bodies sprawled across the floor. She reached him and fell into his arms, folded him into her embrace.

"Thank God you're all right," she gasped, too overcome with relief to say more.

His arms tightened spasmodically around her, then he pushed her from him.

"No," he said.

"It's all right now."

"No."

She stared up into his face. "What's wrong? What did they do to you?"

His mouth opened, but no words came out.

"Hunter?"

"A time to kill..." he said in a thick voice.

"What?"

"The song you were singing," he said.

"Yes. I sang that. But..."

A groan from the floor made her turn. Reid was sprawled unconscious, but Kolb was lying on his back looking at her. A red stain spread across his shoulder.

"Dr. Kelley," he said in a weak voice.

She knelt, felt the pulse at his neck. It was shallow but steady.

He closed his eyes for a moment, then asked, "Where were you—"

"Hunter saved me from the explosion," she explained quickly. "We were hiding out—waiting for a chance to get out of here. Then Reid caught Hunter."

The doctor gave a tiny nod. "Were you listening to us?" he said.

"Yes."

"I saw your computer file."

"My file?" She blinked. She'd been so careful to hide the disk in her pillow. Then the call about Hunter had come from Reid, and she'd forgotten all about the incriminating evidence.

"It's safe," he said. "After the explosion, I came to your cottage and took it. Now you take Hunter. Get him out of here. You can save him."

"I intend to."

He was silent for several seconds. "Emerson dug into my records. He knew..." He stopped and started again. "He forced me to come here. Work for him."

"I understand," she said.

"Go. Before somebody comes," the doctor said.

"What about you?"

"It's not a fatal wound."

"But you said— Are you sick?"

He gave her a steady look. "Stomach cancer."

"I—"

He didn't let her finish. "My car...at the side of the research building." He swallowed, then continued, "A silver Honda."

"Yes. Thank you."

"There's a pass on the passenger seat that will get you out of this damn place." He stopped, sucked in a breath. When he spoke again, his voice was weaker. "Keys...." He gestured toward his right pants pocket.

Kathryn reached inside and retrieved the keys.

"Go. Then I can send a message to the media about Stratford Creek."

She wondered what he was planning.

"Go," he repeated.

"Thank you," she said.

He gave her a long look, then sighed and closed his eyes.

She stood, found Hunter leaning against the wall, his arms folded tightly across his chest and his pupils dilated. Beads of sweat stood out on his forehead. He focused on her as she hurried toward him, but he didn't change his position.

"Are you all right?" she asked urgently.

"No."

"What did Anderson do to you?"

"He...orders to..." His face contorted and he raised his hands, pressing them to the sides of his head. She could see him fighting to say more, but no words came out. And the pain on his face deepened.

She waited with her heart pounding, wondering what the hell Anderson had done to him. When he lowered his hands, she pressed her fingers against his cheek. "We have to leave. Come on."

When she gripped his arm, his whole body jerked. "I…love you…" he said. "I…don't want…"

"I love you, too," she whispered.

"Then…leave me…here." The words were torn from him. When he finished speaking, his whole body was shaking.

"I won't go without you." She tugged him away from the wall, watching anxiously as he swayed on his feet. Picking up the cap that had fallen onto the floor, she put it back on his head. Then she felt to make sure her own hat was still in place. Miraculously, it was.

Pausing, she looked at the gun lying beside the doctor. Hunter's eyes followed her gaze.

"No gun…" he said in a hoarse voice, his fingers closing tightly around her arm.

"Okay." He was obviously in no shape to handle a weapon. And maybe he thought that having the gun would increase their chances of getting shot.

Hunter let her lead him across the lab. At the door to the hall, she paused, listened, then stuck her head out. The corridor was empty, so she hurried them toward the exit. Thank God the building was off by itself. And the lab was deep in the interior. It looked like nobody had heard the shots.

"James Harrison," Hunter gasped out as he stumbled along beside her. "Remember James Harrison?"

"Of course. The man who tried to kill me."

"Kathryn," he said in an agonized voice. "What…if someone had given James Harrison drugs that…that filled up his mind and made him follow orders."

"That didn't happen," she answered quickly.

"Kathryn...listen to me. I can't..."

"Please, Hunter," she begged as she pulled open the door. "You have to be quiet. Someone might hear us."

He stopped talking, and she led him around the building. To her relief, a silver Honda was waiting where the doctor had said it would be.

Hunter was silent for a little more than a minute. Then he started to mumble again. He was saying the words to the song she'd been singing while she'd fixed breakfast. Only they were all jumbled up. God, had he totally lost his mind? she wondered with a sick shudder.

When she opened the back door and picked up the blankets she found on the seat, he stood with his legs stiff, his shoulders rigid.

"Get on the floor," she told him.

He made a strangled sound but obeyed, and she pulled the covering over him, eyeing the camouflage critically. In the dark, it might work.

Inspecting herself in the mirror she adjusted her cap so that the visor hid most of her face. Then she started the engine.

Hunter was still mumbling under the blanket as they pulled onto the road.

God, she needed help. Even if they made it off the base, Emerson would send men after them. They needed a place to hide. If she called some of her Light Street friends, could they tell her where to hole up?

Blocking out Hunter's rambling speech, she picked up the portable phone on the console and dialed an emergency number at Randolph Security. Jessie Douglas picked up on the first ring.

"Kathryn, thank God," she said.

Jessie was a social worker with the Light Street Foundation, and Kathryn wondered why she was the one answering the call. "What are you doing on this line?" she asked.

"Cam has been trying to figure out a way to get in touch

with you for days. He did some research on Stratford Creek, but it was too late to warn you. We've been praying that you'd call us.''

A profound feeling of relief washed over her.

"I'll put you through to Cam," Jessie said.

It took several seconds to transfer the call. Then Cameron Randolph's deep voice came over the line. ''Kathryn, are you okay? Where are you?''

"Driving toward the main gate of Stratford Creek. Hunter and I have a car and a pass that should get us through.''

''Who is Hunter?''

''The man I was hired to work with. It's a long story.''

''You can tell me about it soon. We have a unit stationed in your vicinity, headed by Jason and Jed.''

''They're up here?'' she asked incredulously, picturing the two men who had both been covert agents before joining Randolph Security.

''Yes. Jo wanted to go in and get you. I pointed out that if we got caught on the grounds of a U.S. government preserve we'd risk getting shot and branded as traitors or saboteurs.''

''I understand,'' she whispered.

''They should be in position a couple of miles down the main road. Turn left when you leave the grounds.''

''Thanks.'' She hesitated, then asked in a strained voice. ''Could you have a doctor available?''

''Are you all right?'' Cam asked anxiously.

She glanced at the back seat, seeing the large bulk shaking under the blanket. A shiver of fear went through her as she lowered her voice. ''It's Hunter.''

''Is he wounded?''

She gulped, gripped the wheel, fighting not to let the fear swamp her. ''Shell-shocked, or something like it. I can't say any more.''

''I understand. Good luck.''

''Thanks.'' She was overwhelmed as she hung up. While

she'd been at Stratford Creek, her friends had been putting out an enormous effort on her behalf.

Hunter was still talking to himself in the back seat.

"We're almost to the guard station," she told him. "You've got to be quiet, and don't move."

Thankfully, he stopped his babbling as the car slowed.

A sentry stepped smartly into her path as she approached the guardhouse. The gate beyond it was closed, blocking her exit.

As she came to a stop, she willed her hand to steadiness and rolled down her window.

"I'm sorry, ma'am, you can't leave the grounds," the sentry said as he approached the car.

"I have a pass," she replied, struggling to keep her voice even as she prayed that Hunter would keep quiet, prayed that the guard wouldn't glance into the back seat and ask what she was hiding under the blanket.

Quickly, she handed the laminated plastic card through the window.

He inspected it, then gave her an appraising look. "I'm sorry," he said again. "There's been an incident. All passes have been temporarily suspended. Didn't you hear the directive from the chief of operations?"

"I was out jogging," she improvised.

"Please step out of the car and come with me."

She looked again at the gate. If she'd thought she could ram her way through it, she would have. But she knew that a frontal assault wasn't possible with the doctor's car.

"Come with me," the man said again, leaning down to open her door. When she sat frozen in place, he reached inside and efficiently unbuckled her seat belt.

Before he could straighten, the back door of the car shot open and Hunter sprang out. In a flash of motion, he leaped toward the sentry. Catching him by surprise, he landed a powerful, two-handed blow on his back.

The guard went down, just like Anderson. Kathryn watched in a daze, hardly believing the sudden reversal of fortune. Hunter might be practically disabled, but every time she needed him, he came through for her.

She was still standing there, wondering what to do next, when he turned and sprinted inside the guardhouse. Moments later she heard a whirring noise, and the gate began to swing open on well-oiled hinges.

"Go!" he shouted to Kathryn as he stood breathing hard and holding on to the edge of the door frame, looking as if he would fall over without the support. It was obvious that the sudden violent activity had drained him again.

"Not until you get in the car," she shouted back.

He made a grating sound of protest. "You cannot stay here. Colonel Emerson will send men. And…and Anderson knows you are not dead. He knows…I want to get you…away."

She folded her arms across her chest and bluffed through her teeth. "If you don't get in the car, I'm not leaving."

His features contorted as he remained clutching the door frame. Either he was holding himself up, or he was trying to keep from moving forward.

"Do you need some help?" she asked, starting toward him.

"No." He sucked in a strangled breath, then let it out in a rush. Slowly, dragging his feet, he walked toward her. The misery on his face made her throat constrict. He looked like a man in great pain, or a man walking the last mile to his execution.

"Everything's going to be all right now," she told him quickly. "As soon as we meet up with my friends, we'll get you to a doctor and find out what Anderson did to you."

He shook his head as he slid into the passenger seat and leaned back against the headrest, eyes shut, teeth clenched.

The moment he closed the door she gunned the engine. They shot through the open gate, turning left as Cam had directed.

She glanced in the rearview mirror, half expecting another vehicle to materialize out of the darkness. But hers were the only headlights on the road, in front or back of her. It looked as if they were in the clear so far. And if Jed and Jason were really just around the bend, she and Hunter could make a swift escape.

They were on a stretch of rural highway that wound through deep woods. There were no street lamps, and her headlights stabbed through the dark, illuminating a sharp curve ahead. Narrowly avoiding a tree that loomed in her path, she slowed her speed as she leaned forward, searching for signs of the rescue team. Probably she was still too close to the grounds, she told herself.

Beside her, Hunter sat rigidly, his hands clasping and unclasping in his lap.

"Can you tell me what's wrong?" she asked.

"No. I cannot tell you."

"Is it something you don't want me to know about?" she asked gently.

She heard his breath rattle in his throat. "Kathryn, listen to…me," he gasped out. For long moments he was silent, breathing rapidly. Then he began to speak again. "Listen hard," he said in a voice that was thick with agony. "What if someone—what if Anderson pumped drugs into Harrison—drugs that made him do what Anderson told him to do. What if Harrison…wanted to tell you about it, but he couldn't say it?"

"What?"

He gasped, twisting in his seat, his hands clamped to the dashboard. "Drugs. Can't tell…you," he managed, then made a strangled sound of pain that seemed to well up from the depths of his soul.

"Hunter?"

"I…love…you. Think! Think!" he demanded, turning toward her, his eyes fierce, his face distorted by some inner agony she could only imagine.

Staring into the darkness beyond the headlights, she tried to make sense of what he had been saying since Kolb and Reid had shot each other. She'd thought he was out of his head. What if he was desperately trying to give her a message?

"Drugs…Harrison…a time to kill…"

Suddenly, in a blinding flash, the pieces of the puzzle dropped into place. God, Emerson had told her from the beginning that they'd used drug therapy on Hunter. Apparently he hadn't been lying. They used drugs to reinforce his orders. And tonight Anderson had given him an extra big dose, along with some specific instructions. Instructions to kill *her*. And instructions not to tell her what had been done to him.

Her gaze slid to the man sitting next to her. The man she had come to trust above all others. She was hoping against hope that her theory was wrong. Yet as she looked at him, she knew the truth. His body was shaking, and his hands were clasped tightly in his lap as if he were trying by brute force to control his actions.

Anderson had given him something all right. A lot of something. And Hunter had been fighting it with every cell of his being, fighting not to follow the directions zapped into his mind. And doing his damnedest to let her know she was in danger—from *him*.

The anguished look on his face and the tension in his strong hands told her he was losing the battle for control.

Fear shot through her. What the hell was she going to do now?

Her foot bounced on the accelerator. If she slowed the car, maybe she could jump out. Run for help from her friends who were supposed to be just up the road. Unless Hunter caught her first.

But it was already too late. Beside her, Hunter made a sound that was part protest, part growl, and lunged across the space between them.

Chapter Fourteen

Hunter's body twisted. His large hands angled toward her neck, brushed her skin in a parody of a caress. She tried to dodge away from his grasp, but there was nowhere to go in the close confines of the car as it hurtled along the darkened road.

"Don't," she gasped. "You don't want to hurt me."

"I don't," he sobbed out. Tear tracks ran down his cheeks. The hands in front of her shook, and his face twisted with the force of his resistance as he tried to pull away.

But the compulsion had been too deeply embedded in his mind. He had been fighting it since she came into the lab, she knew, and now he had all but lost the battle to resist.

"I...must," he gasped as his powerful fingers closed around her flesh. Even as he began to squeeze, he made a moaning sound.

"Hunter, don't," she said with her last bit of breath. Desperate to free herself, she jerked her foot off the accelerator and slammed it onto the brake pedal.

Her hands on the wheel kept her in place. Unprepared, Hunter was thrown forward. For a few seconds the pressure on her neck lessened. Then it was back, tighter than before.

The car skidded sideways as she raised her hands, trying to pry his fingers loose, but she might as well have been prying at large metal hinges that had snapped shut. Her fists pounded his chest and shoulder, but it was like pounding against a brick wall.

She could hear his breath rasping in and out of his lungs, even as she struggled to drag in air. But there was no oxygen getting to her brain.

She felt the car dip as the wheels on the right side left the road. Maybe they'd slam into a tree, she thought with some part of her mind while her vision swam, and the blackness of the night closed in around her.

As she felt consciousness slipping away, she dimly heard Hunter make an agonized sound of protest. Then the tension on her neck was suddenly gone, allowing her to drag in a grateful draft of air.

With a mighty effort, Hunter swung away from her and yanked on the door handle beside him. As the door slammed forward, he threw himself from the car and into the darkness.

She screamed, even as her foot found the brake again and mashed down. The car ground to a halt, and she leaned against the wheel, hearing the shrill sound of the horn as she gasped for breath.

"Hunter," she sobbed out as she threw her door open and scrambled from the car into the darkness. Standing made her head spin, and she had to grab the top of the vehicle to stay erect.

Her throat felt like raw meat, and it was agony each time she swallowed.

She had seen a flashlight in back when she'd covered Hunter with the blankets. Opening the back door, she fumbled along the floor, found the light and switched it on. Then, still drawing in strangled breaths, she turned and staggered back down the road, training the light on the shoulder as she searched frantically for Hunter.

Behind her she heard footsteps pounding. Moaning, she tried to run but only succeeded in stumbling. Strong hands caught her, and she started to struggle.

"Kathryn, it's all right. It's Jed. It's all right," a familiar voice assured her.

Finally, the words sank in. "Jed, thank God," she wheezed, the effort to speak making her throat ache.

"I saw your headlights. Then you stopped, and I heard the horn. What happened?" he asked.

"Hunter threw himself out of the car. Back there." She pointed in the direction from which she'd come.

"Why?"

She hesitated, wondering what kind of explanation she could give that wouldn't sound like she'd lost her mind. Then she remembered that the Light Street Irregulars were used to dealing with crazy situations. "They were experimenting on him at Stratford Creek. They put a—a compulsion in his mind that made him want to kill me. He was trying to stop himself. The only thing he could do was try and get away from me."

"Then he still could be dangerous. You stay here."

"No."

Jed started off, training his own light along the shoulder and into the underbrush.

She hurried to catch up.

About twenty-five feet down the road, they found Hunter lying in a tangle of vines that looked like they'd cushioned his fall.

She ran toward his limp body. "Hunter!"

His head moved, and he stared at her.

"Are you all right?" she asked urgently, coming down beside him on the leaves.

"Get...away...from me," he gasped in a broken, desperate voice.

She reached to grip his arm as she gazed down into his horror-filled face. "I know what happened. I understand what you were trying to tell me, what Anderson did to you. I figured it out," she said. "He didn't believe Reid. He thought I was still alive and that he could make you finish the job. But it's all right. We can help you. It's going to be all right.''

''No.'' He tried to shake his head and grimaced.

Jed was beside her, kneeling. He pulled a phone out of his back pocket and spoke in a low voice. ''Get the van up here immediately. And be prepared to—''

Before he could finish the sentence Hunter reached out and yanked the pistol from the holster riding at Jed's hip. With no hesitation, he turned the barrel toward his own head.

''God, no,'' Kathryn sobbed and lunged at him, yanking his hand up as she braced for the impact of the bullet.

''Kathryn!'' Hunter screamed.

Instead of a shot from the gun, the sound of a distant explosion tore the air, and a ball of fire erupted, turning the night sky an eerie orange over Stratford Creek.

Hunter stared at the fire leaping into the blackness. Jed pushed past Kathryn, wrestled the gun hand to the ground, and landed a solid blow to Hunter's chin. He went limp.

WITH EYES DARK-RIMMED from lack of sleep, Kathryn sat in an armchair that someone had been thoughtful enough to put beside Hunter's hospital bed. Her hands were clenched in her lap. Sometimes she prayed, sometimes she simply watched Hunter's face for any sign of change.

They were at the Randolph Security Research Center, where they had been flown by helicopter two days ago. Two days during which Hunter had been unconscious and she had been in turmoil.

First he'd been sedated because she knew that if he were awake he'd try to kill either himself or her. Then they'd stopped the medication, but Hunter hadn't regained consciousness. Instead, he'd sunk into a coma.

With a sharp pang she watched him lying on the bed, his strong body clad only in a hospital gown, his arms strapped to the sides of the bed. Cam had insisted on the straps for her safety, if she was going to stay alone with

Hunter. If he woke and the drugs had damaged his brain, he might go after her again.

She touched one of the thick restraints, then glanced toward the door. If Hunter wasn't all right, it didn't really matter what else happened, she thought. With fingers that were amazingly steady, she unbuckled the straps and clasped one of his large hands in her smaller ones. Turning his palm up, she saw the half-moon gouges where his nails had dug into his flesh as he'd tried to keep from attacking her. Softly, she kissed the healing wounds, thinking about the tortures he'd put himself through to save her.

She had never met a man like him before. She knew she would never meet another. He hadn't grown up with all the cultural cues and restraints that hemmed most people in. For better or worse, that made him unique. Although Emerson and the other devils at Stratford Creek could have broken his spirit or turned him into a monster, she was betting that she'd gotten him out of there in time, and that they hadn't had him long enough to do permanent damage. Her heart told her that must be true. So had her own observations, because every time he'd had real choices, he'd proved his goodness—his moral superiority.

But now she was faced with something she didn't know how to handle.

Her fingers clenched around his strong hand. "Hunter, I love you. Please, come back to me," she whispered.

But he lay without moving. And she felt the knot of fear in her stomach tighten. She'd been in a kind of limbo since they'd brought him here. Mostly she'd sat in the chair beside the bed. Sometimes she'd flopped onto a nearby cot when she was too exhausted to remain erect. She'd watched his pale face, touched him, talked to him. But he'd remained unresponsive. And from the expression on the faces of the men when they came in to check him, she knew that his failure to awaken was a bad sign.

Lifting his hand, she pressed his fingers against her

cheek. They were strong, and warm. Like the man who lay there unconscious, she thought.

"Hunter," she whispered softly as she looked at his still face and began to repeat things she'd told him many times since they'd brought him back to her. "Hunter, everything's all right. You didn't break any bones when you...fell out of the car. You're only a little banged up. You're going to be fine." She gulped, then, and quickly went on with her periodic news bulletins. "Dr. Kolb blew up the lab to stop Project Sandstorm. The media swarmed up to Stratford Creek like bees to a honey pot. It's the latest government scandal. The reporters got the whole story, except the part about you." She paused to draw a shaky breath. "Emerson let them think that you were in the lab. Swinton and Anderson are in custody for conducting illegal experiments. Emerson is saying he only followed orders. I think he's going to end up testifying on Capitol Hill. And something else important. The police caught James Harrison. He can't hurt me now."

Hunter didn't answer. The small, comfortable room at the end of the hall was quiet except for his breathing. Leaning down, she laid her head on his shoulder, watching the rise and fall of his chest, refusing to give in to despair.

Perhaps exhaustion made her doze for a while. But she knew the moment his breathing changed, knew that something was different.

Suspended between heaven and hell, she raised her head and watched his eyes flutter open. For several seconds they were unfocused. Then they found her and filled with panic.

"No!" His whole body jerked as he tried to push himself away from her.

Anguish rose in her throat. *God, no.*

Even as a terrible sense of loss threatened to swamp her, she reached for him and held on for dear life. His fingers squeezed her arm painfully, spasmodically.

"Hunter, it's all right. Everything's all right," she repeated over and over, praying that she spoke the truth.

He went very still as if listening intently for some sound that he couldn't catch. "It's gone," he said in a hoarse voice.

"What's gone?"

He turned his head, focused on her face, really seeing her. "I—" He sank back against the pillows, sweat glistening on his pale skin.

"Talk to me," she begged, her heart pounding.

After a long, long time, he raised his hand to his forehead and pressed his fingers against his flesh. "The pain is gone. From the drugs."

"Was it very bad?" she whispered.

"Yes. I felt like my head was splitting in two, and it got worse when I tried to tell you what Anderson had done."

"I'm so sorry he did that to you." She wrapped her arms around him and held tight, as she dared to hope that he had come through the worst.

"They used drugs when they first started my training. Then Dr. Kolb made them stop. He said they were going to fry my brains. I hadn't had them in a long time—until Reid brought me to Anderson."

"They're out of your system now. Nobody will ever do that to you again."

He nodded, then looked thoughtful. "Dr. Kolb blew up the lab to end Project Sandstorm. It's finished."

She raised her head, stared at him. "How do you know all that?"

"You told me. Over and over. You told me the police captured James Harrison."

"Yes, but I didn't think you heard," she managed.

"I heard," he said with a deep sigh. "I thought it was a dream. I thought if I woke up, I would try to..." He gulped. "I tried to stay asleep."

"You shouldn't have done that. We were all worried. I was so worried."

She saw a shadow cross his features.

"What's wrong?"

"I tried to kill you," he said brokenly.

"It wasn't your fault! Anderson pumped you full of drugs and instructions."

"I should have—"

"You did everything you could. You tried to tell me what he did to you. Then you threw yourself out of the car. You grabbed Jed's gun."

"I had to." There was still uncertainty in his eyes. She couldn't stand his self-reproach. Leaning toward him, she brushed her lips softly to his. She meant it to be a light kiss because she knew he should rest after the ordeal he'd been through. But he demanded more, reaching up to pull her into his arms.

"Kathryn." Her name was a shaky sound as he settled her onto the bed with him. She forgot about restraint as he slid his hands up and down her back, over her hips, pressing her to him with the uncensored abandon that she had come to expect from him. When his hand worked its way under her loose knit shirt and found her breast, she exhaled in a low, pleading sigh that matched his deep exclamation.

"I want to feel your skin. All of your skin next to mine," he gasped.

"Yes." She helped him pull the shirt over her head. Standing, she kicked away her sweatpants and panties, then remembered with a strangled laugh that she'd better lock the door. When she turned back to Hunter, she saw he'd torn off the hospital gown.

She returned to the bed, kissing him, touching him, showing him what he meant to her, even as he did the same.

"I love you," she told him. "So much."

"Yes. So much."

Caught in a spiral of passion, they drove each other to a high plane where the air was almost too thin to breathe.

"Do it the way you did the first time," he gasped. "So I can see you. See your beautiful body above me when I'm inside you."

The request seemed to vibrate through her. She shifted

her position so that she was straddling him, her legs clasping his hips as she came down on him. She liked it this way, too, because she could see the pleasure on his face as their bodies joined, as she began to move above him.

She wanted to make the sheer euphoria of it last. But the joy of being with him like this again was too intense. Urgency overtook her, and she drove for her satisfaction, her breath coming in gasps. He shuddered beneath her and she followed him over the edge into a place of rapture.

For long moments, she lay limply on top of him. His hands stroked through her hair, then stilled.

Rolling to the side, she reached down to pull the covers over them, then nestled beside him. But his silence and his stillness worried her, and when she raised her head so she could look into his eyes, she saw that his expression was sad.

"Didn't you like that as much as I did?" she asked softly.

"It was wonderful. But I am very selfish. I wanted to be close to you like that one more time," he answered, his fingers playing with the edge of the sheet.

"Hunter, you're the most unselfish man I ever met!" The tears that had been threatening her earlier gathered in her eyes and began to spill down her cheeks.

"I am not good for you, Kathryn," he said in a raspy voice. "You must leave me."

She couldn't believe she had heard him correctly. "I wasn't planning to leave you."

"You have your life to live."

"So do you! I thought we would do that together."

"I—"

"You said you loved me," she reminded him, hearing the quaver in her voice. "Did you stop?"

His face contorted. "Of course I didn't stop." He sucked in a quick breath and let it out. "But..."

Behind her, she heard the doorknob jiggle.

Both she and Hunter tensed, and she laid a hand on his arm.

When the knob didn't turn, the door rattled. "Kathryn, are you all right in there?" an anxious voice called. It was Cam.

"We...we're fine. Hunter's awake."

"He's all right?" Cam asked.

"Yes. We're talking," she said, flushing as she imagined her friend checking on them a few minutes earlier.

His footsteps departed and she turned back to Hunter. "What's changed about your feelings?" she demanded.

"Not my feelings. Everything else."

When she questioned him with her eyes, he continued, "At Stratford Creek, I always knew there would be no future for me. Emerson was going to send me on a mission to Gravan to assassinate its leader. Whether I succeeded or not, I knew I wasn't coming back."

When she made a sound of protest, his hand stroked gently through her hair. "I accepted that, and I knew the time with you was precious, that it was only for a little while."

She reached for his hand and knit her fingers with his. "I didn't know which country you were going to, but I figured out what Emerson had planned for you."

"You did?" he asked, incredulous.

She nodded gravely. "Yes. That morning, after you moved out of the guest cottage. I was thinking about you, wanting to tell you I was sorry about the way I behaved when I came back from the lab. Then I thought about the whole Stratford Creek project, and it made a kind of awful sense. If you had a man who didn't exist, you wouldn't have to bring him back from his dangerous mission. But I didn't accept it. I realized that somehow I had to get you out of there."

His head turned toward her, and his fingers stroked her lips. "You are a remarkable woman. And you deserve everything good in life."

"Damn right! And I think I've found the thing that makes me happiest," she told him.

"What about—" He stopped, started again. "I think a man is supposed to support his wife. Take care of her. I can't do any of that. I have no skills to earn a living. I don't know the right things to do and say. I have no place in your world."

She pressed her fingers to his lips. "Where did you get your view of domestic life? From 'Father Knows Best' reruns?"

He shrugged. "Is 'Ozzie and Harriet' better?"

She gave a little laugh. "They're both a little out of date. Women today aren't looking for men to support them," she told him vehemently. "They can do that themselves. What every woman dreams of is a man who will love her as an equal, a man with the same values as hers. A man who will share the joys and the responsibilities of life with her. A man who's strong but not afraid or embarrassed to show his tender side. I've had a lot of time to think about it while you were sleeping. You fit that description better than any other man I ever met."

He looked overwhelmed as she continued, "And I promise you, you have skills my friends will value."

"Killing?" he asked in a hoarse whisper.

"Undercover operations. Jed, the man who decked you when you grabbed his gun, isn't so different from you. And Jason has a similar background, too. They were both secret agents with training a lot like yours. Now they work for Randolph Security, one of Cam's companies. And when you meet our friend Thorn, you'll find out he has an even stranger background than you. You'll be surprised at how well you'll fit in."

"I could...work with them?" he asked, unable to conceal his astonishment.

"Yes."

His eyes told her that he still wasn't convinced. "You

told them where I come from? You told them everything about the Stratford Creek project?'' he asked carefully.

She nodded.

"They don't think that makes me…" He turned his head away, and she saw him swallow painfully. "A copy of a man. Not a real person.''

Her expression was fierce as she caught his chin in her hand and guided his dark eyes back to hers. "They'll accept you on your merits, just the way I have. And they'll help you learn about the world, just the way I have. We can do things gradually. Each thing when you're ready."

She felt some of the tension seep out of him as he shifted his position beside her. He had never had a home or a family who cared, but he was about to find out what it was like to be part of a warm extended family of people who were there for you in good times and bad.

He raised himself on one elbow so he could look down at her. "To have you for a wife would be a miracle.''

She gave him a playful little grin. "Not to be pushy, you understand, but is that a proposal?''

"A what?''

"Are you asking me to marry you?'' she said, half teasing, half serious.

He flushed as he realized the implications of his words. "I want to. More than you can ever know. But I think we should wait.''

"Why?''

"I want to make sure that it's the right thing for you.''

When she started to object, he shook his head.

"Let me see if I fit in first.''

She nodded. Hunter was cautious. And honorable. But she'd have plenty of time to make him comfortable with the idea of marriage.

He brought her hand to his lips, tenderly kissed her fingers. "Dr. Kolb said you looked like Ben Lancaster's wife,'' he whispered. "Ben Lancaster had excellent taste.''

"Thank you.''

"I don't know much about her, except that she was beautiful. But she isn't the same as you. No other woman has the warmth and strength you have. No other woman could have seen Swinton's laboratory and still loved me."

When she tried to deny the statement, he shook his head and plowed on, "No other woman has your bravery. No other woman could have gotten me out of Stratford Creek." Tears misted his eyes. "No one else would have cared enough about me. Why did you care so much?"

Her own vision swam. "At first I knew you needed me. Then I knew I needed you, too."

They lay holding each other silently for several moments, then he spoke again. "Would you...would you go to the desert with me? See the places I remember—the memories from Ben Lancaster?" he asked in a tentative voice.

"I'd like that."

"It's a good place to start, but I have a lot to try and understand now."

"I know. But you'll have my help. And my love."

"I couldn't do it without your love," he said simply. "Meeting you was like waking from a bad dream to find that there was a bright, warm light piercing the darkness around me."

"Oh, Hunter."

He folded her close, even as she wrapped her arms around his neck and surrendered to the joy of the moment, the joy awaiting them in the future.

And there's more 43 LIGHT STREET!

Turn the page for a bonus look at what's in store
for you in the next ''43 Light Street'' book by
Ruth Glick writing as Rebecca York, coming to
you in January 1999.

SHATTERED LULLABY

Only from Rebecca York and Harlequin Intrigue!

Chapter One

Lock the office door.

That was the most important rule when working late at night. With a sick feeling in the pit of her stomach, Jessie Douglas realized she'd forgotten to throw the bolt.

Sitting up straighter, she ran a nervous hand through her blond hair. She'd been focused on the pile of reports on her desk, each one representing a family on the edge of desperation. Like Mrs. Sierra, who needed help paying for day care because her husband had disappeared, leaving her with two young children.

Jessie had been writing a request for stopgap funding for the family, when a sound like stealthy footsteps penetrated her concentration.

Was there really someone out there in the darkness beyond the circle of light cast by her desk lamp? Swinging her chair away from the computer screen, she peered into the black well of the waiting room, praying that her weary mind was only playing tricks. Praying that all she heard was the pounding of her own pulse in her ears.

Maybe the door actually was locked, she told herself hopefully. Or Mr. Rossini, the building superintendent, might have let himself into the office and was trying hard to be quiet now that he realized she was working late.

Sure. And maybe elephants could fly.

Several agonizing seconds ticked by as she wiped her

suddenly damp hands against her slacks and waited for confirmation of a woman's worst fears. Under the new floor tile, an old oak board squeaked, the sound pricking the skin at the back of her neck. Someone was out there, all right. Someone sneaking across the room. Stalking her. Coming closer to her office, step by careful step.

Her eyes darted around the little room. Gulping, she focused on the telephone six inches from her hand. She could call 911.

No good. She'd be scooped up long before help could arrive.

She was on her own, she thought as her gaze fixed on the green metal Statue of Liberty that a grateful client had given her last year. It was pretty tall and heavy for a paperweight. Maybe if she hid it below the desk, she could use it as a weapon.

But it was too late for even that minimal protection. Before she could grab the statue, a figure stepped purposefully from the darkness of the waiting room into the partial light of the doorway.

Too bad she hadn't turned on the overhead light, Jessica thought as she squinted at him, trying to make out his intentions, trying to make the image in the doorway square with the menacing picture her mind had conjured up.

His body squarely blocked her escape route as he stood dead center in the doorway with his mouth set in a grim line, and his eyes narrowed under their straight black brows. But the picture was spoiled by his height—and the way he held his scrawny arms with unbearable stiffness. The whole effect was a study in Latin machismo, she thought with sudden insight. He wanted her to see how tough he was.

They stared at each other across six feet of space, each gathering strength for the confrontation. Yet despite his grim expression and stealthy approach, she felt relief kindle inside her breast.

Good grief, it wasn't a robber or a rapist. It was a boy

from the recreation center where the Light Street Foundation was running sports programs for kids who might otherwise have been home alone after school or on the streets. If she remembered correctly he was ten years old.

"Luis?"

He nodded tightly as he dragged in several lungfuls of air.

"You're pretty far from home," she said, keeping her tone conversational.

He answered with another nod. He must have gone to a lot of trouble to sneak up on her; now he looked overwhelmed that they were actually face-to-face.

"What are you doing here at this time of night?"

He took another breath, then let loose a flow of Spanish so rapid that despite her considerable facility with the language, she couldn't follow him.

"Slow down," she said, pushing back her chair and coming around the desk. *"Por favor."*

"It's an emergency, señorita," he said, staring up at her with huge dark eyes that seemed to dominate his thin face. "You must come with me."

"Where?"

He gestured impatiently. "A house. In the neighborhood," he answered, making an effort to enunciate carefully.

"Your neighborhood?"

He nodded vigorously.

She thought about the dark streets of the inner city, where drug dealers sold their wares and gangs of teenagers fought for turf. Not to mention the rape and murder that had been so well publicized in the *Baltimore Sun* last week.

"What kind of emergency? Something with your mother or your sister?"

"No." His weight shifted from one sneaker-clad foot to the other. "But we have to hurry."

"Luis…I can't just go down there at this time of night. Please, tell me what's wrong."

"You must come!"

"We can call the police if you need help."

She knew at once that it had been the wrong thing to say. His expression turned to panic. At the same time, his small hand darted under the open flap of his windbreaker. When the hand emerged it was holding a shiny little gun. It might be small, but Jessie was pretty sure it was no toy. It looked like a cheap nickel-plated twenty-two-caliber revolver, she thought with surprising clarity as she mentally reviewed the weapons course she'd taken last year.

And it was pointed somewhere in the region of her belly button.

*   *   *   *   *

Don't miss this next 43 LIGHT STREET *tale—*
#500 SHATTERED LULLABY—
Coming to you in January 1999. Only from
Rebecca York and Harlequin Intrigue!

Take 2 bestselling love stories FREE

Plus get a FREE surprise gift!

Special Limited-Time Offer

Mail to Harlequin Reader Service®

3010 Walden Avenue
P.O. Box 1867
Buffalo, N.Y. 14240-1867

YES! Please send me 2 free Harlequin Intrigue® novels and my free surprise gift. Then send me 4 brand-new novels every month. Bill me at the low price of $3.34 each plus 25¢ delivery and applicable sales tax, if any.* That's the complete price, and a saving of over 10% off the cover prices—quite a bargain! I understand that accepting the books and gift places me under no obligation ever to buy any books. I can always return a shipment and cancel at any time. Even if I never buy another book from Harlequin, the 2 free books and the surprise gift are mine to keep forever.

181 HEN CH7J

Name	(PLEASE PRINT)	
Address	Apt. No.	
City	State	Zip

This offer is limited to one order per household and not valid to present Harlequin Intrigue® subscribers. *Terms and prices are subject to change without notice.
Sales tax applicable in N.Y.

UINT-98   ©1990 Harlequin Enterprises Limited

FREE BOOK OFFER!

Dear Reader,

Thank you for reading this *Harlequin Intrigue®* title! Please take a few moments to tell us about the role that mystery plays in your fiction reading. When you have finished answering the survey, please mail it to the appropriate address listed below and we'll send you a free mystery novel as a token of our appreciation! Thank you for sharing your opinions!

1. How important is the mystery/suspense element in a series romance paperback?

   1.1 ❑ Very important   .3 ❑ Not very important

   .2 ❑ Somewhat important   .4 ❑ Not at all important

2. Which of the following types of paperback books have you read in the past 12 months? (check all that apply)

   2 ❑ Espionage / Spy (e.g. Tom Clancy, Robert Ludlum)

   3 ❑ Mainstream Contemporary Fiction (e.g. Patricia Cornwell)

   4 ❑ Occult / Horror (e.g. Stephen King, Anne Rice)

   5 ❑ Popular Women's Fiction (e.g. Danielle Steel, Nora Roberts)

   6 ❑ Fantasy (e.g. Terry Brooks)

   7 ❑ Mystery

   8 ❑ Science Fiction (e.g. Isaac Asimov)

   9 ❑ Series Romance Fiction (e.g. Harlequin Romance)

   10 ❑ Action Adventure paperbacks (e.g. Mack Bolan)

   11 ❑ Paperback Biographies

   12 ❑ Paperback Humor

   13 ❑ Self-help paperbacks

3. How many mystery novels, if any, have you read in the past 6 months?

   Paperback _____ (14, 15) Hardcover _____ (16, 17)

4. If you indicated above that you read mystery paperbacks, what are the most important elements of a mystery book to you?

   _____ (18, 23)

5. If you enjoy reading mystery paperbacks, which of the following types of mystery fiction do you enjoy reading? (check all that apply)

24 ❑ American Cozy (e.g. Joan Hess)
25 ❑ British Cozy (e.g. Jill Paton Walsh)
26 ❑ Noire (e.g. James Ellroy, Loren D. Estleman)
27 ❑ Hard-boiled (male or female private eye) (e.g. Robert Parker)
28 ❑ American Police Procedural (e.g. Ed McBain)
29 ❑ British Police Procedural (e.g. Ian Rankin, P. D. James)

6. How do you usually obtain your fiction paperbacks? (check all that apply)

30 ❑ National chain bookstore (e.g. Waldenbooks, Borders)
31 ❑ Supermarket
32 ❑ General or discount merchandise store (e.g. Kmart, Target)
33 ❑ Borrow or trade with family members or friends
34 ❑ By mail
35 ❑ Secondhand bookstore
36 ❑ Library
37 ❑ Other _____ (38, 43)

7. Into which of the following age groups do you fall?

44.1 ❑ Under 18 years
.2 ❑ 18 to 24 years
.3 ❑ 25 to 34 years
.4 ❑ 35 to 49 years
.5 ❑ 50 to 64 years
.6 ❑ 65 years or older

Thank you very much for your cooperation! To receive your free mystery novel, please print your name and address clearly and return the survey to the appropriate address listed below.

Name: _____

Address: _____ City: _____

State/Province: _____ Zip/Postal Code: _____

In U.S.: Worldwide Mystery Survey, 3010 Walden Avenue, P.O. Box 9057, Buffalo, NY 14269-9057
In Canada: Worldwide Mystery Survey, P.O. Box 622, Fort Erie, Ontario L2A 5X3